# The Bridge Over the River

Johannes Gramich was born in Munich in 1962. He moved to Wales in 1987 and now lives in Cardiff. *The Bridge Over the River* is the first English translation of his prize-winning German novel *Die Brücke über den Fluss*. In it he draws on the experiences of his own family in Czechoslovakia and Germany in the period before, during and after the Second World War.

Parthian
The Old Surgery
Napier Street
Cardigan
SA43 1ED

www.parthianbooks.co.uk

First published in 2008
© Johannes Gramich
All Rights Reserved

ISBN 978-1-905762-43-9

Editor: Katie Gramich

Cover design & typesetting by Lucy Llewellyn
Printed and bound by Dinefwr Press, Llandybïe, Wales

Published with the financial support of the Welsh
Books Council

British Library Cataloguing in Publication Data

A cataloguing record for this book is available from
the British Library

# The Bridge Over the River

Johannes Gramich

PARTHIAN

To my wife Katie and my daughter Eluned


In memory of the countless children, women and men
who were killed or deported from their homelands.

# 1

Down to the park. But not in the lift. There the doors closed
in on you. And you had that queasy feeling deep down in your
stomach before it came to a halt. As if you were being hoisted
upwards and had nothing to hold on to.

She slid her hand along the banister. The door to the
Blumentritts' apartment was open. But Lynette slipped past
and on down the staircase. Lucky this time. She always felt
uneasy when she had to face the tall gaunt man. Good
morning, Herr Professor Blumentritt, she had to say then and
as loudly as possible, whereas the professor responded by
merely giving an approving nod.

Yes, to the park. But not to the big one. That was a long
way off. You had to walk uphill and cross several roads. Mutti
was not keen on that. Only a few weeks ago a girl sent round
the corner to fetch milk had been caught by a black motorcar
and was badly mauled; lately more and more such motorcars

had been appearing, not only on the other side of the river where the inner city lay but also up here. Yes, and if a man you did not know addressed you, you were not to go with him, you had to run away. But why? It was something dark and mysterious, something from the world of the grownups. And what about Jews? Did you have to be on your guard with them? They looked uncanny sometimes, with their black robes and locks. From time to time servant girls employed by rich Jews vanished; they were slaughtered at certain celebrations and the Jews smeared their blood on the doorframe. At least that was what Fräulein Pechwitz said. But Father had shaken his head and said that it was nonsense.

The park that lay close to the house was not really a park. It was a small enclosure with gravel paths, a bench, bushes and flowerbeds. In the middle was a metal framework from which two swings hung. She sat down on one of them. She pushed herself from the ground, stretched her legs forwards, bent them backwards so that she rose higher and higher. The chains were squeaking. She felt the wind in her face, which was pleasant, and turned her head towards the Moldau. But she could not see it: huge, grey houses barred the view. You could never swing high enough to look over the top of those grey giants. But in her head... yes, it was possible in her head. She was flying away on a carpet like the boy in the book she had had for Christmas; this boy wore a length of cloth instead of a cap (he had wound it around his head). Deep beneath her the Moldau was glittering like a silver ribbon, many bridges spanning over it. She was looking down into the streets and small passages between the houses: from up here it looked like a city built for dolls. A blue shield spread out endlessly; it was the sea. Radiant minarets rose up in the hazy distance and caravans were moving through the yellow desert. Yes, a desert – now that was an exciting place. But when she came to think of it, there was nothing more to a desert than sand and stone. A city was made of stone too. She let her legs dangle. The colourful carpet had turned into the hard wood of the swing again; her feet were dragging across the ground so that a lot of dust was stirred up. She saw Herr Novák sitting on the bench. She had not noticed him coming. Suddenly he was there. She started when she saw him.

Herr Novák lived in the house opposite. Father said that he understood German. But he never spoke it. Father always greeted him in Czech, asking him how he was. Herr Novák had grey, silvery hair, was lean and thin, a wiry man; this was especially obvious when he stood next to Father, who was stocky. Though Herr Novák looked youthful with his elastic gait, he was much older than Father, which meant that he was retired and could do what he wanted with his days. The balmy September weather had probably lured him out of his flat, for it was unusually warm for such a late September day and Mutti had not even insisted that Lynette should put on her cardigan. Autumn had painted the bushes. A blackbird disappeared between bright red rowanberries. Herr Novák was looking at something that seemed to be lying behind Lynette. He always looked through her as if she were made out of glass. When she greeted him, he never acknowledged her but walked on, his arms dangling. Whenever Father spoke to him, he was short and curt.

Now he crossed his legs, unfolding his newspaper. The headline was printed in unusually large letters today; Lynette might have been able to read it, if Herr Novák had not returned to the front page straight away. He was bending forward further and further as if he wanted to dip deep into the letters. His glasses were perched on the tip of his nose, which seemed to be pecking at each letter. He looked up, over the rim of his glasses, when a boy ran up the gravel path; quickly, the boy grabbed the other swing. He nodded at the boy, making a funny remark before he returned to his newspaper once again. The boy was looking Lynette up and down but did not say anything. She knew him from school where he would whack the air with his ruler whenever someone came close to his bench; when he did this, he turned completely red in the face. Lynette always chose the next aisle when she came back from the break so that she did not have to pass Petr's bench. She sat right at the back of the classroom. She made herself as unobtrusive as possible so that the teacher would not notice her. Once, when Lynette had been unable to answer a maths question since she had been looking through the bars onto the street, lost in dreams, the teacher had whacked her stick across the back of Lynette's hand. But when they had Czech, she paid attention. This language sounded so soft and lilting, almost like one of the mournful songs Jilka hummed sometimes. Lynette was the best pupil in Czech except for Petr; she couldn't compete with him. She also knew why: he was the only one in class who had a home where Czech was spoken.

Petr was right on top now. The metal framework was shaking and Lynette felt the vibrations. He gave a jubilant cheer; the chains were loose when he reached the top, hanging in the air almost horizontally: he was flying. She was sitting on the swing, watching him. She could fly too but only in her mind, which seemed quite alright to her since there was no gravity in her mind to pull her down and she could stay up there forever. Apart from that, she needed the feeling of safety, security, shelter. That was why she loved it at home in the flat; Mutti almost had to push her out today. 'Stick-in-the-Mud', she had called Lynette, which she hated. 'I'm not a Stick-in-the-Mud,' she shouted, putting her outside shoes on to prove Mutti wrong.

Steps resounded on the pavement. It was Jacques, 'Uncle' Jacques. She let go of the swing, ran to the street, stopped at the kerb and looked to the right, for the cars always came from the left first. Uncle Jacques! He was carrying an old briefcase, bursting with books. The sun was mirrored in the round glasses of his spectacles. In the hallway he began to rummage through his briefcase. When he had finished with the briefcase, he plunged his hands into his pockets. So many pockets; there seemed to be no end to his pockets. He had pockets in his trousers and in his jacket, inside and outside... pockets everywhere. In the end Uncle Jacques shrugged his shoulders, smiling. Lynette stretched out her hand and pushed herself up at the same time till she was standing on tiptoe. *Taussig* she read in ornate writing on the porcelain doorbell. Lucky that she was able to reach it. Otherwise Uncle Jacques would have thought that she was just a little girl but she was not that little any more. Before they stepped into the lift, Uncle Jacques elegantly extended his hand and said laughing: 'Mademoiselle.' He rummaged through his briefcase once again when they were in the lift and after a while he pulled out the key which he held triumphantly between his thumb and index finger.

Mutti was not there; she had gone shopping. Taking Uncle Jacques' briefcase, Fräulein Pechwitz told the young lady, the *gnädiges Fräulein*, that she should be so kind as to take off her shoes this very moment since she had just cleaned the floor. Whenever she said *gnädiges*, it sounded the same as if she had

5

said *knödliges* in her languid Bohemian accent. Like a dumpling... indeed! Well, maybe she had a point, for Lynette knew that she was not quite as slim as other children of her age. That was because she liked eating, especially chocolate. Father liked eating too; maybe she had inherited it from him. He did not go to the Deutsches Haus all the time because of the conversation, which he found tedious; he went there for the excellent *kuddel* soup and nowhere else was the beef of the tafelspitz so soft and tender. Father was a down-to-earth kind of man but when he was describing the *tafelspitz* in the Deutsches Haus, his eyes shone ecstatically. There was no need to chew this *tafelspitz*, no, it melted in your mouth, well, almost. Mutti did not like it when Father went to the Deutsches Haus. She stood in the kitchen for hours to prove to him that her *tafelspitz* was just as good. Father praised the *tafelspitz* she had made each time and once again went to the Deutsches Haus.

'Have you done your practising today?' Mutti asked; she had given her full shopping basket to Fräulein Pechwitz.

'Well, I don't feel like it now; I'll do it later.'

In the children's room Bibi had his soldiers march up for battle. They were wearing simple shakos; only one of them had a cylinder on his head with a horizontal peak in front, reminiscent of French soldiers. A big gun was brought into position and fired. All the soldiers were mowed down by Bibi's hand; the standard bearer was killed also, though he kept on holding the tall post with the flag that showed a wedge of cold blue penetrating two stripes of white and red. The dead soldiers got up again, lining up in orderly formation; and again her brother made the gun thunder. Bibi and his soldiers, Lynette thought, and sat down at the window.

Herr Novák was still sitting on the bench, reading the

paper; he had still not moved beyond the first page. Who knew what important news there was today! The swings were both empty. Petr was crouching down near one of the bushes; he seemed to have discovered something, a weird insect maybe. She heard the flapping wings of a pigeon that touched down further up on one of the window ledges. When it took to the air again, it left a bright white line on the façade. The pigeon was flying towards the white cloud that was swimming through the blue sea of the sky like a shapeless ship. If she could only have her room up there! She would have settled down in the soft cloud bedding and drifted along. It would have been quiet. Down there was the daily hustle and bustle. She would have just been watching it. They were welcome to chitchat down there. Why don't you chatter? Mutti asked when she came home from school, other girls chatter so nicely at your age. A street seller rang his bell, calling 'horky parky, horky parky.' Herr Novák folded his newspaper, got up and went away with quick, elastic strides. While he was walking away, someone came up from the other side.

The figure was coming from the direction of the tramway. She was able to see the outline of the hat but not the face; the sun had already retired behind the rooftops and there was an atmosphere of evening twilight. But she knew that the figure was Father. She would always have recognised Father; she would still have recognised him if it had been darker, if he had been further away and among many people. Father had a certain gait that nobody else had. His right shoulder went down with each step. The reason for this was Father's short right leg. At the end of this leg he wore a tall, bulky shoe. Lynette pushed herself away from the window and ran to the corridor: 'Mutti, Father's coming.'

'Jesus and Mary,' Fräulein Pechwitz said, walking up to the cupboard where the plates and dishes were kept.

It was quiet during mealtime. Only once Bibs dropped his fork, which hit the edge of his plate. Father started, looked at him. He rarely said anything, he only looked at you; there was more disapproval in such a glance than in any angry word. Bibs took up his fork again and ate as quietly as possible. The plates with the cheese and the leftover cold cuts were cleared away and Fräulein Pechwitz brought fruit and two dishes of semolina that she had made especially for Bibi and Lynette. There you could lay out rivers and lakes with melting golden butter and above the cinnamon landscape snow mountains were rising, their tops sugar-capped. Father took his watch out of his pocket; today was Thursday, he went out to play chess on Thursdays. Mutti began to talk to Uncle Jacques. They were speaking in French, which sounded light, like perfume, and Lynette had to think of pastel-coloured blossoms. Father said something in the foreign language too but with him it did not sound as smooth and had some rough edges. It must have been an excuse since he got up from the table.

The *Palace* was the living room. Mutti called it that since it was fairly large and a chandelier made out of Bohemian glass hung from the ceiling. Usually this room was closed off after mealtimes because of Father, who played his violin there. Lynette could see his silhouette behind the door's opaque glass; the violin bow regularly grew out of this silhouette before submerging in it again. Today the door was open. Father was sitting in his armchair, bent over the newspaper. Usually he only glanced at it. She was thinking of Herr Novák. What had happened? When Father had put the paper in the stand, she took it out and read the headline. She knew the man whose name was often mentioned in the report. She had seen him in the newsreel when Father took her to the cinema to see *Pat and Patachon*. Over there in the Reich, people cheered and repeatedly thrust forward their arms when this man made one of his roaring speeches. He stood there, a bit wooden, and from time to time his arm rose as if pulled by strings. And the moustache under his nose, a moustache like a brush, could have been the moustache of a marionette. This man had had a meeting with others and important decisions had been made, concerning the Germans who lived in the borderland. That it had to be this rabble-rouser to whom they had made those concessions, remarked Father, who was just checking in front of the mirror whether his tie was straight.

Bibs was pulling her sleeve. Yes, she knew exactly what he wanted. But Mutti demanded that he had to brush his teeth first, then he had to put on his nightshirt and go to bed. Lynette fetched one of the moss-green volumes, opened it where the coloured bookmark was. Bibi already had a whole series of those books and each year new ones were added, which were given to him by his uncles and aunties. It was easy to buy presents for him. There he was riding through the prairie, this virtuous paleface who came from Germany and was called 'Old Shatterhand'. He was fighting for the American natives who were always noble and good. The others, however, the evil ones, kept trying to get at him but failed to do him any harm, for Old Shatterhand's rifle never missed its mark. She was reading and at the same time thinking of the afternoon when she sat at the window, looking up at the high cloud. She would have loved to snuggle down in it; that would have felt so cosy, like a bath filled with warm water to the brim, and the cloud's ethereal white substance would have been the rustling foam.

Father was walking up and down in the corridor. His steps

**9**

were loud, then they were quiet, then they got loud again. As he walked, he rattled his keys. At last the front door was pulled close. Mutti's voice was chiming, clear and bright like bells: a torrent that had been held back but had broken free now. Lynette was still reading. Bibi's eyes were getting smaller and smaller. But every time when she was about to close the book, they became wide again. Then he called for Mutti.

'And what about you?' she said to Lynette. 'Are you not going to bed tonight?'

'I haven't done my practising yet.'

'You always have a way to get round me!'

Soon her brother was breathing regularly. He fell asleep so easily. He could be wild, rollicking about, this Bibs, but then he was exhausted while she was still laying awake

Uncle Jacques was sitting in the living room, reading. Once in a while he raised his head with a vague gaze as if he were not surrounded by the room's narrow walls but by an infinite distance. Mother was crocheting in the armchair under the soft yellow light of the standard lamp. One of her white, patterned crochet doilies was already lying on the sideboard in the corridor; the doily she was crocheting now was for the dining room where the table looked bare without anything.

Lynette was leafing through the atlas. The world was a colourful place. She was living here where the dot was, right in the middle of the many-coloured mass of different countries. Across the blue sea, the colours did not change so frequently. That was where Old Shatterhand had his adventures. As for herself, Lynette could do without adventures. School was enough of a challenge for her. She thought of Petr and she could not get Novák out of her mind either. Whenever she sensed

10

rejection and hostility, she withdrew; that could be why she was different from other children, who might have chattered eagerly in such a case to win the opponent over. Yes, she was a mimosa plant; mother was probably right there: the leaves of a mimosa plant curled inwards even at the slightest touch. Maybe that was why she understood Father: Father kept to a strict outside etiquette for he was vulnerable inside.

'But child, you still haven't done your practising and it's so late already.'

Lynette swivelled up the stool that mother had left down low after her playing. She put the music on the stand, played the piece, which had been marked, several times. Occasionally she got a note wrong; mother praised her nevertheless. Then the handle of the living room door was suddenly pushed down. Lynette wanted to close the piano quickly, too late: Father had seen her already. That this had to happen to her all the time. She played the piece once again because something was not quite right with her timekeeping. 'This is how it should be, listen,' he said, tapping the rhythm on the piano top with his open hand. Oh, she was so tired and she had to get up early tomorrow to go to school. And now she was sitting here and would stay here for a long time, since she would never ever get it right for him. You could dream so beautifully when listening to music; and something that was so delicate and soon died away after it had left the piano keys demanded such harshness and discipline. When she finally lay in bed, the music notes were dancing in front of her eyes till everything vanished into merciful darkness.

The sun was shining through the reddish glowing curtain linen. It was the Sunday sun: its light was softer and brighter than on other days. Lynette covered up Bibs, who had kicked off his duvet. He lay on his stomach and had his face snuggled into the pillow. Barefoot, she went to the window. She pulled the curtain back, not too far though, so that the sun did not tickle Bibs awake.

Out there it was already busy. A man was walking past, wearing a knapsack. He was followed by a woman with a headscarf, leading two children by the hand. Lynette had seen the children frequently but did not know them; she was sure that they went to the Czech school. They were all wearing thick cardigans and solid shoes. They were probably aiming for the railway station; and from there they would go hiking. She thought of Pension Waldfrieden: how much time and peace you had there. A motorcar roared in the distance. In front of the next house the milkman scooped milk out of the churn while the dogs waited patiently; they only began to pull when the man clicked his tongue. The pigeons were cooing above her. She heard them flapping excitedly. An old woman lived up there on her own; she went out on the balcony every morning to feed the pigeons. Father was annoyed because he could not stand the noise. But Lynette loved their soothing cooing. She smiled, thinking of Bibs; he had said that Frau Abel was feeding the pigeons because she was a pigeon herself. That was well observed for Frau Abel always wore grey; she stooped, jerking her head when somebody walked towards her. You little rogue you, said mother, and looked away so that he did not notice her amusement: poor Frau Abel.

Mother was clattering in the kitchen. She was getting the saucepans ready so that the cooking could begin. The meat had to be boiled for a long time; the preparation of the dough for the dumplings required a lot of work and the dough was wrapped up in napkins that were lowered into the seething hot water. Mother usually got up at dawn. Fräulein Pechwitz was up and about even earlier, so there was already somebody there when the ice block was brought that had to be put in the icebox to keep milk and butter fresh. Fräulein Pechwitz had a room in the attic where she slept. Lynette knew that she could still sleep for a while before she had to get up for school when she heard the key turning in the front door lock in the mornings; then she would turn over happily onto her other side. But today it was Sunday.

Lynette put on a warm dress and woollen stockings. The flat was still quiet despite the busyness in the kitchen. Through the windows, the sun threw bright light beams in which dust was floating. The dust was a bit like snow. Or like bubbles that rose when she dived under water in summertime, though dust did not rise but fell. There was always dust; nobody really knew where it came from. Even Fräulein Pechwitz's duster could not get rid of it.

Lynette lowered the long-handled spoon into the tall glass where strawberries were slumbering redly under the white yoghurt. Father lifted his cup of hot black coffee. He wore a white shirt and tie. Neither Mutti nor Fräulein Pechwitz was able to get the shirt collars quite right for him; they were never stiff enough. His skin had a pinkish tinge from shaving. He always had a thorough shave and his skin felt as soft as Mutti's when Lynette kissed his cheek in the morning. Everything was correct about him, though it was not a weekday but Sunday; today he did not go to the office but to the football. He went there in the afternoon when Hungary played; he always went to the football when Hungary played. Mutti ran the comb along Bibs' parting once again to make sure that it was straight. Then it was time to leave and walk a few blocks to where the church was. Mutti was a keen singer and her tremolo voice was quivering. In Lynette's mind, the servers' ringing blended in with the ringing of the tram. The tram wore a red corset, moving along speedily and almost without any noise. The *Herr Conducteur* appeared when you had settled down. A lady with a broad-brimmed hat was sitting in front of Lynette; the hat left its imprint on the pictures that were gliding past outside. Water was glittering between dark bridges while tall houses silently lined the riverbanks. A boat with two rowers ploughed past and several swans swam leisurely near a pillar; time and again they dipped their long necks into the water's rippled silver. St. Vitus's Cathedral rose gloomily up to the clouds as if it was trying to build a bridge. But not a bridge between the two sides of the city – a bridge that linked the ethereal realm with the firm ground underneath. Beyond the cathedral lay Lawrence Hill in autumnal colours. And between the leaves you could see the Eiffel Tower, Prague's Eiffel Tower that was somewhat smaller than its distant cousin.

Now houses and shops with colourful displays were filling the tram's window. People were hurrying past and there were so many cars that one followed another without a break. A building with columns sat majestically above an imposing flight of stairs.

'Muzeum, Museum,' the conductor called out and joked: 'The second word is German.'

They had to get out at the next stop. There Mutti went to the cloth merchant Seidler who was called either František or Franz depending on whether you read the first name under or above the line. Then the coffee house lured you with its chocolate gateaux that were Lynette's favourite. But she was

**14**

running past the coffee house and further on; there, where the imperial looking boulevard ended in another wide and open street, many people were jostling each other.

There was a metallic din of music and hoarse voices blended into it. It was Czech that they were shouting: 'Aržije Moskva! Aržije Moskva!' She was pushing past a lady. A gentleman pointed at her and said, laughing: 'Look at this little nosy-parker!' Now she was standing right in front where neither a back nor an arm or leg restricted her view. Men were marching past, hurling up their fists. A young fellow with long dark hair and a beret on top of it was waving a flag that was red. Blood was red, so was the autumn with its leaves. From the upper corner of the flag a sickle shone forth that was crossed by a hammer. Why are they shouting like that and looking so angry, Lynette thought, as if there weren't a lovely coffee house right round the corner. Should she take the wild flag-waver by the hand and persuade Mutti to treat him to a chocolate gateau? The men stopped. But they could not have got any further anyway because of the barriers. And it would have looked a bit silly if they had turned round to march up a second time. A man distinguished by a beer belly and a carefully twirled moustache got up on a platform. While he was clearing his throat and getting his notes ready, Lynette looked for a gap in the human wall that immediately closed once again after she had pushed into it. That was the same as with water which also filled any vacuum straight away. She stretched her fists out, forcing her way through the crowd... then somebody touched her arm. It was Mutti: Lynette had to get up, everyone else was already standing. That she had to be so far away with her thoughts all the time, even here in the church.

There was still the smell of food in the flat. Lynette had been playing the piano for a while now while Father was away. When she pushed open the door to the children's room, she saw her brother sitting on his bed; he had one of her dolls in his lap, swaying it and humming gently. He had his head lowered so that he did not notice Lynette straight away. Then he looked up and it was most likely embarrassment that coloured his cheeks red. He pushed the doll away and it fell to the ground. Well, that was her brother: he always pretended to be tough on the outside, probably because he thought he had to be like that as a boy. And now she had caught him playing with dolls. She bent down to pick up Margot. Bibs had crawled into a corner and did not seem quite to know what to do next. His hair fell down to his shoulders; it was wavy and silky: a girl's hair. Mutti enjoyed running her fingers through his hair. Bibi was her favourite. She always accused Lynette of 'pulling a face'. But she only looked like that because she felt sad. Her brother never seemed to be sad. He raved and shouted; that was how he got rid of any anguish and torment. She, on the other hand, suppressed her sorrow and even a bar of chocolate did not help. Her brother could rave so much that his hair was flying around his head while he got deep red in his face; he screamed then and whacked the air with his fists, almost like Petr who did the same with his ruler. Mutti dashed towards Bibs when he held his breath, her arms wide open. But Fräulein Pechwitz only shook her head then, smiling: 'He has the *buhst* again; that's all,' she said and Lynette thought about the word *buhst*, which she had heard nowhere else; Fräulein Pechwitz seemed to have made it up especially to describe this very particular condition of Bibi's.

16

Jilka came at last. Now they would be going to the park. Mutti would have a quiet afternoon to read around in her novels. Sometimes Lynette leafed through the books, looking at the illustrations. There a simple girl was kneeling next to a tall gentleman, who stood in front of a palatial flight of stairs, or, through the window from behind her flowerpots, a young woman was looking down longingly at a gallant beau who was waving his handkerchief. Those were the books Mutti liked best. But when talking to Uncle Jacques, she only mentioned Goethe or Schiller. The two Classics were kept behind glass in neat editions; as with any other treasure, they were hardly ever touched, it was enough to know that they were there. Maybe Father had read those editions once. But now he hardly read anything but books written in other languages. He had conversation classes with a woman from Salamanca; she had left her homeland a few years ago because of the civil war and was now living in Prague. Later on he began to read a thick and famous book that was about some kind of knight.

Jilka strode ahead while Lynette trotted behind with her brother. Before crossing each street, Jilka took them both by the hand, looked to the right and left for any automobiles, but there were none. All the streets were deserted. It was never as quiet as on Sunday afternoons when even the small corner shops, entered by descending several steps, were closed. An old woman with a shrivelled face was looking out of a window; she had a cushion in front of her, on which her elbows were resting. Looking out of the window was her Sunday pursuit and she was most likely pleased now that she could see Jilka and the two children, who were on their way to the park.

The park they were heading for was the big, real park where many birch trees grew with their white shiny trunks but also oaks, sycamores, beeches, chestnuts. It was autumn and therefore a lot of useful things were lying about. The dark chestnuts with their wonderfully grained surfaces as if they had just been polished made magnificent marbles; Bibs put so many in his pockets that the trousers' fabric bulged. There were noses; Lynette pushed their two sticky sides apart and fitted them onto her own nose. Jilka got such a nose as well. There were shells and leafy sails. People in their Sunday best were strolling along. Herr Novák was among them; he lifted his hat, though they could not respond to his greeting since none of them wore a hat, not even Jilka. He said something jocular to Jilka in Czech, laughed more about it than anybody else, then walked on with bouncy steps, swinging his walking stick. Some street urchins were shouting rude names after a lavishly done-up lady who was taking her poodle for a walk; then they disappeared behind an old, decaying wall. Bibs went for the bushes; he kept looking around to make sure that nobody was following. He need not have worried because of Lynette; she knew his *tschipperle* from their joint bathing. That was how Mutti called his little man and to Lynette it sounded like a word which had been taken over from the Czech. When doing *lulu*, Bibs was able to stand while she had to crouch down. But she did not envy him, for women were able to wear colourful clothes, yet men were always dressed in the same old grey stuff.

Bibs broke off a twig and made it whistle through the air. A young man with an open shirt and a cap with a red star on it was sitting in front of a small Russian-style palazzo; the sun and the sky were mirrored by its shining onion dome. He jumped to his feet when he saw Jilka. They had a lot to tell each other while he was putting his arm around her. Jan got a few pennies from the pocket of his jacket where he carried loose change. He gave them to Lynette, jerking his head towards the merry-go-round. Jan did not speak German but Lynette understood what he meant, even if Jilka had not said anything. From the back of her white horse with its golden harness, Lynette could see them both sitting on the bench. The leaves formed a colourfully painted wall, almost like the wall in a room. Then both disappeared behind her back, only to emerge again as the horse moved up and down. After the merry-go-round had stopped, Lynette and Bibs stood next to the bench. Bibs was still holding his twig, lashing mercilessly down on invisible foes who seemed to be lurking everywhere in wait for him. Did they want an ice cream? It was autumn and the season for ice cream was really over but there was still an ice cream man because it was warm and a Sunday. He opened one of the two copper basins, scooping out a white ball; then he took the lid off the other basin: chocolate. The donkey was standing there patiently, its muzzle in a food-filled bag. The ice cream man had dark skin and almost jet black eyes; he seemed to come from far away and Lynette imagined him travelling the streets in winter selling roasted chestnuts when there was no business with ice cream.

Everything was clear and transparent in winter. You were able to see the castle already from the other side as soon as you set foot in the park. The cathedral that could look forbidding in its powerful massiveness stood out stark against the grey sky. And further down, through the bare branches, you could see the city from where the noise came roaring upwards.

You snow flake, you little one, with your white tutu on... they stretched out their hands, catching the snow that melted.

**19**

The white snow filled the space between the dark stems and it all looked very solemn as if the park had put on its ermine coat.

Jan was pulling the sledge. From time to time he stopped, panting, and took off his red starred cap to wipe off the sweat while Bibs and Lynette shouted at him in Czech to carry on pulling them. They had rolled the snow for the snowman in the small park, together with Uncle Jacques. They rolled the snow around the swings and across the flower beds where stems and frozen leaves appeared against the backdrop of brown soil. Uncle Jacques tied an old headscarf of Mutti's around the snowman's head and called the snowman his *bonnefemme de neige*. Every morning Bibs ran to the window to check whether the snowman was still there. Usually it was dark and the snow was glimmering blue under the street lamps' reflection. Then the weather grew warmer. The façades of the houses opposite seemed to have moved closer overnight; the white dress had brown rips, and there was nothing left of the snowman other than a heap of dirty snow with the headscarf on top.

# 2

Bibi was crying; everything disappeared but there was nothing that could be done about it. Mother said that's the way things were. The snowman had disappeared and slowly the holidays were disappearing as well. But school remained. School days lined up before her in an endless row, and every day was just like the last.

In the schoolyard Lynette nibbled at the healthy apple that her mother had put in her satchel, but she was longing for a bar of chocolate. Over there her brother was rollicking about. He still wrote with chalk on a slate board while she already used an exercise book. There was always a lot of red in her exercise book after the teacher had gone through it, especially on the maths pages where numbers were crossed out again and again. You had to concentrate too much when doing maths and she... yes, she preferred to be carried away by her own mood and thoughts. Essay-writing was more to her taste;

there one sentence flowed on easily from the last and you only had to be careful not to misspell anything. There was almost always a *Good* written under her Czech homework. You could say Czech was in her blood. Baba, Father's mother, her grandmother, was Czech; she had always called her 'Baba' as far back as she could remember; maybe she had wanted to say Babitschka but had said Baba instead and since then her grandmother had been called Baba.

Baba hardly ever came to Prague. Maybe it was not the best time for a visit right now though... Lynette quite liked it when grey clouds swept across the sky, casting their shadows on houses and river. It was difficult to walk in the slush; in the huge puddles, the many-windowed house fronts gaped at you. There was a green shimmer around the buds in the little park while the earth exuded a strong smell; blackbirds rustled among the leaves which still clung there from last year. The swings dangled forlornly and the water beneath rippled with wavelets running across its clear face at each gust of wind.

Father grabbed his hat. Bibi's coat was buttoned right up to his chin and Mutti had a fur stole around her shoulders and a muff on her hands. 'It was good after all that we came early,' Father said when he saw crowds of people lining the pavement already. Lynette pulled her woollen hat further down over her face when a particularly cold gust of wind blew through the streets. From time to time Father bent forward and looked down the track in the direction the parade was expected from. Why had Uncle Jacques not come with them? He had stayed in the living room with his books. Mutti had tried to persuade him to come, though she had not been all that keen on going herself, which was probably partly due to her fear of catching a cold. At any rate Uncle Jacques declared that he had to work and this meant for him reading poems, and then writing something about them for his professor. So Mutti waited in the cold with nobody to make conversation; and surely, once in a while, Uncle Jacques would have turned with a remark to her, the Mademoiselle. But suddenly shouting could be heard from further down.

Steps resounded on the cobbled pavement, coming closer. But really it was one single mighty step. In between you could hear the high-pitched beat of the horses' hooves. The soldiers' boots were tall, black and shiny. Their long coats were drawn in at the waist by broad belts. The helmets did not sit on the top of the soldiers' heads as shakos did but pushed further down to cover their necks as well. Under the helmets the soldiers' foreheads and chins appeared angular and hard, as if carved in stone. There was something of Rome in those soldiers, Mutti mused, something proud and warlike that reminded you of Mars, but the soldiers of the Old Austria had looked even smarter with their colourful plumes and golden buttons.

'Yes, Madame,' said an old gentleman who stood behind Mutti, 'those were soldiers for operettas but these here are destined for operas, Wagner, *Götterdämmerung...*'

New columns were approaching; the rhythm their boots were pounding was merciless, unstoppable. The onlookers were shaking their fists; the policemen formed a cordon and they struggled to hold the people back. The faces of the crowd were full of hate and bitter disappointment. Sporadic cheers were heard, filtering through the soldiers' footfall. A bouquet of flowers was thrown onto the cobbled street. The people pushed forward, stretching their necks. There the man, whom Lynette already knew from the newsreel screen, was coming; he stood upright in his horseless carriage, which made him

23

stand out, raised his importance, and Lynette thought of the German folk song *Hoch auf dem gelben Wagen*, High Up on the Yellow Carriage. But this carriage was not yellow but black and elongated. There was no friendly mail coach driver sitting on a coach box, his legs apart and blowing a golden horn. Instead the figure of the Leader rose up next to the driver; the Leader's face was almost invisible between his coat's high collar and his cap which he had pulled down. He held onto the windscreen of his vehicle with one hand while he bent the other hand backwards. Neither his arm nor his body moved so that he reminded Lynette of a figure carved in wood. In her mind she saw the figures of the astronomical clock in the Old Town Hall moving past her; and it seemed to her that, among apostles and allegories, there was also this figure which abruptly turned towards the onlooker with its arm bent backwards before it dipped into the dark again.

Column after column went marching past. This was different from the time when she had pushed her way into the crowd at the end of the imperial boulevard; then the number of men who rallied round the red flag had soon been exhausted but now there seemed to be no end to the parade. Maybe this was a merry-go-round and everybody was waiting for the reappearance of the black stretched limousine. A flag fluttered out of the window of one of the houses further up; the flag was red but there was a white circle cut in its middle, filled by a black cross with crooked arms. People leaned on the windowsill, shouting: 'Heil, heil...' The glass of the window panes trembled when the tanks rolled past. The tanks' chains rattled across the cobble stones, squashing the flowers and turning them into a mushy paste. The tanks' guns were moving slowly from one side to the other; men with rifles were crouching down in hatches. How strange these square steel monsters look between the soft curls of the houses' decorated fronts, Lynette thought. Once she had come here with her school, equipped with a drawing pad; they had studied the buildings so that they could paint them. The roofs were wavy and frequently the walls formed a protruding bump. Some of the solid wood portals led to stairs that went steeply and narrowly up under arches. There were corners, alcoves and oriels everywhere, and the houses had gables that were bent down by the weight of the years. Wall paintings were fading and the moulding that decorated the windows with garlands and blossoms was crumbling. Now tanks were rattling past and the soldiers' boots were beating out their rhythm. Again Lynette thought of the men marching at the end of the imperial boulevard: 'heil, aržije, Moskva, heil, aržije, heil, Moskva…' was resounding in her head while hammer, cross and scythe were hurled together in a wild red dance.

She opened her eyes and leaned her cheek gently against Mutti's coat which felt soft. Father and her brother were still staring at the columns; maybe Bibi was comparing the soldiers to those that were waiting for him at home. Mutti was breathing in and out deeply, wrapping the stole closer around her shoulders. She was looking in the direction of the flat. But even if all four of them had wanted to walk away, it would hardly have been possible; the pavement was heaving with a dense, black human crowd and a cordon of policemen sealed it off from the road.

The castle gazed down out of innumerable windows. She knew that until recently the former Czech president had been living up there near the dark outline of St Vitus' Cathedral. Not far from it was the big park. That was called Letná by

25

the Czech, which meant something like Summer Hill. There the lilac was in bloom; Lynette had seen it herself when she and her brother were taken there by Jilka. While she was thinking of the park, the boots' regular beat turned into a dark, muffled background against which her thoughts roamed.

Then the boots' beat stopped. Up there the castle's gate was closing slowly. Nobody was to be seen there: the gate seemed to have closed itself, without any human help. The long worm with the stretched black limousine at its heart got stuck between the houses. Mutti pointed out the old aristocratic palaces of the Sternbergs and Schwarzenbergs to Lynette and Bibi. Lynette thought the grand houses seemed to be looking down disdainfully at the columns of soldiers which hesitated now, not knowing what to do; they were waiting in front of the high gate which had seemingly barred itself. Of course, times had been bad when these palaces had been built, too, but those past days now seemed soft and mellow, covered by the patina of several bygone centuries.

A tank rattled up the cobbled stones, past the front columns which moved out of its way; the road up to the castle was narrow. The tank directed its gun at the gate. Several crows rose up from one of the roofs. There was no sound apart from the crows' croaking; everything had turned completely silent. St. Vitus's Cathedral had a gloomy, threatening appearance. Lynette remembered how she had once vertically looked up the front of the cathedral – and it had not been the clouds that moved but the towers, the portal, the ground that she stood on. Now everybody was waiting for the tank to fire its gun. Who knew whether partisans were lying in wait behind the gate? Then it would all end as it did in Bibi's room; only these soldiers here were no toy soldiers who got up again. Did all boys secretly love wars? So it seemed to her when she saw his sparkling eyes. But Father's face was worried.

The tank rattled backwards; there would be a huge bang now; Lynette covered her ears. But no... there was something moving at the gate. Slowly it was opening; as it had closed itself, so it opened itself. The tank advanced. Were the partisans lurking inside to blow up the iron monster with a hand grenade?

Everything stayed calm. Column by column, the soldiers began to march again, stepping into the vast area of the castle with its myriad courtyards, gardens and palaces, till the last soldier had disappeared. The Czech flag was taken down and in its place the red flag with a crooked cross resplendent in its centre was raised.

'The swastika,' said Uncle Jacques who sat in the living room, looking up from his books, 'is not new; it's old, an ancient symbol. But these days everything is brought together, mixed up... it's called potpourri, isn't it? In India, I'm sure, the swastika will remain holy. We Europeans take ourselves too seriously; we think that we are the world but you only need to take an atlas, press your thumb on it and Europe is no more.'

Yes, Uncle Jacques... for some reason he had begun to ruminate like this all the time. Also Lynette hardly ever saw him with his briefcase; most of the time he left the flat without it. It was rare now for him to smile when he saw her. She found it hard to believe now that he had once opened the lift door for her with a cheerful 'Mademoiselle'. But Father carried on going to his office, playing the violin, attending his chess evenings. Mutti kept on getting up almost at the same time as Fräulein Pechwitz. Only Jilka did not come any more. So Mutti took them to the park once in a while, which was not the same for there was no Jan to give them money for the merry-go-round or an ice cream. Mutti also fussed around all the time; once they had not wrapped themselves up properly in their scarves, another time the top buttons of their cardigans were not done up. But they still fell ill despite all the fuss.

Whether she had got it from Bibs or Bibs from her... the fact was that they were both lying in bed with fever for a couple of days. No, Mutti's worrying had made no difference. Lynette enjoyed those days in the warm bed and the snug feeling of safety and comfort that went with it. She could let herself go; nobody expected anything from her. Once in a while Mutti came and had a look at the invalids. Then again Lynette could follow her own dreams. The fever tinged these dreams with its vivid colours. How luxuriously cosy she felt when she saw the fidgety Petr with his ruler in the far distance; and the screeching noise of the chalk on the blackboard which went through you so horribly in the classroom was softened by her memory. Such thoughts intensified her sense of a protected cosiness and she happily gave in to them. She soared high up like Petr on his swing till the chains were hanging slack; there she was sitting, completely free, not holding on to anything. At the same time she had the reassuring caress of the pillow beneath her neck.

Tweet-tweet, tweet-tweet... sang a little yellow finch sitting on the other side of the fence. The finch seemed intent on teasing her; she was not allowed in her school break to go where the bird was sitting in a tree. The languid days of her illness had long gone. Those light days had been followed by dark, gloomy ones, not so different from Father's chessboard, where white squares alternated with dark ones.

She was running towards the swing in the small park. All of a sudden Herr Novák was standing in front of her. He had come up from the side and stepped between her and the swing. Slowly he was moving towards her till he was so close that she had to get out of his way. The only place to go was the flowerbed; her shoes sank into the heavy soil. She felt her satchel on her back weighing her down. Far above her, Herr Novák's face loomed up. She avoided the steely blue eyes, looked at the grey moustache that sat above his mouth like a roof; his mouth moved and as it did so it bared its teeth. It spat out saliva and words that Lynette did not understand, that she did not even hear for she was staring at the stick Herr Novák had got out from behind his back. The next moment a trail of fire was laid across her legs. She ran straight through the bed even though she trampled on some of the flowers that had opened today, one of the first truly warm days of the year. She pushed her way through the bushes out of the park. In the house entrance she rubbed across the scratches and the burning fire trail on her legs. Herr Novák stood next to the bench, looking across at her, and she pressed the bell a second time. Where on earth was Mutti? She had probably taken Bibs with her; his school had finished one hour earlier today. And what about Fräulein Pechwitz? Maybe she was resting a little in her room under the roof; Lynette did not begrudge her the rest since she was busy all day... but why did she have to rest right now? Herr Novák began to pace up and down with elastic steps; while doing so, he kept flicking the stick against his empty palm. Like a predator that was about to jump on its prey, Lynette thought and wondered whether he objected to white socks. That was what Germans wore: white socks. Yes, maybe it was her white socks that enraged him so much.

Into the hallway came a girl, not much taller than herself; she was carrying two heavy shopping bags which she put down on the floor next to Lynette. She knew the girl: it was the servant girl of the Blumentritts. She was a blue-eyed, cheerful little thing who talked all the time – chattering, as Mutti would have called it. That was how Lynette should have been; then Mutti would have liked her more. The servant girl was called Anneliese and her plaits dangled round her shoulders when she bent down for the shopping bags. She would need to look for new employers soon, times were changing, everybody made a face when she told them who she was working for, yes yes, and she did not want to be turned out onto the street in the end, so it was better for her to watch out... And while she was chattering, they got into the lift and it rumbled up slowly, too slowly for Lynette who was stretching her skirt down across her legs so that Anneliese would not see anything.

Lynette hesitated at the threshold, peering into the dark corridor. When Anneliese noticed that Lynette was shy she let out a light peal of laughter. Nobody would gobble her up, no, there was no wolf but she would need to take off her shoes, yuck, what had she done to her shoes. Anneliese picked them up gingerly as if she were not the Blumentritts' servant girl but a princess. She told Lynette to wait, she was only going to Madame; there was no need to worry, everything would be fine. Then red-cheeked, cheerful Anneliese disappeared.

Frau Blumentritt, the wife of Professor Blumentritt, was gaunt and tall; she had shiny black hair and her skin appeared to be yellowish and dry, like parchment. She reminded Lynette more of a ghost than a human being of flesh and blood as she walked in front of her, dressed in a dark floating robe, to show Lynette the way to the living room. But Lynette's steps too were softened so that they were hardly audible; her feet sank deep into the carpet which really consisted of several carpets that had been put on top of each other; Lynette saw their edges like steps. 'Do sit down; Anneliese will bring you a glass of milk,' said Frau Blumentritt and she also disappeared.

Lynette sat down on a chair close to the wall. She pressed her knees together, took care that her skirt covered the red streak that was still burning. She had the glass of milk in her hand and grasping it seemed to prevent her from falling, losing herself. She was not drinking it as an excuse so that she still had something to hold on to. There was nobody in the room. Anneliese was helping Madame with packing in another room. Here too stood a box into which a few books had been put. But most of the books were still on the shelves that covered a whole wall. Pieces of paper stuck out of some books, and often the books' spines were torn or completely missing. These were books that were used every day; that was exactly the reason why they induced reverence and respect in Lynette. Her family, on the other hand, kept books behind glass. Among them were stamp albums, mother's novels, a few neat editions of Classical works, and though they were much more magnificent than the books the Blumentritts had, Lynette did not look at them with the same awe.

A candelabra with seven candles stood on the piano. There was a tall bureau with drawers on each side in the room and a landscape with mountains hung in a solemn golden frame above the sofa, which had a silver fringe along the bottom edge. So, this was where Professor Blumentritt lived, though he was not really a professor but a *Privatdozent*, which probably meant more or less the same. Her parents' furniture was walnut too; but this furniture here appeared darker, more forbidding. Small wonder that Professor Blumentritt was so unapproachable and that she felt dejected when she had to greet him.

The shadows of the rubber plant's leaves trembled on the rug. That was how Lynette noticed that somebody had entered the room, for the parquet flooring rocked beneath each step. Frau Blumentritt said in her smoky voice that Mutti seemed to have come back now, that she had heard a key turning in the lock next door. Lynette gave Anneliese the glass that was still almost full and thanked the wife of Professor Blumentritt by curtsying which Mutti had taught her to do on such occasions.

It had not been Mutti whom Frau Blumentritt had heard but Fräulein Pechwitz; now she began to boil the laundry in a huge pot. Where had Mutti gone to? Lynette sat down at the window and looked down the familiar road that seemed alien to her all of a sudden, almost hostile. The houses had got piercing eyes and the metal framework from which the swings hung looked like a gallows. It was strange that everything was shifting all the time; nothing stayed the same. At least Herr Novák had disappeared. Maybe he was roaming the streets looking for more victims in white socks. But Lynette was safe in her room.

Mutti came at last. She was carrying the shopping basket in one hand and holding Bibs with the other. She sighed when she put the basket down in the pantry, running her fingers through her hair. 'The Provazník didn't have any semolina; I've been going to him for seven years now and he has always had semolina. And now he suddenly didn't have any. But of course, I know why. They can be crafty, the Czechs, there's a bit of a Schweik in every one of them. That's why we had to go to another shop which was far away. But Frau Blumentritt has been looking after you; they're fine people, Professor Blumentritt and his wife; what a difference it makes when people are educated.'

In the evening, when Lynette got into the bath, Mutti saw the red streak, which Lynette had hidden for so long. She called Father; and Lynette felt ashamed when they both bent over her. It seemed to her as if she were to blame for that red streak. Father shook his head, cursing Herr Novák, but when Mutti asked what they should do about him, Father did not know either. It was probably best to keep quiet since the whole atmosphere was already very heated. Hatred was flaring up everywhere: these were bad times. It was not really their fault, of course; they had never chosen the time they had to live in. Uncle Jacques had done the right thing – he had gone to Paris a few weeks ago. He had left Mutti a couple of volumes of French poetry and had waved Lynette good-bye from the back window of a black taxi. And now Uncle Jacques was surely strolling down a broad, light-studded boulevard while the bath water filled her limbs with luxurious lethargy. Slowly the fizzing foam drifts were collapsing with Uncle Jacques, dissolving into the night's black background.

After the bath Lynette was allowed to stay up for a short while. Father was sitting at the table in the living room, a stamp album in front of him. He was putting in the new stamps; among them was one of the Leader gripping a rostrum. Mutti bent over her doily, her shoulders hunched up; again and again she glared around the room as if she needed to reassure herself that at least here everything was still in its place. The V-neck of her dress showed the skin on her chest, puckered and blotchy. A moth was knocking against the shade of the standard lamp.

'What a day,' Mutti said, sighing, and told Father about Herr Provazník, who had not wanted to sell her any semolina; she had her hands folded in her lap. Father closed the album, nodding at Mutti. The Czech waiter in the Deutsches Haus had been made redundant. Maybe it was not just because of the *tafelspitz* that Father went there but also because of this waiter. It does take such a lot to make a really good waiter, Father said. Either waiters were too servile or not attentive enough. But this waiter looked after every guest without ever being obtrusive. And he had brought Father the newspaper together with the coffee without the need for Father to say anything for he knew when Father wanted his coffee and which paper he preferred. That pleased Father, whom Mutti maintained was vain.

Then Father said suddenly: 'There's an export manager's job going in Teplitz. Maybe I should apply for it, though it seems a pity to leave now... of course, life in Teplitz would be quite different from life in Prague...'

Mutti started, not answering straight away. She was dreaming of her novels, Lynette thought. Mutti was floating towards him, the gallant beau, who was standing in front of a flight of palatial stairs, waiting for her... She was gazing at the singer, striding through the velvety realms of a stage where everything was dissolving in melancholic beauty, coming towards her...

Mutti shook her head and shrugged her shoulders, then said quickly, her words tripping out of her mouth like the ringing of small bells: 'You talk of Teplitz, Mani. But it doesn't have to be

**34**

Teplitz. Think of Aussig! Aussig isn't far from Teplitz. There are good piano teachers for Lynette in Aussig too. I only have to ask Karl. And there's a theatre in Aussig. There's everything there, though we haven't got the time anyway. How often do we go out? You have your chess evenings, your conversation classes. But there's a chess club in Aussig too. And you can brush up your Italian with Herr del Vesco. Yes, and there's Herr Stelzig. You've hardly seen them lately, that will be different once we're in Aussig. And then Aussig is a German town, you feel safe there. And in Aussig...'

'Yes yes, I know,' Father said, stopping her, 'you never really wanted to come to Prague.'

# 3

The men from the moving company were big, strong fellows with massive hands. But they held the porcelain very gently and it was Fräulein Pechwitz who broke a cup. Fräulein Pechwitz appeared to be very excited. Mutti had already assured her that she could stay with the family. She did not have anybody else: poor Fräulein Pechwitz. And as she prepared breakfast in the kitchen, she told the story of her life once again. Lynette had heard this story many times before.

Her father had been a rich industrialist. When she was a child, they had dined at a table which was so big that it would only just have fitted into the *Palace* room; Fräulein Pechwitz put her kitchen knife down to indicate, with both her arms at full stretch, the size of the table. And he travelled a lot, her father; he brought her, his only daughter, the most beautiful presents from such trips. This sounded almost like a fairy tale and, like a fairy tale, it had different versions so that Lynette was curious to see how it would go on. Yes, said Fräulein Pechwitz, that's how it was but then one day they had been turned out of their house. Her father had hanged himself and her mother had died of a broken heart soon afterwards. This was the version of the story that Fräulein Pechwitz preferred today. But sometimes her father had shot himself and her mother had spent the rest of her days in a lunatic asylum. Whatever the version, the story always had a tragic ending. Anyway, her father had gone bankrupt. He had always been honest, hard-working. But the Jews had had no pity. They had wanted money, only money. They would have sold their own grandmother for money; that's how they were, the Jews. Lynette thought of the Blumentritts who had probably been in England for quite a while by now. She remembered the many books and the candelabra with seven candles on the piano; she had not seen many luxurious things in their flat, except perhaps for the carpets. The emphasis had been on learning and not on material gain.

'I had to get work then,' said Fräulein Pechwitz, 'washing has made my hands coarse. Is there a man who likes a woman who has coarse hands?' But now she was happy that she was here, that she had a family and she had grown so fond of the *knödliges Fräulein*. That's how she talked while boiling the breakfast eggs. For the last time in the old flat.

The rooms seemed to expand as they were being emptied. Lynette's steps resounded; and when she spoke aloud, there was an echo to her voice. Light flooded the parquet flooring; it did not stop any more at the dark lines where the furniture had stood until recently. The men put up a ladder to take the chandelier from the ceiling.

'Please be very careful,' Mutti said, 'it's genuine Bohemian glass; Bohemian is the best.'

She asked Lynette to go down to the basement with her when the men had safely packed the chandelier. There stood a box with Lynette's things. Mutti thought perhaps they could give something away so that they did not have to move all this stuff. The box was her treasure box, Lynette thought, her very own treasure box, for memories were treasures. Mutti had opera tickets between the pages of her novels; but sometimes there were crumbling rose petals instead of tickets or a poem that Mutti had copied in steep, narrow writing using not the Latin but the German script. These were all things that reminded Mutti of something: that was why they were precious. But this box here was filled with Lynette's memories. They were memories of a girl and not a woman whose memories reached deep back into the past, for a woman already had a good part of her life behind her, whereas with her it was still stretching endlessly into the future.

A stuffed bear with greasy, scarred fur lay there, his snout threadbare. A little monkey clanged its cymbals after Lynette had wound it up. The Lauritsch grandmother had once given her the farmyard with the painted animals. There was a crumpled dress in the middle of it all. She spread it out in front of her, smoothing it out slowly. It was the fancy dress that had turned her into a lily of the valley. Mutti had sewn it before she had gone to school even. She grasped the cap's petals and saw herself back in the Waldstein palace again. The perfume of a lilac bush wafted over a wall. But maybe it did not smell of lilac then and it was something added by her imagination. Long tables were lined up in the great hall while darkness filled the arcades with its bluish tinge. Little flowers, mushrooms, butterflies, fairies, dwarfs were pushing their way to the tables and had their plates filled by their mothers.

There were colourful drinks and countless gateaux, yes, even chocolate gateaux. There was no end to the food; it was like the fairy tale of the *tischleindeckdich* where the table continuously spread itself with new feasts. Outside, the lights and lanterns swayed in the light breeze. A small orchestra was playing *Alle Vöglein sind schon da* and *Winter ade*. Lynette saw a water nymph rising out of a seashell while horsemen were chasing a fleeing enemy in another fresco. The putti on their pedestals had armed themselves with bow and arrow. Warfare had made the builder of this palace rich; he had been a pushy man, somebody who had wanted to get to the top whatever the cost. Still... there was beauty in these gardens and the hall, at least during that balmy spring night. All the sweat, the blood had been forgotten. Heroic figures were looking down from the walls; they had never lived but in legend. The lilac's perfume was rising up from her memories, blending in with the smell of mothballs which was increasing in strength until there was only the smell of mothballs and she was kneeling again in the basement in front of the crumpled dress.

'I want to keep it, Mutti,' she said wistfully since they were about to move away from Prague. The way she felt at this moment she would have liked to stay; she had got used to the city.

It was cold next morning. But there was not a single cloud in the sky and it would surely be another hot day. The sun had burnt the grass in the small park dry in some places. The bushes appeared less full now than in spring; a few leaves were already changing colour. The mud beneath the swings had turned into yellow dust. The sun had not risen above the roofs when Father locked the flat's front door; the house opposite still lay in darkness. Inside this house Herr Novák was sleeping his pensioner's sleep. At least he would not be worrying her from now on.

Fräulein Pechwitz carried the 'Grub Sack', as Mutti called the bag with the food in it, including their breakfast. Apart from this bag, they did not have any luggage; the moving company had taken care of everything else. They went on foot. It was not all that far to the station. There was no point in getting a taxi since car rides made Father sick. Once, when his boss had taken him for a ride in his saloon car (which he could not refuse) he had got out of it completely pale in the face. It was probably the petrol smell blending with the smell of leather that made him sick. The tram passed, ringing, and shortly Lynette saw faces behind windows; these were all people who had to get out early to work down in the city. A grocer was pushing up the shutters of his shop with a pole while another shop, a few roads further on, already had trays full of fruit displayed outside. Two tired men in uniform staggered along; they seemed to have spent the night celebrating. The yellow station stood out against the Moldau's velvety blue background.

'No, no return, singles please,' Father said at the ticket window.

St. Vitus' Cathedral rose up above the glittering water. In front of it flourished the big park with its greenery. Only now did she realise how long it had been since she had been there. Why had they not talked Mutti into going over to the park during the last days? The last time they had been, there was a wonderfully sweet scent in the air, for the linden trees were

**40**

in bloom. They had rested on a bench on their way home; from here she saw the city lie, far beneath her, with its countless domes and towers onto which the evening shed its light, so that it looked as if the whole city were coated in a delicate layer of gold.

The train rattled on and the next bend made the cathedral, the Moldau and the park disappear. Bye-bye, Prague! The train was in no hurry; it moved along at a leisurely pace. There was an abundance of time; her head reclined, Lynette let herself be carried along by the train's lazy rhythm. Now the train stopped again. It was a small station; the yellow paint was flaking off its walls. Weeds grew between the pavement slabs and chipped earthenware pots were overgrown with geraniums. It all looked a bit neglected, including the stationmaster who was stuffing his shirt into the front of his trousers. There was nothing wrong really with letting things slip a bit, Lynette thought – everything did not have to be so clear-cut and proper all the time. The portly stationmaster, who might have already stood here during the time of the Old Austria, lifted his signal and the train, very slowly, chugged itself into motion once again. Father spread open the newspaper. Bibi was jumping from one seat to the next, howling, as he thought the American natives did in the moss-green volumes. Father lowered his newspaper and looked over the top at Bibi who became quiet, sitting down next to Mutti. From the food bag she drew out an apple, which she gave to him. He began to chew the apple, to *schnurpseln*, as Mutti expressed it.

Rocks rose up high on one side and made the compartment dark. Sometimes night descended till the train left the tunnel and dipped into the daylight again. The Moldau ran along on the other side; it wound itself round the hills and the train track that followed its course became bendy. Nothing held Bibi back now. At one moment he pressed his face against the compartment's window, at the next he rushed out into the corridor, depending on which side the locomotive was emerging. Thick white smoke rose up from the chimney like cotton wool and the red wheels made the connecting rod jump. He wanted a train set for Christmas, a locomotive, just like this one. Lynette held him back when he was about to storm out into the corridor where a frail looking woman was approaching. Then she stood next to her brother who was looking out of the window and greedily taking it all in. She did not fuss around that much: after all, she had travelled this way once before, albeit in the opposite direction. She did not remember it, of course, but surely it had taken the train just as much effort then to steam around all those corners as it did now.

When the countryside opened up, the locomotive hid itself behind the long row of wagons. Lynette saw flat land sliding past; there were hops which climbed up high poles and rye, ready for reaping, stood in the fields. These fields were lined with red poppies. In between lay fallow fields where cow parsley grew in wild abundance. She would have loved walking through there now; some of the tall flowers would have reached above her head, swarming with butterflies and shimmering beetles whose long, sensitive antennas sounded out the world.

At the next station, a girl and a young man came into the compartment. Lynette had seen them already on the platform where they had cuddled up to each other. Now they were silently sitting next to each other in two seats, shyly surveying their new surroundings. The girl had pale-coloured eyes and her hair was blonde but not golden; it was lighter, like white

42

gold. Lynette would probably be sitting like this next to a young man one day; but there was still plenty of time till then.

Two stops further on, both of them got off the train. In the end they had talked quietly to each other in soft-sounding Czech. And Father had begun to read a thick book that he had been reading now for at least a month; it was called *Der Nachsommer* and Lynette imagined that throughout this book a tired sun shone sideways, different from the sun outside where nothing moved in the silent heat; only a bird of prey was circling high up in the blue sky.

Soon Father put the book away again. In the next compartment a woman talked so loudly that even Mutti, who was not as sensitive to noise as Father, started. The woman talked continuously; only once in a while could you hear a quiet 'yes' from a man who appeared to say it more out of habit than with real approval. Lynette bent forward, closing her eyes; though she tried to listen carefully, she could only make out several islands in the musical stream of words. She did not understand much because the woman was from the country and pronounced things differently from the way Lynette had been taught at school. Of course, Father understood every word; that was why he had been unable to carry on with his reading.

'Look there,' Lynette called out. Water stretched out under a bluish haze. Everything was so still and quiet and the water mirrored the silvery-leafed poplar trees which stood on the riverbanks. A barge was moving slowly past with the water receding smoothly under it, forming gently dispersing waves. An angler sat on the bank on a folding chair. Here and there a fish made bubbles rise... no sooner had the fish surfaced than it had gone. The water was smooth again: quiet, without a stir.

This river was not the Moldau any more but the Elbe. The Moldau had accompanied the train at the beginning when the track had been close to the rocks. The Moldau knew Prague and the park with the sweet scent of its linden. No doubt the ice cream man was there again. Lynette's imagination turned her old school into a building with open windows that had no bars and the trees' branches seemed to grow into the classroom where it was light as if no house giants rose up on the opposite side of the street. Even Petr seemed gentle now. Soon she would go to a different school that was called 'Realgymnasium'. There was not just one teacher who taught everything but a different teacher for each subject. And anyway, teachers were called 'professors' there. Again she thought of Professor Blumentritt. But he had been a professor at the university, the Karolinum where Mutti's two brothers, Uncle Karl and Uncle Franz, had been students. Surely Professor Blumentritt had got some new employment in England where the landscape was said to be green, gently undulating with broad trees in between, resembling a huge endless park. And for her too something had come to an end that would glide further and further back and something new would come in its place but she did not know yet what it would be.

Looking outside, she noticed that it was getting hilly again. Ash trees climbed up steep slopes. A small white church shone on a hilltop forest in the middle of green. In the valley apples and pears hung; though they were not quite ripe yet, they were heavy, bending the branches. In some places the soil had receded, baring the mountain, revealing rocks of dark sandstone. Bibs jumped up because the train was racing a motorcar that was going along on the road that meandered between the rail track and the river. The train pulled ahead but at the next stop the car overtook it again. A young woman who got on the train smiled at Father who put Bibs on his knee and played 'horsey-horsey'.

Again and again different hills came into sight. But no, that was not quite true; they were the same hills, only the distance which was continuously changing made the hills look unfamiliar each time Lynette looked at them. The first houses appeared; they had wooden balconies and balustrades. There were gardens dotted here and there. Factory chimneys rose up high; far away, on the other side, lay Schreckenstein castle on a rock. The train stopped. Bibi was about to rush out of the compartment but Mutti held him back by the corner of his cardigan. They had not quite arrived at the station. The locomotive set itself in motion once again and chugged along slowly. Roofs and walls came into sight. A few forlorn ash trees. Sooty pillars supporting the roofs of the platforms.

There was hardly anybody on the platform. Only some little old women wearing headscarves sat waiting, their baskets before them. Lynette had seen little old women like this in Prague where they sold herbs at street corners. The train finally came to a halt with a screech. A hefty woman in an elegant blue costume and white shoes minced out of the station waiting room. She waved. It was Auntie Bertha.

# 4

'So, there you are at last,' Auntie Bertha said loudly, treating them to a peal of laughter.

She opened her white leather handbag in the car and gave the children a sweet each. Uncle Wenka smiled tiredly behind the steering wheel. It went without saying that Auntie Bertha had a motorcar; that was *comme il faut*. There was enough room for everybody since Father was walking to the flat, accompanied by Fräulein Pechwitz. 'It's not that wonderful a flat Uncle has found for you but you can still look for something better later,' Auntie Bertha said, opening the front door.

The men from the moving company were already there, though they had left later than Lynette and her family. Vans were clearly faster than lazy, dallying trains that were bound to their winding tracks. Some furniture had been moved into the flat already and the men were having a break, snacking on some food they had brought into the kitchen. Lynette opened the piano and her hand slid down the keyboard. It seemed to her as if the sound had changed, which was probably because it was standing in a different room now. Auntie Bertha told the men what to do. I'm sure that the dresser should have gone on the other side, Lynette thought, and Mutti suppressed a sigh but did not say anything in front of Auntie Bertha.

Lynette ran into her room. This room was solely hers; her brother would have his own room from now on. She was pleased that the window looked out onto the street again and not onto a courtyard. The far distance was filled with treetops. It was a wall of green leaves, tall and lush, different from the small park in Prague that had looked forlorn between the grey house giants. Mutti told her that this was the Town Park. She was allowed to go there since in the flat she would only have been in the way at the moment.

She walked towards the green wall in which chinks opened up as she approached it. Full blossoms bent the heads of rosebushes that were planted in a long bed in the middle of the lane leading into the park. She jumped up the steps to a pavilion that was empty and imagined that it was her castle. The town seemed to be far away here. The façades of houses disappeared behind the beeches, birches and ash trees; they shimmered distantly through the greenery and once in a while you could hear a motorcar rumbling past. The ground undulated and rose up to a gentle hill which was a welcome change, especially when Lynette thought of the big park in Prague where everything had been quite flat as if flattened by a steam-roller. Further into the park, a stream was murmuring, before being swallowed up by subterranean realms.

On the way back Lynette discovered a small corner shop.

She walked past it at first but realized then that what she had glimpsed in the window was the head of a black man on a board; this head was well-known and the advertisement for a brand of coffee. She had got a bit of money from Auntie Bertha. As she opened the door, a bell rang, which was attached to its top, and Lynette walked across the creaking floor to the counter. Behind it was a top shelf full of bottles; some bottles had fat bellies and long necks; others looked square and stocky like small fortresses; and there were also bottles that had familiar shapes. The bottles' labels were colourful with foreign-sounding names and had gathered a film of dust that also lay on the shelf. The bottles were most likely cognac, rum and such things, just like Father had, hidden in a sideboard in the living room. Further down on the shelves Lynette saw containers of flour, sugar, semolina. There were scales with many weights, getting gradually bigger and bigger. Lynette could hear a scratching and a shuffling and eventually a small man who was hardly as tall as Lynette appeared. His eyelashes fluttered when he looked at her and Lynette felt immediately at home in the small shop. His melodious German made Lynette realize that he was Czech and when she said something in Czech he blinked even more. She told him that she was going to live here from now on. Right over there, and she pointed in the direction of her flat. Filip was his name, Herr Filip or Paní Filipu. He carefully wrapped the chocolate bar in silver foil. Herr Filip did not have one of those big, iron tills that printed the prices on a paper roll and, as if by magic, sprang open, ringing, to receive the money. He wrote the due amount very tidily and a bit laboriously in a tall book instead and put the money into a box which he got out from under the counter. Then he lifted

48

up a hidden bridge in the counter and quickly rushed to the door to hold it open for her, the young Fräulein, wishing her all the best while his eyelashes fluttered.

The thought that the mild Herr Filip was just round the corner made her step light. The entrance next door had mighty arches that reached up to the second floor. Lynette wondered whether the people who lived there came from the Giant Mountains, though it was by no means certain that the people from the Giant Mountains were really giants.

Lynette came back just in time to help Fräulein Pechwitz to put the covers on the duvets, which were filled with down, and to spread the sheets across the mattresses. Fräulein Pechwitz had a bad back again today, so she was grateful for every bit of help. And getting the bed ready was very important for Lynette to withdraw to it in the evenings and to be snug and cosy in its safe softness. It was strange that people hardly ever mentioned bed when you considered that they spent a good part of their lives there – life's shadowy, twilit part. And on early mornings everyone was forced to leave this refuge and take up the challenge of another chilling day.

An alarm clock blared. It was Father's alarm clock; he got up first. He had to travel a long way to his work. First he had to get to the station and from there he caught the train to Teplitz. And it took a while for Father to have his thorough shave and to make sure that his shirt collar and tie were properly arranged. Lynette listened for Bibs' breathing; he breathed through his mouth so that the air vibrated along his palate, causing a soft snore. But of course... she could not hear his breathing since they did not sleep in the same room any more. So far Bibs' breathing had always annoyed her and kept her from falling asleep; now all of a sudden she missed it and thought that that was why she could not go to sleep. Fräulein Pechwitz clattered the dishes and Father unlocked the door (he never slammed the door closed when he went but always turned the key). Mutti walked in, opened the curtains and called out that the sun was already smiling, though it was only dim light that reached Lynette's bed. Her brother was allowed to carry on sleeping; his school was just across the street and Mutti took him there. Lynette went to school on her own, day after day till it was autumn.

It was very cold outside. The morning lay like lead in the streets. The outlines of the trees were red and yellow, resembling flames. The rose bushes were almost all bare by now with some wilting leaves as colourful yellow dots. Gardeners raked the leaves from the path. The worker with the frizzy full beard on his weather-beaten face was among them again. Lynette called him 'Rübezahl' after the spirit from the Giant Mountains, who had the same full beard and a weather beaten face when he took on human shape. The Kleische stream was bubbling and a blackbird pecked red berries. When Lynette saw a squirrel scurrying along white beech stems, collecting storage for the winter, she had to remind herself that there was a war on. Odd that a war could be so peaceful, she thought.

Uncle Karl had told her. He had been living with them for a week, had moved in with his sister. Lynette did not see much of him for he slept deep into the mornings and in the afternoons he was in his office. A few days before he had had a 'night shift', that was how he expressed it; this meant that he had to leave his bed early in the morning to have breakfast with Lynette. It had probably been an urgent case, possibly a

Jew. Mutti said that he had to be more careful; he could not threaten to throw the Party men down the stairs when they came to advise him to join the Party. Those people were in power now, and it was wise not to challenge them, said Mutti, who shook her head, sighing. Now another worry was added to the many worries she had already, for each time the doorbell rang, she thought that they were coming to arrest her brother. A few days ago when he started his 'night shift', he declared while tapping open the shell of his breakfast egg that there was a war on now. In the early hours of the morning a speaker on the wireless had triumphantly announced that Germany had finally begun to retaliate. Wherever had Uncle been then? In his office at work, he would have probably said. But Lynette and Mutti thought that the Café Falk was a more likely place.

Yes, Café Falk, Lynette thought and saw the chocolate gateaux in front of her as she came out of the park. A broad avenue stretched down to the horizon from where the Ferdinand Rise, a wooded hilltop, looked over the town. Lynette walked past the house with its two men who were holding up a balcony; their upper bodies and arms were taut and tense under the weight. You have to carry your weight, and I mine, thought Lynette, whose back was burdened with a satchel full of books. But it was not the same at all since the men were made of stone and did not feel their burden. Around the next corner, Lynette saw the school coming into sight. The school building was made up of three square blocks with a clock at the top of the central block. The hours were lines and the hands were lines too, only a bit longer. The longest line was threateningly approaching the clock's zenith. Well, she had to hurry up so that she would not be late again.

She had been dawdling since she had been thinking about almost everything except how late it was.

She walked through the bare corridors that smelled of disinfectant. One door was like the next. She was lucky that the number of her class was displayed on the wall but by now she would probably have found the right door without this help. Lynette sat in the last row. The years in Prague had taught her that it was best there because you had a good chance of the teacher leaving you in peace. When Lynette looked out of the window (there were no bars here) she could see young trees in a semi-circle, supported by sticks. The chalk Fräulein Lämmert used did not screech; it seemed to Lynette that even the chalk and blackboard were more modern here than in her old school in Prague.

Fräulein Lämmert was slim and tall. She craned her wiry neck when she had asked something and nobody held up their hand. Her skin was brown and leathery; this was considered healthy now. Only Lynette looked pale and the others called her 'pasty'. But could paleness not be a sign of refinement too? The ladies in Mutti's novels always had pale skin when they were led up a palatial flight of stairs by their gallant beau. Lynette wore her hair loose, though it had become fashionable now to plait it so that it would not get in the way when you skipped and sprinted in the open air to achieve fitness and trimness. She liked it when her hair curled in the rain since it was not so boringly straight and straggly then. Bibs had asked Mutti to have his beautiful, wavy hair cut short. Now nobody could take him for a girl any more. His hair had reached down to his shoulders. But now he was shorn; he wore shorts and a knotted cravat, so that he did not stand out from the other boys of the Party's youth organisation, who also wore shorts and a knotted cravat.

The teacher had once again begun to explain the origin of first names. This was one of her passions; and Lynette did not really object to it since she had only to sit there and listen. Helga, so Fräulein Lämmert explained, came from the Scandinavian where it meant something like 'the holy one'.

Adelheid, however, was a German name through and through and its translation into modern High German as 'of noble kind, of noble rank' exceedingly honoured the fortunate bearer of this name, though it was most regrettable that it degenerated all too often to the silly 'Heidi'. Gerda... was from Old Icelandic where our magnificent Edda epic came from; Gerda was the 'protecting one' who was strong and self-confident. There was some giggling when the teacher looked at Gerda who sat in the front row, trying to pull her plaits over her face because she had turned red.

Fräulein Lämmert stopped in front of Lynette. And Lynette saw the swastika shimmer at the end of a pin on her flat chest. The swastika was still a holy symbol, thought Lynette, remembering Uncle Jacques. As she thought of him, India made a triumphant entrance in her imagination; and she saw peacocks displaying their feather wheels and a sepulchral ivory monument was solemnly mirrored by still waters. But what kind of name was Lynette? It had more dubious influences but things were not all that bad for when you went back far enough you were able to find Celtic origins to this name. 'When you hear Lynette you think of somebody slim and slender,' said Fräulein Lämmert, before stalking back to the blackboard on her long skinny legs.

In her break Lynette looked into the mirror. A round face with full cheeks looked back at her. They seemed to have grown fuller after Fräulein Lämmert's remark, making Lynette angry with Mutti. Why had she called her Lynette? But then... she should not have been so offended by Fräulein Lämmert. Who was she anyway? Don't take everything so seriously, she told herself and concentrated her thoughts on the next lesson: they had art.

The art teacher's name was Morousek and he was Czech. Most of the time he sat in his cabin which stood in the classroom and which he seemed to use as a kind of secret studio, for he himself was a painter of pictures which he exhibited, and sometimes he even sold one. You could tell that he was a good-natured man because he always called 'Watch out, I'm coming!' before leaving his cabin. He did not mind the giggling that followed this habitual sentence. And when he looked at their drawing pads, he said 'Be brave! There's no need to be afraid of the space' or 'Don't be afraid of colours'. But Lynette failed to get something down on paper that was daring, bold. Each line seemed about to collapse into itself and it was not much different with the colours. It was almost as if lines and colours feared the empty void of the pad. In Lynette's imagination pictures blossomed, lush and beautiful, but they turned pale and cramped on paper.

Later, in the park, sitting on a bench, she had lots of time to dream of those pictures in her imagination. A lady sauntered past with a skirt that was tight around her hips. She was accompanied by a uniformed man whose scrawny head jerked constantly from one side to the other so that he resembled a bird of prey. Lynette stretched her legs; the midday sun warmed them and she would have loved to sit here forever, the school satchel at her side. Rübezahl abandoned his rake and unwrapped his lunch: a few slices of bread with lots of cold cuts. That made Lynette think of Mutti. She must have returned with Bibs by now and would be waiting with the food ready. If Lynette was late, she would want to know the reason. Lynette would be quiet then, for how could she have explained herself? Once again Mutti would complain about her daughter who was so inward-looking that you really never got anything out of her.

In the afternoon children played noisily in the streets. From behind the curtains Lynette watched the girls skipping rope and playing hopscotch. Lynette stayed in the flat. She sat down at the small desk in her room and opened an exercise book. An ancient Germanic magic spell had to be rendered in today's language, which made it sound strangely plain. She was glad that Fräulein Lämmert's gaunt figure disappeared when she closed the German exercise book. Her biology exercise book was larger than her other exercise books. She sharpened one blue and one red crayon. In your body everything began in the middle where your heart lay. From there, the arteries led to your legs and arms and head. And in your blood swam nutrients, waste and dreams, for without blood nothing would stir in your brain, not even dreams. She compared her drawing in the exercise book with the picture in the biology book and was quite proud of herself. In summer they would be moving on to study plants. She leafed through the colourful pages of her botany book and thought of her small plot of land down in the courtyard. The brown, lumpy soil turned into a flowering garden instantly. And everything was growing so big in her imagination that she could duck down in the flower fields while Fräulein Pechwitz walked slowly to the washing line, a basket full of laundry pressed against her side above her hip. Then Lynette suddenly jumped out of her hiding place, startled Fräulein Pechwitz and then laughed. Lynette was fed up with doing her homework and went to the kitchen where Fräulein Pechwitz was busy. As soon as she saw Lynette, she began to talk. Lynette thought that she might be carrying on interior monologues all day. And when Lynette was there, these words did not stay in her mind but were turned out through her mouth.

Fräulein Pechwitz had learned Latin many years ago. Her father had been ambitious and had sent her to a lyceum for daughters of the upper classes. But she never really got on with Latin and her father had her go out into the garden to cut supple shoots from the hazelnut. In the drawing room she had to bend over across his knees and felt the coarse fabric of his suit against her thighs. The rod lashed across her buttocks, cutting into her skin. But her Latin did not improve because of this for she was not lazy, that was not the reason. Her father, however, always seemed to want to force things till he went bankrupt and had to realise that nobody was able to determine their own destiny. Yes, yes, of course... the Jews were guilty. But even the Jews had been sent by God. And what did being 'guilty' mean? You could not say anything definite about it. Nevertheless, the *knödliges Fräulein* should be on her guard with Jews. And Fräulein Pechwitz also knew how to recognise them: their noses gave them away... they had these typical noses that nobody else had, those Semitic noses.

Why was Fräulein Pechwitz always going on about the Jews? Most other things she said sounded quite wise. Lynette thought that it was because of all the bad experiences she had lived through; that was probably what had brought her this fixed idea but also her wisdom. But nobody could pin down those bad experiences since the story of her life kept changing

56

and apart from the strict father there also existed a gentle one who never raised his hand against his daughter and did not go bankrupt either but died early from an ugly disease.

A few days later, when Lynette was once again sitting with Fräulein Pechwitz in the kitchen, the doorbell rang. It was Auntie Bertha. With her hands folded behind her back, she strode from room to room. But her striding was only an impression she gave, for she was too small and sturdy to make any expansive movements when she walked. There was a sense of importance in her walking and it was this sense of importance that turned her mincing into something like striding.

'I've only come to see how you're getting on, whether you've settled in already,' she said. 'Are you happy with this flat or would you not rather move to a larger one?'

She stopped in the dining room, shaking her head; two apples had fallen out of the fruit bowl. And when she saw Lynette, she said: 'I don't like the dress she's wearing at all. Well, Antschi, what on earth have you botched together there... don't be angry with me, you know that I'm always straight and open. A young girl like this needs to wear something pretty which fits and suits her. You know what... I'll take her to my tailor; as it happens, Uncle and me are just on our way to town.'

Auntie Bertha laughed while saying all this. That probably meant that Mutti should not take it all as seriously as it sounded. But Mutti started nevertheless; she kept silent and stood in the doorframe shaking her head.

Uncle Wenka started the engine; Auntie Bertha sat next to him on the cushioned seat, upright, as if on a throne. Uncle wore a bow-tie as always and his hair was carefully combed back. He had been smoking while he waited but now he stubbed the cigarette out since Auntie Bertha told him off because of Lynette. He has the most amazing eyes, thought Lynette, who saw him in the rear-view mirror; his eyes were dark, wide and big with a gentle moist shimmer in them.

Lynette reclined in her seat and saw Goethe Street flying past, though of course, it was not called that any more. Young couples walked along, holding hands, and a little girl screamed. Two perambulators as big as fortresses were being pushed by two small, delicate-looking women. A gentleman rushed along very busily with a briefcase tucked under his arm; he had long thin legs and when he lifted one leg to step on the pavement, Lynette briefly thought of a heron. On the right hand side, the cast-iron bust of Master Wagner appeared on a plinth, led up to by a flight of stairs. And this square was followed by the imposing Town Theatre with its pillars and candelabras.

The Market Square was a wide open space with two empty flagpoles. On one side stood a building with a small tower, the former Town Hall that housed the Magistrates' Court now; next to it the swanky Municipal Savings Bank rose up. There were a few motorcars parked in the middle of the square and Uncle Wenka stopped there too.

'Well, are you coming then?' Auntie Bertha asked. But Wenka shook his head, and, along with a cigarette box, also took a notepad and a pencil stub out of the inner pocket of his jacket.

The tailor was small and bald but by no means thin, as Lynette had imagined tailors to be until now; he fussed around Lynette busily and not without a strong sense of self-importance. While sticking the pins into the fabric, he chatted about the most recent town gossip with Auntie Bertha; she was sitting in a soft armchair holding a cup of coffee. Lynette had to stand and was not allowed to move so that the fabric did not slip. She felt like a dummy in a window display. And there seemed to be no end to it: here more measuring needed to be done and down there you had to stick in another pin which the tailor held between his lips. It was almost as if he was not making the dress for Lynette Taussig, a fairly chubby schoolgirl, but for some famous singer or actress. Surely, she thought, even with Zarah Leander there could not have been more fuss. Would she ever feel comfortable in this dress? She felt weird in it and wistfully she remembered Mutti's comfortable dresses that Auntie Bertha thought were 'botched together'.

'Your dress will be ready next Wednesday,' Auntie Bertha said, 'you're going to come with me again then to try it on.'

In Café Falk Uncle Wenka took the newspaper from the hook on the wall. He opened it out; the paper covered him almost completely. Sometimes he fidgeted around a bit, bending forward, deep down into the paper. Auntie Bertha had a good look at the other well-dressed people, her head slightly turned as if she wanted to hear what they were talking about at the neighbouring tables. It had got dark outside by now and there were countless chocolate boxes with golden and silvery ribbons in the window display; the window illumination made these ribbons glitter, which looked magical against the background of the dark night. Lynette thought of Christmas; it was not all that far off any more. A tram glided into Market Square and stopped. The people had all turned into black shadows now, pouring out of the tram's shining inside. She would not have to join these shadows afterwards for she had travelled nobly and exclusively tonight in a motorcar. Her chauffeur, who was Auntie Bertha's husband

and her uncle at the same time, was still reading his newspaper. Uncle Wenka always appeared to her as slightly unreal. She could well imagine him as a wax figurine, standing in a glass cabinet. Yes, that was how it seemed to her: Uncle Wenka was surrounded by a glass bell. Now he got up, held her coat open for Auntie Bertha. His movements seemed delayed while doing this as if he was holding back, which made Lynette think of dreams or movements under water.

'I hope you said thank you to Auntie Bertha; that's what she likes,' said Mutti when Lynette told her about the café and the dress. Auntie Bertha was difficult, she said. She wanted to be worshipped; in this respect she was like a man, for all men loved to be worshipped, Father above all. But you could feel nothing but pity for Auntie Bertha's husband. Him and his agency. To be fair to him, he had found the flat, that had worked out well. But apart from that he wasn't up to much. If it weren't for Father's mother, Baba, who secretly gave her daughter money from time to time... Keeping a motorcar wasn't exactly cheap either. But of course, Auntie Bertha wanted to be chauffeured around in a motorcar because she had to show everybody that she belonged to the upper thousand of the small town, though that wasn't even true. On the whole Uncle Wenka was really quite capable and could have had a decent income so that they could have made ends meet without Baba's help if his thoughts had not always dwelt on his plays, poetry and other writing. There was nothing to be said against writing but there were not many who turned into a Schiller or a Goethe... it was an uncertain, unpredictable business. 'One is better off with something more reliable and solid,' Mutti said, scrubbing the table.

In the evenings Mutti got her novels out again or went to

the Town Theatre when an opera was being performed. It did not happen very often because these days some sort of political play was always on. But when there was an opera, Mutti was always accompanied by Auntie Bertha. And after returning home Mutti complained that Auntie Bertha did not have a clue about the music's beauty, no, she had even nodded off once. But in the breaks she was wide awake, scrutinising the dresses of the other ladies who mostly went to the same tailor, considered to be the best in the town.

The tailor made a bow and an assistant carried the big, tied up box to the car. Lynette held her hand on it during the drive and contemplated how it would be if she went to school in this dress; everybody – possibly even Fräulein Lämmert – would be surprised. But there was no way she would wear it to school since she would not have been herself any more then but someone else.

That was why she put on her favourite dress which she had worn so often that its fabric had become thin and shabby. It consisted of many subdued colours and it looked as if it had been woven by autumn out of many leaves. She wrapped a red scarf around her neck before she left the flat. The entrance arches of the house next door looked even bigger today and Lynette thought that this was due to the clear, cold air which made everything appear more stark and wide. The trees' branches were leafless and clear cut against a blue sky; its very blueness seemed to make it less harsh. From all sides the houses encroached on the park, whereas until recently the colourful shield of the trees and bushes had kept them out. Lynette's breath formed a pillar in front of her, which collapsed only to grow again. Yes, she knew that this was due to the work of her lungs; usually it went on invisibly but left its traces in this cold weather. The pillars were getting bigger, followed each other more quickly when she stepped up her pace so that she would get to school on time.

The seat next to her would be free today; that meant that she had the whole table to herself. The eyes of her school neighbour, Feilchenfeld, had been of a light watery blue that could be colourless when the sun shone into them. She and Lynette had only exchanged a few sentences, had mostly smiled at each other in the mornings. They were both shy; and when both were equally shy then nothing much happened. Miss Feilchenfeld's parents were rich, and she lived in one of the villas in Bismarck Street. It was always a good thing to have money, especially with circumstances as they were now for some people. With their money Miss Feilchenfeld and her parents could afford to buy a nice house across the Atlantic whereas for others the journey itself was already too expensive.

When Lynette stepped into the classroom, she hesitated briefly but then walked on. There was somebody sitting on the seat next to her after all; it was Miss Domansky who had sat in the front until now. Just like Lynette she tried to hide in the corners during the long gym lessons and in the breaks she too stood mostly by herself. So it was not all that strange that she had taken the seat next to Lynette in the last row now. The last row was where the enlightened people sat, who had withdrawn from all the pushing and elbowing, Lynette mused; she and Anne belonged to them.

'Fräulein Lämmert always spits when she talks,' said Anne, 'it's almost as if you were sitting under a shower.'

They stood next to each other in the schoolyard during break. They watched the others fooling around. Watching them like this had always saddened Lynette and she had felt singled out from the others, her loneliness appearing to her like an ugly brand that immediately drew everybody's attention to her. Being together blotted out their singleness, though each of them had always been trapped by it until now. They parted after school. Anne lived towards Pockau where her parents had a house. Next day they sat next to each other again and did not leave each other's side all morning. Both of them had dark hair but Anne was thin and tall. The other pupils called them 'Pat and Patachon' and giggled when the gym teacher found them in some corner.

The first snow fell and Lynette realised that she was getting older since she was not quite as excited by it as she used to be when she and Bibs pulled the sledge in the big park in Prague, together with Jilka. Then it got warm again, the snow melted, turned into slush; water hung in drops like tears from trees and bushes. A warm wind swept along, shaking the branches. At Christmas the town looked grey and pale. But when the night of Saint Sylvester approached, fat snowflakes were dancing down from the sky.

# 5

In her new dress she felt like one of the angels who hung from the Christmas tree. Though it did stick out and was a bit of a nuisance and she always had to watch out that it didn't get creased. But Auntie Bertha had looked at her like a true benefactress and Lynette read a 'That's how I like you' in her eyes. She had come much too early and wanted to leave almost straight away. But Mutti eventually persuaded her to stay, which Auntie Bertha had been secretly expecting. She had arrived early intentionally, Mutti assumed, so that she would be there during the preparations and could inspect everything.

Fräulein Pechwitz attached the paper garlands to the chandelier. Mutti brought out the pink piglets, placing them in the middle of the laid table; the piglets were meant to bring luck. Uncle Wenka sat in Father's armchair and his sole company was a glass of cognac which he cradled in his hand. Father had already left after lunch to call in on the del Vescos.

He still had not come back. Lynette thought that he wanted to get away from the hurly-burly here and was quietly playing chess right now or making conversation in Italian.

'Here are some paper streamers for you,' said Mutti, and Bibs and Lynette made paper spirals coil across the back of the sofa. One of Bibs' paper streamers descended on Uncle Karl who was just coming into the room. The streamer was supposed to go above the door and Bibs had stretched up on a chair to get it there. Now Uncle Karl took the paper streamer to the sofa above which was a picture of the painter, Magnus Rühr. He put the streamer across the picture frame. 'It looks much better now,' Uncle said, stepping back to admire it.

Karl is a little devil, Mutti said: the way he was standing there now with his short hair and his round glasses made him look exactly like someone who had just passed his final exams at the gymnasium. Our Karl will always be a bachelor, Mutti thought. And Lynette was quite happy with that, for who else would have played rummy with them for hours? Though he only did that on Sunday afternoons after he'd had plenty of rest.

Here come Mary and Joseph, Mutti joked. Auntie Lili put the crib with her child in the *Palace* and Uncle Franz sat down next to Wenka. Lynette glanced at little Irmchen who was sleeping. How sweet she looked when asleep! Lynette bent over the edge of the crib where the child lay under a piece of fabric that was strung up to form a tent. She touched one of the small hands, which were not much bigger than the hands of Lynette's dolls. What was Irmchen dreaming now, Lynette wondered. Maybe she was dreaming of the *schlaraffenland* where milk streamed out of snow-white hills. Lynette gave Uncle Franz an annoyed look for bursting out into loud laughter. But Auntie Lili reassured her: Irmchen liked it when there was some noise because she felt then that she was not alone.

'Jesus… how you've changed,' called out Auntie Bertha, stepping into the room.

'Well, some put on weight afterwards and some lose it,' Lili said, smiling. She always had freckles on her noise, even now in winter. Her eyes were dark, almost black, but gleamed with a certain brightness despite their darkness. She wore a dress that made her body look even slimmer. Lili's movements were elegant and for a while Lynette saw herself as a young woman who looked like Lili.

Lili was just in the corridor when a key turned in the lock of the front door. Lili smiled at Father who stood in the doorway with his hat and coat on. He did not respond to her smile, looking at the floor. Yes, he was quite self-conscious; Lynette noticed it clearly. But it would not have been like Father if he had not pulled himself together immediately. He apologised for this momentary slip; he had just been going through some of the moves of the last chess game in his mind; that was the curse of chess that it never let go of you.

'There you are at last,' called Mutti, who was on the verge of wringing her hands in despair, for the soup did not improve with being kept warm.

The soup was served in pretty, onion-patterned dishes; they were part of the dinner service that Mutti had inherited from her grandfather, the old Präger who had owned the Präger Farm.

'Have you settled in now?' Uncle Franz asked. 'It surprised me that you moved here though Monsieur's job is in Teplitz.' Mutti nodded and was silent. Father (who was known in the family as 'Monsieur' probably because he worked in exports but also because of his distinguished, almost urbane manners) answered: 'I don't know why everybody seems to object to Aussig all the time; there are nice cafés here and a beautiful theatre. Teplitz isn't more elegant either but people think it is, only because it's a spa – just a little spring bubbling away there.'

Fräulein Pechwitz served the main course which was *lendenbraten* with Bohemian dumplings and cabbage. As accompaniment she poured the Gewürztraminer which Father had kept chilled.

'A lot of things have changed here,' Uncle Franz said. 'The last time we saw beggars squatting everywhere but this time I haven't seen any, not one.'

'You're right, a lot has changed,' Uncle Karl said. 'Aussig is still called Aussig but apart from that, almost everything has been renamed. They seem to think that by changing names they can change the people. And they only want the names which are convenient to them. Look at Ignaz Petschek who made his fortune in the coal trade. But he was generous with his money; just think of the tuberculosis sanatorium he built. And Masaryk – he was only head of state three times in a row, that's all. Well, and you'll probably just about have heard of Goethe. And now Goethe Street, Masaryk Street and Petschek Street are all called Adolf Hitler Street. It's almost as if Hitler is as important as Petschek, Masaryk and Goethe, all three of them. Well, Franz, what do you think of that in your capacity as a teacher of German language and literature?'

Monsieur tapped the table with his finger, saying as nonchalantly as possible that they had come together to celebrate and not to talk politics. And the street mentioned, well, it had had many names. 'It almost seems like yesterday,' he said, 'that Masaryk Street was called Dresden Street. And before that, I remember it clearly, it was called Kaiser Wilhelm

Street for a while. And before it was called Kaiser Wilhelm Street, its name was Pockau Street...'

Irmchen began to cry. Lili got up, smiling, pushing her chair back. Of course, children got hungry too. And Lili stilled her hunger whilst she turned her back to the table. Karl wanted to say something but Mutti put her finger across her lips. Softly Lili was humming a lullaby and Lynette remembered its words: 'Fly, ladybird, fly once more – our father's in the war.' And mother, yes, she was in Pomerania. Where did Pomerania lie? Well, it didn't matter, for this Pomerania had been burnt down. Was mother still alive? Did she flee? And the ladybird, wherever was the ladybird to fly? These were questions that did not bother Irmchen much. Well-fed, she fell asleep.

'Well, what I meant to say before,' began Uncle Karl who was in a boisterous mood suddenly, almost like a pupil who wanted to tease his teachers a bit, 'I meant to tell you about the sausage factory. We have a new sausage factory here in Aussig. Yes, they've built a sausage factory where the synagogue used to be.'

Now Franz turned red in the face. He would have loved to bang the table with the flat of his hand but withdrew it when he saw Monsieur who pursed his lips and leant far back.

'They've all kicked us around,' Franz said loudly, 'but that's over now at last. Or don't you know what they did to Doktor Schöppe? They threw him into prison because he wanted the same rights for us as the Czechs had... that was his crime. And what about our fifty-four fellow countrymen who were shot because they went on peaceful protest marches for our rights? Have you forgotten them?'

'I think it's time for the dessert,' Father told Fräulein Pechwitz, who stood in the door nodding at what Uncle Franz had been saying.

**68**

The chestnut cream was excellent and Uncle Franz had seconds; he began to talk about school (he was a teacher at the gymnasium, after all), having his glass repeatedly filled with wine while his voice got louder and louder. His loudness was still a habit from the last war when he had had to shout so that the soldiers were able to understand his orders in the trenches. And Lynette thought that it was probably of some advantage to him as teacher that he was able to shout and get a grip on his charges rather than being too quiet and softly spoken.

Uncle Franz seemed to like it at school and it was quite possible that he felt at home everywhere as long as there was a challenge. 'What a weird war this one is,' he said loudly. 'There is no fighting... where are the Tommies and Frenchies? Things were quite a bit different in nineteen fourteen.'

'You should be glad,' Auntie Lili said, putting her arm round his shoulders, 'because you can be here with us. Don't tell me now that you prefer to be in the war.' She smiled, implying that she knew what he really wanted.

Uncle Wenka tapped his glass with a knife. He had been sitting so quietly next to Auntie Bertha that everybody had forgotten about him. Now he was getting up. Slowly he unfolded a piece of paper that he held far away from his face. His eyebrows raised, he began his recitation.

'Oh boy! What can one say to this,' Auntie Bertha called out while he was reciting and she shook her head laughing. According to him she was a woman with no *fear* who loved her cards, her schnapps and her *beer*; she also liked complaining a *lot*, for her it was always either too cold or too *hot*. Of course, there was always a rhyme with Uncle Wenka. He had not written anything about Father. He probably had not been brave enough for Father was always surrounded by this aura of authority. Auntie Lili and Uncle Franz were next because of their Irmchen. Little Irmchen cried so much since she realised how terrible the world was; her screaming clearly spelled out where she wanted to go, that is back into the warm belly of her mother. And thus little Irmchen was not much different from all other sensible people. Uncle Karl was a moth who was attracted by light and some other things. Franz wanted to know what was meant by 'some other things'. But Wenka did not give anything away, for after all he was reciting poetry and poetry had to stand for itself. Bibi had become a 'Boyo' who, by wearing a knotted cravat, was preparing himself for the life of the grown-ups when tie and collar meant everything. Wenka did not forget Lynette either. Her new dress... what else? It was as if the tailor had slipped itching powder down her neck but a real lady had to learn to be patient first. And Wenka had not even been at the tailor's. Auntie Bertha must have told him, Lynette thought. Was Auntie Lili a lady? If she was a lady, then Lynette wanted to become one too. The last stanza in which he said thank you to Madame, that was Mutti, sounded very courteous and civil. 'To our dear sister, Mutti and wife who has spoilt us with such a wonderful meal tonight, to Antschi,' Uncle Franz exclaimed loudly, lifting his glass.

Uncle Wenka sat down after bowing to his audience. He had remained serious during his whole recitation; his mouth was now closed, tight and narrow. Nothing moved in his face which always looked the same, with the same moist shimmer in the eyes. Sometimes it seemed to Lynette as if Wenka wore a mask, a mask that was made out of sadness.

'Good grief,' Auntie Bertha said, 'where does my man get all these ideas from... dear, dear, dear, dear...'

Mutti got up, thereby ending the meal, for with dis-

**70**

tinguished families you did not just leave the table after a meal; instead, the meal was ended by the Lady of the House. And of course Madame, that was Mutti, presided over a distinguished family. And Fräulein Pechwitz too came from such a family, for her father had been an industrialist, though... you could not be sure about anything with her, apart from the fact that something uncertain which might be called fate had expelled her from the house of her parents and the security of her early life.

Uncle Wenka sat down in the armchair. His delicate figure seemed to lose itself in this massive piece of furniture. He lit a cigarette, looking far away into the distance. Lynette thought that he might be contemplating what verses to write next year or he was musing over one of his works that were always in the process of being written but were never finished.

Bibs was playing with his train set (Little Jesus had remembered the wish he had made when on the journey from Prague to Aussig). Between the rails lay pine needles that had an aromatic smell. And this perfume, blended in with the odour of the wax candles, made the Christmas scent which was something magical. But Christmas was over, and now the men lay flat on their bellies watching the toy train – even Father lay there. Only Wenka was still smoking in the armchair which was much too big for him.

Suddenly the train stopped. Bibs desperately pushed the switch of his control box up and down. Tears were gathering in his eyes before Uncle Karl removed the tinsel that he had put on the rails, laughing. That was mean... but Uncle Karl himself was sometimes like a big boy and you had to forgive

**71**

him pranks like this one. The train was buzzing round in circles once again. But Bibs was sulky. 'I don't want to be called Bibs any more,' he shouted, 'I want to be called Heinz; I'm not going to answer to Bibs any more, Heinz is my name.' After stating this, he stomped out. But the men did not seem to be much bothered by his dramatic exit since they had the train to themselves now. They had it move forwards and backwards, then they sped it up till it jumped off the rails and lay on its side with its wheels still turning.

Lynette went over to Lili who was listening to Auntie Bertha telling her something. And Bibi, no, Heinz, joined her. When Mutti saw them, she called: 'Watch out, little ears are listening,' which annoyed Lynette since she was not that 'little' any more; Mutti must have said it because of her brother. As soon as Mutti had mentioned the 'little ears', Auntie Bertha stopped what she was saying and asked Lynette: 'I wonder who you're going to marry?'

She had never really thought about marrying. And the next year which was about to begin... who knew what would be in store for her in this coming year? Of course Irmchen was sweet but she also screamed during mealtimes. And then boys did not really like Lynette that much. If she had been like Lili, slim and always full of smiles... then things might have been different.

'He who doesn't marry or inherit, poor will stay until he's buried,' said Mutti. 'That's what the maids and labourers at the Präger Farm said, your great-grandfather's farm... but is it true? Mani didn't have a fortune and we haven't inherited anything either; the farm floated away long ago thanks to Uncle Josef's schnapps bottle; a single man like him can destroy what's been built up by many generations.'

'The main thing is that you're happy, that you enjoy life...

what would you want a fortune for anyway?' said Auntie Lili. 'It's alright for you to say that, you're still young,' said Mutti. 'But as you get older, you quite like it if you're cushioned by a bit of money.'

The corner turned dark. Uncle Franz had switched off the standard lamp and now it was only the chandelier that shed light from the ceiling. But soon Father came and pulled the cord and the corner was dipped in brightness again. Uncle Franz did not come straight away for he went to the corridor first, then to the kitchen, from there to the dining room. And Father followed him at some distance. That's how it went on and on, always in a circle: when one had turned the light off, the other one switched it on again. It had been the same in Prague when Uncle Franz had not been married yet and visited on his own. Father was too polite to say anything. Only when the visitors had gone again, he complained to Mutti. Father wanted it bright. He paid for this brightness from his own money. Any dim nooks and crannies had to be lit up; everything was to be reached by light so that it showed itself clearly without sinking into twilight. But for Uncle Franz the pale wedge of light that shone through the frosted glass into the corridor was enough; it was perfectly feasible to work in the kitchen with only one of the two top lights burning and why had the lamp in the dining room to be on when nobody was in it? Now he sat down, satisfied, lighting a cigarette. When there was suddenly light in the kitchen, he raised his head. Well, he would stay put for a while. That was just as it had been in the war; then he had also smoked to pass the time before the next attack; he had not only got used to speaking loudly then but also to smoking. Father sat down far away from him; he could not stand smoking.

In the meantime, Karl was lowering the piano stool, opening the top and beginning to play dance music, after he had poured himself another full glass. He has learnt this tune in the Café Falk, Lynette thought. Hop, one, two, three... hop, one, two, three...

'Come on, Bibs, dance with your dear sister.'

But Heinz did not move and now Karl realised that he had got it wrong.

'Heinz I meant to say, not Bibs. Whatever made me say Bibs?'

Even now, her brother did not move. Lynette was certain that he would have danced with Lili; she would have led him from far above, whirling him around, if she had not just left the room with Irmchen. But maybe he did not want to dance with any sissy at all since he was now a tough man who lined up in formation with his knotted cravat on. Even if the scent of women allured him, he would not give in.

Lynette began to swirl around so that her dress billowed out and the air under it was pleasantly cool. 'Just look at this lass,' Auntie Bertha called out, 'who knows, she might be a dancer one day; maybe even in a coffee house.'

The music was hurled out by the piano, note by note, quicker and quicker... hop, one, two, three... hop, one, two, three... The way the rhythm took over her movements... that was a really weird but beautiful feeling. She lost herself for a few moments and was thus freed from any burden. There was something overpowering streaming through her head, which felt pleasant to her. It was streaming and streaming, and soon she felt giddy as if lifted off her feet by water. Everything flowed together and Uncle Karl turned into Herbert, Anne's brother. Herbert had been sitting at the piano, leaning to the side. His left hand was searching for a melody that might not have existed. And he wore round glasses too, just as Uncle Karl did. For a short while, it seemed to Lynette that Herbert was Uncle Karl, only younger, and Herbert again would soon grow and become Uncle Karl.

'Dear me... you're sweating, better put a cardigan on,' she heard Mutti say.

Lynette sat down in the chair next to her, gasping for breath. Mutti always looked so worried; for her life consisted only of an almost endless series of duties, tasks, troubles. But when Lynette thought of Frau Domansky....

She was a small, lively woman with a pageboy cut. Frau Domansky had been barefoot when greeting Lynette; what joy it was for her to see somebody from school, yes, any friend of her daughter, Anne. And Lynette would be welcome at her house any time. But instead of offering Lynette tea or milk, as Mutti would have done, she swept out of the room in her silk dressing gown that was embellished by bamboo and a magnificent display of far-eastern flowers. That had been in the afternoon; Frau Domansky still wore a dressing gown in the afternoons. Later a young man came; his blond hair had a clear parting and he wore a tidy suit though he had loosened his tie and opened the top button of his shirt. His age was probably somewhere between Herbert's and Uncle Karl's, so he was quite a bit younger than Frau Domansky. There was something easy-going, boyish in the way he moved, which was not without a certain charm. The man looked familiar to Lynette, though she was not able to tell where she knew him from. Only when Anne said that he worked at the Municipal Savings Bank did Lynette remember who he was. This was the same young man who stood behind one of the counters in the swanky building on Market Square. Mutti usually preferred him to the other gentlemen who were older and a bit morose. She babbled away in her clear, high voice and the young man smiled, well-behaved. Frau Domansky went upstairs with him now. There was something strangely detached about her when she came down again after a while to mix two cocktails and her eyes were shining; she moved as if under a certain, invisible constraint. Laughter spilled down from upstairs: her laughter sounded shrill whereas his laughter was more like a giggle. And Herr Domansky was in Berlin. He had built a good career; it had worked out this way since he was a Party member. And now he was in some Ministry which was of course important, for all Ministries were important. But Frau Domansky did not want to leave Aussig because of her children. They should not have to grow up in a big city. Yes, it was only because of her children. Lynette wondered whether Herr Domansky believed her. Maybe he had somebody else as well, though Lynette could not really imagine it when she looked at his picture that had slipped in its frame. He seemed to be a dull, stocky man and there was something blunt and heavy in the way he looked at you.

'I've got it all ready,' said Fräulein Pechwitz as she came in, carrying a tray of high-stemmed glasses. Father had already unlocked the bar and put the Tokay on the sideboard. The wine shimmered golden and tasted sweet; the Tokay was meant for Heinz and Lynette. They loved sweetness and found the taste of the glistening champagne that also stood ready too sour still. It was probably the thought of the sweet Tokay that had made Lynette stay up so late overcoming her tiredness; only at Sylvester were she and Heinz allowed to have some Tokay.

Outside the bells were beginning to ring. Father took his

watch out of his pocket. He had refused to turn on the wireless. They did not need a radio to tell them when the new year began. The wireless was a foreign body that tipped all the outside rubbish into their living room. If only at Sylvester Father wanted to be saved from it. It would all be different tomorrow; then wonderful concerts would be broadcast and Father would sit in the armchair, listening. Now Father opened the champagne; he did it gently so that it would not bang, for any loudness was vulgar to him. 'Happy New Year,' Father said, 'and may the new year bring peace.'

Uncle Franz opened the window. It had stopped snowing. Several stars twinkled like ice crystals in the sky. The snow resembled thick fur and lay on roofs and windowsills. You could hear the bells even more clearly now as if they had moved closer. It was like a round of many voices: the fullest sound came from the venerable Town Church. But you could also hear the bells of the protestant church and the bells of the distant Chapel of the Virgin Mary. Mutti even claimed that she could hear the bells of the Castle Church of Schönpriesen; maybe she's right, Lynette thought, for that was where Mutti came from.

Lynette pressed her back against the wall since there was a cold draught. And Uncle Franz must have felt as she did since he closed the window.

# 6

Next morning Fräulein Pechwitz opened the window again. There was a smell of stale cigarette smoke in the room and the paper streamers looked pale in the daylight.

Lynette shivered since she had got used to her warm, cosy bed. The soothing morning hours in bed were the most beautiful time; she stretched and glided, dreaming along the border between waking and sleeping. Today she was surprised that her head felt heavy – but you couldn't get a heavy head from one glass of Tokay, could you? No, it was because she had stayed up so late; she wasn't used to it. She yawned, covering her mouth with her hand.

'Good morning,' warbled Mutti, who was working in the kitchen. And her brother was waiting for Lynette, holding one of the moss-green volumes in his hand. She still read to him, though he was able to read by himself now. 'How!' said Heinz when the door suddenly opened and Uncle Franz looked into the room; 'How!' Lynette said too and they both giggled. Who was faster saying *Hadschi Halef Omar Ben Hadschi Abul Abbas Ibn Hadschi Dawuhd al Gossarah*? Then Mutti called them for breakfast.

Irmchen was still sleeping. But Lili and Uncle Franz were already sitting at the table. Lynette had had to sleep in the same room as Heinz last night since there would not have been enough rooms otherwise. Lynette was sure that Lili would have loved to go to a hotel but Uncle Franz was too conscious of the money. Their train was leaving in the afternoon. So they would stay here till then; and Uncle would smoke and annoy Father, who wanted to enjoy the New Year Concert, with his loud talk.

The midday meal was served at twelve o'clock on the dot. Father liked fixed times he could hold on to. Lynette, on the other hand, was still able to let herself go; nothing much was asked of her as long as she went to school in the mornings. But now she had holidays anyway; she did not have to go out but could sit around in the warm, cosy flat.

She opened the top drawer of her chest where she kept the things she had got for Christmas. She leafed through the small, leather booklet in which she had entered the addresses of all her uncles and aunties. But she was not related to Anne and maybe that was why she stopped at her address. Anne's father had come and taken his children to Munich which he visited for the sake of the arts. Herr Domansky seemed to have a weakness for art. Lynette imagined Anne striding through wide halls with magnificently framed pictures on the walls. On Lynette's desk lay the postcard Anne had written. It showed a pillar with a Statue of the Virgin Mary on top and in the background rose up two sturdy towers wearing homely hats. She put the address booklet back and carried on rummaging in the drawer till she found a large black book with a red spine and red corners. The pages were all empty. This book could be her diary, Mutti suggested. A diary was something where she could write down her thoughts and feelings which nobody else was to know. But she could also put in special happenings and experiences day by day so that not everything was lost later. Opening the book and reading about all that at some later time would be like walking through a museum where things from the past were displayed in glass boxes. The things themselves were dead but your imagination endowed them with life.

She put the book on her desk and fetched her fountain pen. What was she going to write? She thought of the sweet Tokay, her heavy head and that Heinz should have been reading himself by now. But she was not sure whether all that would really interest her later. Had anything unusual happened? Before Christmas she had gone to town with Mutti once more. Then they had walked across the Materniplatz, which had been renamed of course. Together with its name, its appearance had changed too: the square had been turned into a stony desert. The lindens, sycamores and flowerbeds had disappeared. The beautiful Elbe Fountain with the soothingly streaming water and the delicate female figure were gone too. The Town Theatre seemed to have moved further away as if it had retreated from the square in horror. Columns of soldiers lined up in front of it regularly now, standing to attention while speeches thundered from the loudspeakers.

Nobody should ever forget how beautiful the Materniplatz had once been, thought Lynette. That was why she wanted to describe the square as well as she could. She hesitated a long time before she wrote down 'Once there was' in her tidiest writing; that was how she began. But it wasn't really a diary. She was writing about things that had happened to the town, changes. People who recorded something like that were called chroniclers and a chronicle was what they wrote; Lynette knew that from her history lessons. A chronicle was something that lasted. And Lynette felt pride when she smoothed down the very first page, writing in large letters at the top 'An Aussig Chronicle'. She made roses entwine themselves around the letters so that it would not look so plain; she coloured the roses in carefully with red and green crayons. She was going to write her name under the title in a special, solemn ceremony. But when she put the nib of the fountain pen down, she pressed too hard and some ink got splashed. She covered the stain with blotting paper which made it go paler but also larger at the same time. She would have loved to tear the page out. But then she would have had to squeeze the title on top of the next page. Perhaps, she thought, it was best to tear out the whole entry she had written already? But then the whole book would have looked lopsided and ugly. She had made a mistake and there was nothing she could do about it.

As she carried on writing her name down, she began to feel freer, more at ease. She had been out for perfection. But ink had spilt and now any pressure and the burden that followed from it was taken off her shoulders. All of a sudden she enjoyed writing since she did not need to be afraid of making mistakes any more. She simply crossed the word out when she had slipped. She wrote about Herr Filip who also belonged to this town. She described his fluttering eyelashes that were butterflies and how he pulled rather than tore the silver foil from the roll. Then he smoothed the foil down, putting the chocolate bar on it; he folded the paper with utmost care, thoughtfully, and dedicating himself completely to this task. Other chroniclers did not mention such things. But it was important to write about them since nobody else did.

Should she be writing about her birthday that was in February? But that was something private which should not be part of a chronicle. Then white carpets of snowdrops blossomed between bare trees in the Town Park. It was almost as if the flowers were to make up for the snow that was bound to come again, probably at a time when everything was getting warm and bright, with nobody expecting snow any more. Mutti put freesias into a vase. Freesias were her birthday flowers. Lynette never really knew what to make of them. She felt ashamed since the flowers looked so clear and pure, with their pastel-coloured blossoms. They were spring, innocence itself; there was not even a hint of anything dark, any twilight. Freesias would have been the right flowers for Gerda, Lynette thought, but not for her; roses or carnations would have suited her better.

Anne came. Mutti wondered why she did not have more friends. There were hardly enough chairs for all the friends in a household when other girls of her age had a birthday party.

'But you're here,' Lynette said, 'and Uncle.'
She meant Uncle Karl. He had closed 'the place of drudgery' for today; that was what he called his office. One day without files and clients... that meant he was able to breathe freely for a whole day. But he did not have a present for her. He had intended to go to the Café Falk yesterday to buy a certain box of chocolates that Lynette had always fancied but

something unexpected had come up. Instead of a present, he asked Lynette to lend him her autograph book. After all, he was acquainted with Magnus Rühr who had painted the picture that hung above the sofa. Mutti, Father, Auntie Bertha... they all knew Rühr; he was a painter who was well known in the town. So Lynette would soon have a genuine Rühr in her autograph book next to her relatives' well-intentioned attempts at drawing.

A letter from Freudenthal stood propped up against the vase. It was a thick letter and Mutti looked between the pages and in the envelope but in vain; there was no bank note. Uncle Franz promised her that she could choose a book when he came next time. The letter, for reasons of expediency, was directed to Mutti, Karl, everybody. Lynette began to read the letter out loud, first hesitatingly but then faster as she proceeded from page to page. Mutti was surprised that Lynette could read the letter so swiftly, for Uncle Franz had quirky handwriting, though he usually appeared to be frank and straightforward. He curled his letters up but Lynette said that it was easy to read them since she only had to de-curl them.

'She knows what to do,' said Karl laughing; then he sat down at the piano to play *Hoch soll sie leben*. They all lifted their cups of hot chocolate and took a few sips in honour of Lynette. She blew out the candles on the rich gateau; she liked rich gateaux best. But before satisfying her sweet tooth she had to unwrap her presents. Father gave her a watch, a pretty golden watch. Lynette thought that he had given her the watch so that she would become more aware of how time was passing; the watch should make her notice that the amount of time you had was not infinite and that you could not forever dip your hands into it, hoping to pull them out filled to the brim. Father was economical with his time; he had to accommodate a lot in his days. But Lynette... she loved to fritter her time away. Now she had to try on a dress that Mutti had made for her. Heinz gave her a chocolate bar that had been very carefully wrapped in silver paper; it obviously came from Filip's shop. She got perfume from Anne. The perfume smelled sweet and Lynette thought of the linden in the park in Prague. But it was not a linden perfume: it was something from the Far East. Lynette put the flask away and while doing so she had a strange feeling because Anne had given her perfume.

Karl shuffled the pack of rummy cards. They had to make the most of having four players since Anne had joined them. Lynette uncovered all her cards, laying them out on the table; she had won. Heinz could not stand it when he lost. But today at least Uncle Karl succeeded in calming him down. Then Anne won. And again the cards were shuffled; Lynette felt her cheeks glow with the excitement of the game. Heinz won and Karl made fun of him by pretending to sulk as Heinz always did when he lost. But even Karl won in the end. And so it went on, while it was slowly getting dark outside. Lynette would have liked the hands of her golden watch to stop. To stop at this hour so that tomorrow never came when she would have to go to the cold hall to do exercises on equipment that smelled of iron....

After doing gymnastics Lynette always had blue bruises that turned green, then yellow. Her skin was soft, yielding. Gerda's body, on the other hand, was tight, as if laced up; it was all strength and firmness. With a sudden jerk she hauled herself up; swinging on the rings she was well aware of the admiring looks of the class. The gym teacher, a small, solidly built person, had them line up. And Lynette too looked upwards but her look went past the swinging Gerda towards the small windows that were filled with a metallic sky. In summer a wide sky rose up above her when Lynette stood on the school's track and field ground. The green of the forested hills in the distance had something soothing about it. Sometimes two butterflies danced across the grass and Anne said that this dancing was their love play.

The gym teacher always called Anne and Lynette her 'two beauties'. That was supposed to sound funny but was really quite contemptuous. She judged everybody on how fast they could run and on how far they could jump; that was why she despised them, at least Lynette. Anne with her long, slender legs would have been able to run fast if she had not been under Lynette's influence. At least, that was how the gym teacher saw it. Lynette pondered whether the gym teacher would have liked her more if she had been bright and lively. Then perhaps she would have ignored Lynette's physical shortcomings. But Lynette could not change who she was: someone restrained, difficult to make out, especially for a woman teacher whose very job meant that she saw nothing but mere external motion in everything. Sometimes Lynette smiled when she felt hurt. Lynette was sure that the teacher took such a smile for arrogance. And now she stood on the track and smiled again. Some boys were waiting up ahead where the sandbox was; they had cheered Gerda who had landed, with her plaits flying, far inside the box. Lynette felt strangely exposed in her vest, longing for a corner to crouch into. An ugly feeling was taking hold of her stomach, deep inside her: it was this queasy feeling of being suspended in the air, a feeling that she knew from getting into a lift and which she therefore called 'lift feeling'. She started to run and felt better for it. She stepped right onto the wood, pushed herself off and found herself sitting in the sand. She waited for the boys to shout something at her or to laugh but it remained quiet. This silence was the worst. She brushed the sand off herself and when another pupil pushed the rake through the imprint of the two basins she had left she just wished to sink into the ground.

Just as the main dish was followed by a dessert, running, throwing and jumping were rounded off by a game of dodge ball. The teacher appointed two captains; Gerda was one of them. The captains chose their players, one by one, separating the wheat from the chaff. And Lynette was part of the chaff, at least when it came to physical education. It seemed to her that she could not stand any 'education'; she preferred simply to grow, which happened naturally from within yourself and without any coercion.

She and Anne stood by themselves at the end while both captains were surrounded by their teams. Somebody called out Anne's name when it was Gerda's turn to choose. Far above, clouds were sailing past. Everything was open and blue up there. The clouds were frothy, resembling the white spray on waves. That was where the wild Waterman lived... Lynette hummed the melody of the song about the wild Waterman. They had sung it at school in music. And Lynette imagined that the Waterman looked like the music teacher: stocky and heavy around the hips. But as was right and proper for somebody whose element was water, this image soon got blurred and dissolved into the beautiful Lilofee in Lynette's fantasy: she herself was the beautiful Lilofee. The wild Waterman pulled her down under the waves where his palace,

**86**

built out of shells, awaited them. From this deep water she saw the sun glittering up there; its glittering was getting more muted further down, turning into a mere shimmering. Proud Gerda and the gym teacher bowed before her shell throne and Lynette smiled benevolently as rulers did. After the audience, the Waterman with his trident escorted her upwards where she was received not by comforting darkness but by the shrill day... 'Hey, Fräulein Taussig, would you be so kind as to come over here,' she heard the gym teacher shout.

Lynette learnt that the other captain had finally taken her into her team. And Lynette was the first to get to feel the leather ball that burnt like fire. Now she had to leave the field for Valhalla; from there she could take part in the tumult of the mortals' battle without being vulnerable herself. Gerda was the last one onto the field. Her plaits flew, and the boys who stood around the field cheered her on. Lynette got hold of the ball, threw it and hit Gerda's foot though she tried to lift it swiftly out of range. The teacher gave Lynette a short, astonished glance, then she clapped her hands twice which meant that the lesson was over.

She had had some satisfaction after all today. She did not tell Mutti anything; she sat at the table silently and did not chatter. But Heinz made up for her silence by having loads to tell: not about school but the time he had spent with the other boys in the Party's youth organisation.

After the meal she got her chronicle out. Now the chronicle had turned into a diary after all. But what else was a diary if not a chronicle that also reported about private things? And then, Gerda and the school's sports ground also belonged to this town, just like Filip and the wild Waterman who lived mainly in Lynette's fantasy but were hardly less real for that.

Then she played the song of the wild Waterman on the piano in the evening when Father came home. He did not stand next to the piano today to listen to the pieces she had been given as homework. He looked really pale; it was quite likely that he had fever but he had been to work nevertheless. He did not answer when Mutti tried to persuade him to go to the doctor. What was wrong with taking some sick leave? Others took sick leave every few months. But Father had never taken sick leave. He went to work every day even if he felt wretched. Work was important for him: he did not want to leave anything to others. Or maybe he did not want to make an exception, for if you made an exception you were bound to make another exception and so on... in the end you would become lenient towards yourself. And being a businessman, especially in the export branch, was tough. You had to stay calm and strong when making difficult decisions. Once he had not insured a large shipload. Mutti had told them about it since Father was more taciturn than usual then. He hardly slept at night, said Mutti, till the ship had reached Batavia. Then, of course, Father was well off: the insurance sum had been saved and the bottles had reached their destination. But everything could have turned out completely different if a storm had brewed up. Even then Father would have remained calm and firm, Lynette thought. Sometimes it almost seemed to her as if he had built up walls around him to protect himself from anything that was intrusive and coarse. And it was because of those walls that nobody could really get close to him, not even Mutti. Sometimes the walls were suspended for a short while, like last Saturday evening. Then Heinz and she had had a pillow-fight with their father.

He just raised a pillow above his head when the door opened and Mutti came in, sighing. The pillow was hurled through the air nevertheless; Heinz dodged it and the pillow hit the wall. 'Honestly, Mani,' Mutti said and picked the pillow up. Father was a *glosblutzer*, said Fräulein Pechwitz. In Bohemia almost everybody had something to do with glass. But whoever saw him in his office would not have known that he traded in glass; there was not a trace of glass there. He stood at the desk and dictated letters to Fräulein Mandel, his secretary: letters in Spanish, Italian, French, English. And since he wrote letters that went out all over the world he himself received letters from everywhere. He cut out the stamps, detached them from the paper and put them in envelopes. On all the envelopes he wrote the name of each country. He also bought mint stamps, the ones that mainly increased in value, from the shop, putting them in albums. At the very beginning of one of these albums there were stamps from a time so far in the past that the writing on them was not in Czech any more but again in German. Many of these stamps showed a head and face with paternal whiskers: seen from the side, from the front, crowned with a laurel wreath and then as a mere silhouette. That had been the Emperor; Bohemia had been part of his Empire. Mutti said that Bohemia had been his favourite crown land. Father kept these stamps in his best album which was bound in leather and bore an inscription in golden, curled letters. From time to time he solemnly leafed through this album; Heinz and Lynette who sat at his left and right were allowed to look at the stamps with him. On the most precious stamps the Emperor appeared to be fresh and youthful, with a ribbon attached to his laurel crown. Later he gained in dignity, reminding Lynette of busts of Roman Caesars. In the end the Emperor sat on his horse bent down by age but still upright. The Emperor, so Lynette thought, had been deeply rooted in time; he had not ruled because he was thirsty for glory but because he had been predestined for it and because it had always been like that. She imagined the Emperor as a quiet man like Father who started when a door banged. And the Emperor, too, had done his duty day by day without making a lot of fuss about it. He was overhung by melancholy that muted any loudness. It was already the melancholy of decay; slowly the old order had been dying, even before the war had begun. The war had only been the outward sign of a process that had happened from inside because it had to happen. And now everything had begun to dissolve and flow away, with everybody trying desperately to hold on to something.

Above the teacher's desk hung the picture of a man with parted hair and a trimmed moustache. It was the same man whom she had seen in a carriage in Prague. He relentlessly stared down the aisle between the benches as if he had the only valid answer to all the questions. During his speeches he yelled, ranted and raved. He poured out his venom and loved it to be loud, for without this loudness the world would hardly have taken any notice of him. Not long ago in that place above the desk (and maybe in the same frame) there had been a picture of Masaryk. And if the school had been a bit older, a portrait of the Emperor would have hung there before that.

'By what name was the leader of the Germanic tribes in the battle of Teutoburg Forest known to the Romans?' asked Fräulein Lämmert. There the legions had been slaughtered, attacked by redheads and blond heads from all sides.

Lynette's sympathy lay with the Romans. She imagined herself as a Roman lady who rested on a chaise longue, supporting her head with one hand while the other hand picked sweet grapes from a bowl. That was what you called *savoir vivre*.

'Lynette, Lynette,' said Fräulein Lämmert, 'what kind of name is that!'

It was strange, Lynette thought, that these people who had only contempt for the Romans, whom they considered to be weaklings, used the Roman salute all the time. She had found a picture of it in her brother's Latin book. Fräulein Lämmert jerked her arm up high as soon as she entered the classroom. Then they all had to stand to attention beside their benches and stretch their arms out stiffly, calling out HIS name. There was something mechanical in this as if they were all little figurines with keys in their backs and these wound-up keys were suddenly let loose when Fräulein Lämmert entered.

In music Lynette belonged to the two or three chosen ones who were allowed to sit in the front and read the score while the gramophone was playing. The music teacher stood at the grand piano; his face was shiny with sweat since he had hammered out a few examples of melodies on the keyboard. His mane of hair made him look like Beethoven and the round, bloated face was reminiscent of Schubert. But he did not have any likeness to Wagner. Lynette thought of Master Wagner's memorial at the Town Theatre; it was surrounded by bushes and flowerbeds. Had Father not told her that he had played the *Meistersinger* overture, back in Türmitz where he had joined an amateur orchestra? In those days he played the double bass. Then she thought sadly of the Materniplatz that had lost its name long ago and had become dreary and desolate.

In this square, military units fell in on HIS birthday while music by Wagner resounded from loudspeakers. The poor men stood under these loudspeakers, freezing in their grey uniforms, the thin ones more so than the ones who had some fat. The music was losing itself between the stones and in the indifferent spirals of the men's ears. No, that was not where this music belonged, Lynette thought, and neither should it have been played in this music room with its hard chairs whose wide armrests used for writing slotted into place in front of you. A hall that was completely veiled in velvet and silk would have been appropriate; and the listeners should have been able to recline and dip deep into the twilight of this music. Glittering, the sun was refracted by the full green of the music's stream that reached down into regions where the wild Waterman was at home.

'I beg you, give me a rest from Wagner,' said Uncle Karl and finally turned the radio off, 'everybody needs something light-hearted from time to time, something to relax. And this music first thing in the morning... it's a bit much.'

Of course, it was not morning any more; it was noon but Uncle had his own way of dividing the day.

Mutti told them about Bismarck Street. There she had had to dip her thumb into the black ink and press it on the paper of the identity card as if she were a criminal. Her face looked thin in the photo that showed her wearing a fur stole. It was much too warm for a fur stole by now but nobody would notice it in the picture.

The ranges of hills that surrounded the town lay in a hazy distance. The leaves silhouetted on the path by the sun moved gently. Roses blossomed and a delicate-looking small man bent over one of the flowers. The man reminded Lynette of the drawing in Father's thick book where a bare-headed man was depicted between full rosebushes, holding a watering can. A band was playing in the pavilion. The musicians sat under a wooden roof and a conductor stood in their midst. It would soon be Whit Sunday, and already there was a holiday atmosphere. Women and girls in white dresses perambulated past and it felt to Lynette almost as if she were again in the big park in Prague where Jilka used to take them. Lynette still spoke Czech then. But now nobody spoke Czech any more; you could only hear German. Herr Filip did not speak Czech either now. His German sounded strange, as if it was about to dissolve in pure melody at any moment. Since the customers who came into his shop all spoke German, he spoke German too. What did Filip care about big politics? He was happy if he got more customers by speaking German. There were never many people in his shop anyway; it was almost always empty when Lynette put her pennies on the counter.

Now Lynette saw Herr Filip sitting on one of the benches that surrounded the pavilion. What was he doing here? He was always so hard-working... But perhaps he had decided that enough was enough and had put up a sign on the shop door, saying: 'Closed because of the nice weather'? But when the man briefly looked in her direction, she realised that it was somebody else.

Men in uniform appeared, wearing high polished boots; they stalked around with their chests thrust out; one or two medals dangled from some of them. These were men who were empty inside, Lynette thought; they were in need of uniforms and medals in order to be somebody at all. There were other men who moved awkwardly in their uniforms, which hung on them as if they belonged to somebody else.

93

She noticed that they avoided the women's gazes, for they seemed ashamed of their present clothing. A soldier wearing round glasses and whistling a popular song reminded her of Uncle Karl. But no... she could not really imagine Karl as a soldier. Perhaps that was why he had not been called up, a fact which almost bordered on a miracle since, without Party membership, he should have been one of the first men to report for duty. Lynette was sure that he had some useful connections which helped him delay things; that was part of being a lawyer. And anyway he had been called up once already over a year ago; he had not worn the uniform of the Reich then but the uniform of the Czech army. He had even been a lieutenant. He had told Lynette and Heinz about it during a Sunday afternoon when they had got bored playing rummy but still would not leave him in peace.

He had only become a lieutenant, of course, because he spoke Czech. Only if you spoke Czech could you become a lieutenant in those days. Uncle was not a native speaker; he had learnt it. He said you were still growing as long as you were learning something. He had also worked with a shoemaker to learn how to make shoes and he had been an apprentice to a bookbinder too. 'It's important,' he said, 'that you can make something with your own hands; it's wonderful if you can make something which you're able to touch and look at... but this endless paperwork...'

Apart from speaking Czech and standing to attention, Uncle had learnt something else with the Czech military. One morning he received the order to deliver an important message. Only high-ranking officers had motorcars and the stable boy had neither brushed nor fed the horses; he was German – there were lazy and unreliable folk among the

Germans too. A bicycle stood propped up against a wall and the captain said that he could use this bicycle. Uncle felt the blood drain from his face since he had never sat on a bicycle in his life before. He tried to hide his horror, saluted the captain and pushed the bicycle across the yard. It was a hot, dusty day; the country road was deserted. It meandered between gentle hills up to the gate of the neighbouring barracks where they were expecting Uncle's message. An oriole warbled in a grove and from beyond the red roofs a small village shimmered; the red roofs shielded the pale houses protecting them from the sun. When the barracks had disappeared behind the hills, Uncle perched gingerly on the saddle to ride along a bit on the even road.

But already when he pushed the pedals down a second time he lost his balance and fell. He brushed the dust off his trouser leg and pushed his bicycle along again for a while since a horse and cart was approaching on the other side. The cart was loaded with hay; the farmer greeted him from the coach-box and two girls sitting on the cart let their brown legs dangle. Second attempt, Lieutenant Lauritsch. A good soldier had to be hardy and not give in. This time he pushed the pedal down four times before he fell. Third attempt, aborted: he heard an engine roaring in the distance and it was slowly getting closer. It was some time before he was able to see the motorcar at last, for in this silence even the sound of a dragonfly carried a long way. He contemplated whether he should find a place to hide since it might have been the captain, who often made little excursions to the village where he was attracted not only by the fresh rolls but also by the fresh cheeks of the baker's girl; at least, that was what they said in the barracks. However, it did not turn out

95

to be the captain after all but a fully packed motorcar that was probably on its way to the border. He could smell the petrol fumes a long time afterwards. Come on now, get ready for the fourth attempt. Learning to ride a bicycle had become his task, his duty; every soldier had to do his duty until victory or ignominious defeat. This time he got his feet on the ground before falling. Uncle still did not surrender. He took his cap off and wiped the sweat from his glasses. Luckily, his uniform was still intact and not torn. Uncle went for his fifth attempt. The handlebar swerved in all directions; it had to, for him to be able to keep his balance. But the longer he sat in the saddle, the steadier the front wheel became. And when he rode, shaky still, through the gate of the neighbouring barracks, it seemed to him as if the guard looked up at him in acknowledgement and as if trumpets sounded. But perhaps the guard only raised his head in surprise that somebody was coming in on a bicycle. And the sounding trumpets were perhaps nothing more than the yellow flickering between the dusty ground and the blue sky that blared in the ears of the exhausted man. When he returned he had learnt to ride a bicycle and entered his barracks, sitting high up on his saddle.

And now he was a civilian who sat with his sister's children, looking at his watch. 'Well, so late already,' he said, 'I've got an appointment. I must be going now. Believe me, I'd rather stay with you. It's so comfy here.'

He lay on his bed, with his legs drawn up. His shoes were at the foot of the bed, not in an orderly fashion, side by side – that would not have been like Uncle: one shoe was turned over, and the other one was about a step away. That was how Uncle had taken off his shoes before lying down on the bed or, to be more precise, on the day cover that Fräulein Pechwitz always spread over the bed towards noon.

'Ach, the Café Falk, it's not what it used to be,' Uncle said. Buses came from the Reich and the tourists pounced upon the gateaux like locusts till the last crumb had disappeared into their greedy mouths. They did not seem to have such gateaux in the Mark Brandenburg. That was where the Protestants lived, whose ministers had knocked any enjoyment out of them long ago. But Uncle would not have begrudged these people their enjoyment of the gateaux if they had not been so terribly snooty. All that talk about the Balkans and so forth. For them, the Balkans were everywhere where garlic was eaten. But the Balkans were a beautiful region of the world, just as every region had its own charm and attraction. Not to mention garlic, the most magnificent of spices, the ultimate expression of any great civilisation. Why did they not just stick to their potatoes which they preferred watery and salty? Oh well, my lass, good that you remind me: you'll get your autograph book, I'll definitely see Rühr this evening.

Instead of getting up to prepare himself for the café he stayed put and again took up the pack of cards which he began to shuffle. Lynette observed Uncle, for he was to figure in her chronicle. Everything about him was to be recorded: his round glasses and the boyishness that suddenly overcame him when he boisterously played a card, whistling. And thinking about Uncle, Anne's brother appeared before her inner eye and both of them melted into each other so that she was unable to tell the difference between them. At the same time she had a beautiful, restless flickering feeling that warmed her from inside; she enjoyed this feeling to the full.

Meantime night had completely draped the window in black

**97**

garments and she could see the room light and herself sitting between Uncle and Heinz reflected in the windowpane. Her image was slightly blurred which she liked since she did not want to see herself in every detail. It dissolved at the edges, faded away. Looking at herself, it seemed to her that she was somebody else. Perhaps life was not much more than a continuous dream in which you were just dreaming yourself, she thought, just as she heard Heinz call out that it was her turn now.

Frau Domansky gave Lynette a hug, as if they were two old friends. Her eyes had that strange shine again. Books lay on the dinner table; next to them stood a cup half-full of mallow tea. There were pale water stains on a German Renaissance chest. Everywhere in the corners dust gathered, forming little grey clusters; Mutti would have called them 'dust mice' and Fräulein Pechwitz tracked them down under beds and sofas where they were hiding. But here these mice were thriving in the open and Frau Domansky did not seem to be much bothered by them: she just let them thrive.

'Anne has just gone shopping but maybe Herbert can go out with you; he can show you the redcurrants,' she said, calling him. She called as loudly as if he were on the other side of the town and not in the next room, from where he emerged with round shoulders, looking tired.

'This is the way out,' Herbert said, opening the glass sliding door.

A spacious, overgrown garden lay spread out in front of them. Beyond the wooden fence with its sparse cypress hedge, fields and meadows stretched out as far as a range of hills; from there you could follow paths up to the Striesowitz Mountain. She would have loved to live around here and not in the narrowness of the town where she had only a small plot of land down in the courtyard. The grass in the garden reached up to her hips and was full of seeds. Shrivelled-up apples hung from a tree. In a greenhouse that had several cracked glass panes, red shiny poppies grew in pots; the blossoms looked fuller than the ones Lynette had seen in the nearby fields and meadows. The greenhouse stood sheltered between the house and a decaying wall. Nobody could see it from the outside; and because of her unusual way of life, Frau Domansky employed neither a maid nor a gardener. Gossip would have spread quickly and that would not have been good, especially with Herr Domansky being something high-up in Berlin.

The redcurrant bushes grew in the garden's sunniest place. Nets were spread over them to protect the berries from the birds and this was the only looked-after area, with the exception of the greenhouse perhaps. Herbert said that he cut off the old stalks every year. Otherwise he was monosyllabic and Lynette did not mind since that meant she did not have to say much either. He lifted the nets and they began to pick the berries, putting them in a bowl. They fetched sugar from the kitchen; it was hard and crusty and Herbert had to crush it first. The sugar turned something that tasted sour into a fruity sweetness.

She told Herbert the story of *Der Hagestolz*; she had read the story at school in Fräulein Lämmert's class. It was about an old bachelor who lived all by himself on an island in a mountain lake.

'It's by Stifter,' Herbert said, 'I know the story well.'

Lynette was surprised since she did not expect boys to take an interest in stories. They were both lying on deckchairs on the terrace, blinking into the dazzling summer sun.

'My father reads Stifter too,' said Lynette, 'it's a terribly thick book. He began reading it when we were still in Prague; he's got so many other things to do, you know. He works for the Mühlig-Union and he manages the exports there because he knows lots of languages. Yes, seven languages, if you count Latin but why shouldn't you? – Latin's a language too.'

There she was: showing off about her father. And she was really quite different from him: soft and self-indulgent. She would hardly have studied at night to pass the entrance exam for university as an external student. During the day he had had to work as an apprentice, lifting heavy cheeses from the shelves to wipe them. That was what he told her when she complained about school. Working hours had been long in those days and you had had to work till noon on Sundays. The paraffin lamp blackened the ceiling while Father rubbed his eyes, poring over books. Yes, that was what Heinz and Lynette should remember when they complained about school. And because things were so much easier for them, they should at least bring home a good school report.

*Physical Education* headed the school report. Things had changed quite a bit since Father had studied as an external student, for in those days your intellectual abilities had still been important. Fräulein Lämmert had written in narrow letters, using the German script: *Pass*. The writing was like Lämmert herself, Lynette thought, thin and intense. Lynette had been given a *Good* in all the other subjects, even in German which was taught by Fräulein Lämmert herself. Rounding off the school report, her general observation was that Lynette was always on her own, did not join in with the others. No, that was not quite right, for she was always with

Anne. Perhaps she should have joined the school choir; she felt that she was more likely to belong to the school choir than to anything else. But Anne had told her that the music teacher ruled the choir like a tyrant, shaking his sweating Beethovenian mane while roaring wildly.

Father nodded slowly, getting his wallet out of his jacket. He gave her a bank note; she would take it to Herr Filip later. She would put the change in her piggy bank; she was saving money but did not know what for. The future was uncertain and Mutti said that it was always a good idea to put some money aside. Father pored over Heinz's school report for a long time: it was not very good. But her brother did not really do a lot apart from listening to her reading from the moss-green volumes. In the world of these volumes, nobody had to sit still and the good and valiant ones were those who lived through adventures, fighting evil. That was probably what he daydreamt about and Mutti had to keep telling him in the evenings that he should be doing his homework. He was still not able to read and write properly. And he was supposed to go on to the gymnasium later that year! After the holidays he had to sit an exam that would decide whether he would be admitted to the gymnasium. Father shook his head and put Heinz's school report down with a sudden movement. When Mutti packed the suitcases for the summer holidays, Father put Heinz's exercise books for writing and his reading book into one of the suitcases.

Havelka's servant was waiting at the station platform and carried the suitcases to the carriage. Lynette sat down with her brother and had a view of the servant's broad back; Father and Mutti took the seats on the opposite side.

The servant clicked his tongue and off they went into the summer holidays. The carriage was soon engulfed by forest and they were going along in the shade that the tall trees cast onto the road from both sides; tree trunk followed upon tree trunk. The sunlight got caught in the greenery and seemed less harsh down here after it had been filtered by the treetops; it had a shimmering glaze to it, reminiscent of stardust. And then the forest suddenly opened out, so that Lynette and Heinz saw the Pension Waldfrieden in the clearing at the same time. The house almost looked a bit bewitched as it emerged from the forest. Soon they were all sitting outside at the table that stood between three elms. The table was generously supplied with gateaux, for Havelka was a confectioner. Towards evening the Stelzigs arrived. Herr Stelzig and Father got their violins out and played a duet outside, under the three elms. Herr Stelzig had composed the duet himself and when Father nodded in recognition, he reached into his briefcase and pulled out another duet which, of course, he had also composed himself. Mutti went into the house to fetch a cardigan. She made a wide berth around the German shepherd dog which tugged at its chain, growling. When Father walked into the house with firm steps soon afterwards it did not growl. Father returned with Heinz's exercise books and his reading book; the poor boy had to practise reading now till he could read fluently, at least the few pages that were the work for today. The young del Vesco and Lynette sat next to them, playing chess on Father's chessboard. Father took over from Lynette and was able to hold him to a draw. Against the light of the descending reddish sun, the dark fir trees looked like the wooden pointy laths of a fence. An owl somewhere said: too-whit, too-whoo. An almost full moon glowed smoulderingly and stars sparkled everywhere; someone seemed to have strewn a whole apronful of them across the night sky. The sparkling was nowhere near as bright in Aussig where the lights of the houses and the streetlamps made the stars pale. A glow-worm hovered in the air against the darkness of an elm trunk.

'It's beautiful sitting here, isn't it?' said Frau Stelzig. Her dark eyes and round face had something Italian about it though she came from the region around Olmütz. But who knew what lay hidden deep down in the past? Perhaps an Italian had come up to Bohemia, an architect who built baroque churches; and as such things happen, he fell in love but wandered on and left the girl with a child. And this Italian had given Frau Stelzig her eyes and her hair. And as chance would have it or fate or whatever you wanted to call it, her daughter married Herr del Vesco who was an Italian as well. So everything was joined up again.

Next morning they got up early, drank coffee and already had a piece of cake. That was a 'Bohemian Breakfast', said Mutti, when you ate a piece of cake straight away in the morning. Then off they went to the forest. Lynette felt the morning chill against her knees. But soon the forest heated up as the sun rose up to its zenith. Lynette believed that she could almost hear the twigs crackle in the heat and the smell of the wood blended in with the fir needles' fragrant aroma. Wherever the forest opened up there were wild strawberries competing with flowers and herbs for space. The strawberries that shone brightly between jagged leaves were tiny. You had to be hard-working, picking them for quite a while before even covering the bottom of a basket with them. Lynette wiped the sweat off her forehead. Father strode skilfully across branches and twigs though he had a shortened leg and a bulky shoe. Mutti spread out a blanket; she had brought lemonade. Now they had a rest. Father began to talk slowly while a woodpecker was knocking close by and a jay flew to and fro between the tree trunks as if it wanted to show them its russet and steely-blue plumage.

Father wanted to know whether they were familiar with poplars. Poplars had thin branches that clung closely to the tree stem. They should never climb any poplars; otherwise, the same might happen to them as it had to Father. A branch had broken and he fell on the rough stone that smashed his hip. He had been about the same age as Heinz then. For a long time he had lain on his sickbed, in a fever. The doctors had given him up but Father recovered. He had to walk on crutches, yes, the doctors said he would never be able to walk without crutches. But they did not know Father. Every day he tried to walk without crutches and there you go: one day he succeeded. It was a great sensation in and around Augiessl that Taussig could now walk without crutches. He had been forced to learn to be strong; and the accident had had its good side in other ways too. If it hadn't been for his shortened leg he would have had to go to war as a young man; then he might have suffered the same fate as brother Karli, who never returned. And his shortened leg had still another advantage, which Father laughed about when recollecting it. They had been little scamps, the whole lot of them. They had climbed over a fence into a garden where a tree laden with dark cherries stood. Father did not climb it, of course, for he was not able to climb any more. Instead, he kept a lookout in case somebody was coming. Nobody would lay hands on him because of his maimed leg. So he looked down the street.

There was only one street. The whole Elbe valley and the town of Aussig were spread out down there; hills enclosed the valley on the other side. The river glistened and the street wound its way up via Hottowies. Father went to the primary school in Türmitz that had a castle as well as a neat church and he could see the top of the steeple from up here. As he kept gazing down the street, the outline of a uniformed man suddenly obstructed his view. The man ran as fast as a gendarme of a mature age was able to run uphill. Father put his fingers in his mouth and whistled twice. The other two boys jumped down from the tree and landed on the grass with a thud. They climbed over the fence, with cherries tumbling out of their bulging pockets. They ran full pelt, so that the gendarme could only see their backs. Father hobbled after them till he heard somebody panting for breath and felt a firm grip on his arm. Off they went to see Baba; the gendarme already knew Baba and Mani too. Lynette imagined Baba's garden to be full of stocks and wild roses, and at the back there was possibly a sunflower that was just as high as the low-built house. Baba stood in the doorframe, arms akimbo. The gendarme took his cap off; wiping the sweat from his forehead, he complained that Father would not tell him the names of the other boys. Why should he, Baba said, what kind of boy would give away his playmates? That was just like Baba. No gendarme could have intimidated her, no matter how many polished buttons he had on his jacket. The gendarme just left in the end. But next time he would catch the other boys, he said, before leaving. Yes, the next time they held a wasps' nest at the end of a long stick, waiting for a cart to come along. When they threw the wasps at the horse, it reared; the coachman had to take a firm hold of the reins

105

since the leisurely trot had turned into a wild chase. What a scamp Father had once been... though she could not imagine Father as a scamp when she saw him now sitting in the forest in a stiff shirt, brushing grass seeds off his suit.

On the way back Heinz hurried on far ahead; he thought that he was Winnetou, chased by evil palefaces. But he fell amongst briars. It was not too bad since he was wearing *lederhosen* but his legs got scratched nevertheless. That was why he was pulling a sullen face in the photograph; Herr del Vesco took the picture when they stepped out of the forest. Young del Vesco, who was thin and lanky, sat cross-legged in the front. Lynette looked down so that you could see more of her full, dark hair than of her face. There was something suspicious in Mutti's expression and she pulled her head slightly back. Father looked into the camera directly; he appeared firm and confident, a bit impatient almost. There was nobody else in the picture, for Frau del Vesco had stayed with her parents. And Herr Stelzig preferred to sit under the elms to write another duet since he had some time now and was not harassed by his daily school duty.

'Everything comes to an end some time,' he said philosophically on the last day as he watched his luggage being loaded. Did he also think of his duets when he said this, Lynette wondered, for they lay dead in his folder now while the last note had faded away yesterday evening.

The servant clicked his tongue and the horses started pulling; slowly the Pension Waldfrieden disappeared in the forest. The locomotive covered mile after mile and, with each mile, the dreary school life that Lynette dreaded came closer. Perhaps the train would suddenly change direction. She hoped that this might happen at every station they stopped at, though she knew that it was not possible. The landscape was soon dominated by fields and meadows instead of the dark forests of the Erzgebirge. The Elbe was not glittering today, for it was raining. It was a heavy, seemingly endless rain that welcomed them here after it had been sunny in the Pension Waldfrieden. The chimneys of the Schicht Works seemed to touch the sky; that was how low the clouds hung.

How small the flat was, Lynette thought; the white walls seemed bare to her now, she missed the wood panelling and antlers. Outside, the traffic rumbled past, day and night, up and down the broad road named after Masaryk, Petschek and Goethe earlier but which only bore HIS name now. Uncle Karl was not in; 'flown out', as Mutti said. But at the side of her bed she found her autograph book, which she had almost forgotten – it was so long ago that Uncle had taken it to the Café Falk. Now she opened it, turning page after page, relishing the feeling of suspense that tickled her stomach. Auntie Lili had drawn a pretty meadow full of flowers, which seemed light and freckly, like its creator, to Lynette. Mutti had made a special effort by painting a watercolour of a multi-turreted castle; under the watercolour it read *Meinem Dornröschen*, To My Sleeping Beauty, in Mutti's handwriting, which was thin like cobwebs. There was even a picture by Uncle Jacques. It was a beautiful still life of a tall vase with lilies. What a wonderful picture Magnus Rühr must have painted for her, she thought, full of anticipation, turning to the next page where she found his name written in carefully drawn, calligraphic letters... but that was all: there was nothing else on the page but his name. That was what artists were like, Mutti opined, they always did what you least expected of them. But perhaps he was just fed up with painting since he had to earn his living doing it. Or he hadn't been inspired, for artists needed inspiration. They got it in cafés or young women's rooms. But then they had to move on... that was what art expected of them, for inspiration was scared away by a fixed relationship with a woman and possibly even children, by anything permanent like regular working hours. Consequently Uncle Karl was an artist too.

'Me, an artist?' he said. 'I wish that was true; but in times like these you have to be a magician, not an artist. I can't do magic and still take the money the poor devils give me; that's how they buy themselves hope for some time. It's swindling really. Artists are more honest but people turn up their noses at them.'

# 7

The leaves in the park changed colour again. And it was not all that long ago that they had hatched out of their budding shells. The park had turned into a sea of colours with a predominance of red. It was a symphony which autumn had composed out of all these colours and red was the symphony's keynote. Or perhaps autumn was a painter and maybe the great Rühr should have kept the autograph book for a little longer; then he could have gone to the park where his inspiration would have entranced him to lay down a swirling dance of colours on the page with a light stroke of his brush.

It was dark in the mornings now and the duvet was so warm and soft. It seemed to go against the grain to get up when it was still dark outside. Lynette snuggled up to her pillow, closed her eyes; a stream of cosiness went through her. But then somebody pulled her duvet away: it was Mutti, getting-up time, school....

If only it had been a Sunday, she could have played the piano (nothing in particular but whatever came into her mind) or written her chronicle. Heinz fidgeted on his chair. His hair was short and tidily parted. He was a Latin pupil now, attending the town's gymnasium where Uncle Karl and Uncle Franz had been before him. All the boys went there and she too would have loved to have gone to the gymnasium because she could learn Latin there. But this option had vanished, together with Czech and the Republic. Perhaps the new men in power thought that only a male brain could master Latin sentences, though her brother did not seem to be all that clever either. Father had coached him every evening, sometimes deep into the night. When her brother complained that he was too tired to study, Father had told him that no matter how tired you were, you were never too tired to learn. Her brother had just about scraped through the entrance exams to the gymnasium. He studied Latin which he enjoyed far less than she who took up his text book again and again to ask him questions. Perhaps she would not have enjoyed it quite as much if studying Latin had been expected of her. But as things were, a clear sun-flooded world shone through the Latin vocabulary in her mind. The men and women who lived in this world had decayed long ago and you could find their remains in stone sarcophagi. But Lynette imagined that she walked over a mosaic floor and she felt the sandals' leather on her naked foot. Between the pillars stood a man in a toga, holding a scroll. How very strange that he wore a pair of round glasses....

'Come on, it's high time for you to go,' she heard Mutti say. Lynette had been dreaming again. Her brother was a Latin pupil now and did not want to be taken to the school gate by his mother. She and her brother parted at the house entrance with a curt 'bye'; he went to the right, she to the left. Everywhere the leaves were falling but entwining around the next-door entrance, the gate for giants, they still grew vigorously since they were chiselled in stone. Lynette saw Rübezahl in the park; he stood there propped up on a rake. It was a long time since she had seen him last. She had thought that he might be in France, somewhere near the channel, where, well-shaven, he had joined the other soldiers who kept guard there, in case the English should ever dare to come out of the safety of their island.

Splendid façades rose up on the other side of the street when she stepped out of the park. These houses dated back to the Old Austria and made an especially melancholic impression on Lynette, which was perhaps also caused by the autumnal atmosphere. In class she repeatedly craned her neck to look into Anne's exercise book. When she made her eyes into narrow slits she was just about able to read what Fräulein Lämmert had written on the blackboard. Her sight was getting worse; she needed glasses, like Uncle Karl and Herbert. But maybe it was not all that bad the way she saw the world, the reality that surrounded her slightly blurred. Perhaps that was why the park was especially colourful this year, since the colours did not keep to any borders but ran into each other. So far she had been able to see the decorations and the protruding windowsills of the façades clearly but now they seemed to be dissolving. When she was in the courtyard for her break she looked at the square blocks of the school building; their outlines were not all that sharp any more but contrasted mildly with the sky.

Anne stirred up the leaves with her feet, making them rustle; the leaves had fallen from one of the trees whose supporting sticks had been taken away now. The tree had grown and as the tree had grown so Anne had shot up. Only Lynette remained small and plump. But they were not called Pat and Patachon any more because those films had gone out of fashion and had been forgotten. The most popular actors were not comedians any more but youthful, strong men as depicted on small cards that were collected by Gerda and the whole class. The men all looked somewhat alike: they had the same powerful chin and the same firm, relentless way of looking at you. Lynette was never able to remember their names. But that was what men had to look like: determined and not bespectacled. Herbert was different, an eccentric, and perhaps that was why he kept surfacing in her thoughts.

Her brother, on the other hand, wanted to be part of it all. He told Lynette, still full of excitement, how he had gone camping with the other boys from the Party that summer. They sat around the campfire under a starry sky and their group leader had played the guitar. It sounded like an adventure and very romantic, yes, it seemed like something that could have come out of the moss-green volumes. His eyes beamed when he told her about it. This was the New Time, its very beginning, and everything that happened at such a time was exciting. Anything outdated and fusty had to be thrown mercilessly overboard. This clearing was a prerogative of the young who were beginning to feel the strong winds of a great future. Heinz had to be tough and hard on himself as a man. Lynette wondered whether he really believed in what he said to her. She still remembered him back in Prague when he had loved nothing more than crawling into a corner to play with her dollies. But that was long ago and now he wanted to be a real boy, to be one of the gang, every boy wanted to be one of the gang and maybe she would have wanted the same if that had been within her grasp.

On Sunday Mutti was taking Heinz's velvet jacket out of the wardrobe when the doorbell rang. Father went to the door and opened it. She heard her father talking loudly, which was against his usual habit. Then he closed the door. Heinz's group leader had called and demanded that Heinz should come along on Sunday mornings too. But this fellow had no right to demand anything. It was all up to the parents, was it not? And Father wanted his son to go to church with Mutti.

Lynette noticed how disappointed her brother looked. He would probably have preferred to go with the group leader. He did not say a word on the way to church. It was cold; on days like these Lynette would also have liked to have a fur stole like Mutti's. They walked past the façade of the monastery church with its figurines and rich décor. The Town Church, in contrast, looked plain and stern. Singing rose up the tall pillars and the priest prayed the same Latin prayers as had been prayed for centuries; they sounded like magic spells. This had a soothing effect on Lynette and she let her thoughts drift. The smell of incense emanated from the silver vessels that were swung by the servers. She saw carefully clad men walking to the front; they were not all that much older than herself. One of them resembled Herbert. But it was not Herbert, of course, since Frau Domansky would hardly have gone to church with her children on Sundays as all the other townsfolk did.

Fräulein Plötzl who taught Lynette needlework at school went to the Holy Communion too. Lynette always asked Uncle Karl whether she could pass on his regards to Fräulein Plötzl since she looked more favourably upon her work then, giving her better marks. Fräulein Plötzl saw Lynette stand in line to take communion and when mass was over she asked Mutti after her lawyer brother, Herr Dr. Lauritsch. Uncle, of course, had gone away. Nothing had held him back when the first snow fell; he got his skis from the basement, packed a suitcase and went to the station in trousers that just reached down to his knees. The Tatra Mountains had been his destination. That was a pity, said Fräulein Plötzl and sighed; she would have loved to invite him to a coffee morning. Karl had been lucky, Lynette thought, that he had got out of it. Fräulein Plötzl was a bit of an old maid and probably thought that such a coffee morning was a big attraction for a well-to-do lawyer like Uncle. Instead, he preferred to lie in bed with his shoes off; liked to leaf through Wilhelm Busch's comic verse-tales *Schnaken und Schnurren* and you could hear him laugh out loud from time to time. At least that was what he would be doing after returning from his skiing trip, which would be after Christmas but still before the New Year.

He celebrated New Year in the Café Falk. Lynette was sitting with the rest of her family at the breakfast table when he came in with a loosened tie, his unshaven cheeks stubbly. The night of Saint Sylvester had been quiet for Lynette and her family. Father had played a few pieces on the violin, Mutti had read out poems, Lynette had played the piano for a while and Heinz had scratched something out on his learner's violin that sounded ugly but brought him a lot of applause, especially from Mutti. He had only begun playing a few months before and the applause was probably to encourage him to carry on. Father winced when Heinz failed to reach a note but he did not say anything. There was Tokay and champagne at midnight. They all emptied their glasses quickly and quietly before turning in. It had been a lot different last year when Father had stayed up for a long time with Wenka, Karl and Franz.

Auntie Bertha had not come either; she did not want to celebrate without her dear husband, the good Wenka. But Wenka was in France and so was Franz. Franz lived in Paris, billeted with a distinguished lady whose drawing room was at his disposal. Wenka, on the other hand, had to stay in the common room of some barracks that had been swiftly put up close to the channel. Wenka had been called up whereas Franz had volunteered. Wenka was a simple soldier, a *muschig*, as Mutti called him contemptuously; Franz was a captain. But not even the epaulettes on Uncle's shoulders could undo the fact that the freckly, always smiley, Lili had been burnt to death, as had Irmchen. Perhaps in Paris he would have forgotten them or tried to forget them. Lynette wondered what it felt like to be burnt. She clearly remembered the flaming matches from the children's book and then the heap of cinders that had been a little girl once; next to it the cats were sitting, their sad tears pouring down. Lili had been so easy-going and carefree and that was why she might not have been careful enough. A match that she had thrown away was perhaps still glowing... but nobody knew what had happened exactly. From that time on Mutti held every extinguished matchstick under water for a long time. Fräulein Pechwitz had to do the same; and Mutti kept the new matches on the top shelf in the broom cupboard so that she had to get the ladder first in order to reach them.

This was still going on in February when the candles on Lynette's birthday cake had to be lit but Mutti had forgotten to get the matches ready. There was a big fuss. Fräulein

Pechwitz had to go and fetch the ladder and Auntie Marchen giggled when Mutti came in with the matchbox at last. Uncle Adalbert stretched his long sinewy neck and frowned but Marchen still could not stop giggling. She took her glasses off her nose and rubbed the tears away. When *Hoch soll sie leben* was intoned, she joined in merrily and had only one relapse that was audible as a chortle. Marchen had found that strange, Lynette thought, all that fuss for a single matchstick. But it was not really surprising, for Marchen had little patience with minor things like housework and cooking. Everything was untidy in her house in Böhmisch-Leipa: the clothes hung up to dry in the middle of the living room and the coffee grounds going mouldy in the coffee pot. Auntie Bertha who went to Leipa regularly to check that things were alright was appalled by all that. But Auntie Bertha had little else to do apart from keeping her place tidy, whereas Marchen worked as a teacher. Marchen was a 'bluestocking'; that was what Mutti called her when she was annoyed with her for some reason. Marchen was very dainty and small; she seemed especially small when standing next to Uncle Adalbert who was tall and lanky. Baba was his mother too but it was different with their father since Mani and Uncle Adalbert did not have the same one.

Uncle Adalbert was completely different from Lynette's father. Adalbert was a driver of locomotives and always on his way to different places, while Father sat in his office most of the time. Uncle had gone as far as Romania and Bulgaria in his locomotive. Its smoke streamed backwards over his head and Uncle's helper shovelled coals into the boiler so that the steam made the wheels turn. Outside, glistening cupolas with onion towers drifted past; in front of them men and women in national costumes danced cheerfully. That was how Lynette had seen it in the pictures that Uncle Adalbert had brought back. But these were just pictures, for life was surely not all that different there from what it was here. The traffic rumbled trough the towns, chimneys rose up into the sky and a girl who was perhaps as old as Lynette stopped on her way to school to look at a bird that hopped free and without any worries through the undergrowth.

One picture showed Uncle Adalbert with his shirt open standing in his locomotive with his long hair being blown back. It was beautiful to travel from one place to the next though... she preferred it quieter. Uncle did not get a lot of money out of his travelling either; that was one of the reasons why Marchen worked as a teacher. Their pretty house in Leipa and its wide, wild garden needed to be paid for. And though Uncle Adalbert certainly did not work fewer hours than Father, he did not earn as much. That was why he had joined the 'Reds', who demanded equality. But people were different, Mutti said, and whoever wanted to make them equal had to press them into moulds, which could not be done without force. There were only a few polite questions that seemed very formal to Lynette when Father came home in the evenings. Father always observed the proprieties; he sat with the visitors for a while before he withdrew to play the violin.

Yes, Adalbert, Father probably thought while pulling the bow across the strings. He and his workers ought to have a go... why not? But it wasn't that easy. It did take a lot to run a factory, otherwise it went bankrupt. Then the workers would be on the street and would not have anything at all. Then there was what had happened to the big cargo of bottles for Japan... the Soviets in Russia had made an offer that

**117**

looked like a bargain. But then it turned out to be dear since every tenth bottle burst when they were filled up whereas it would only have been every hundredth bottle with the Mühlig-Union. The Japanese would think twice before ordering from the Soviets again. Adalbert had difficulties now since he had been a member of the Reds when they still existed. That was why he had become even skinnier and leaner than he had been before. But the Lauritsch Karl would help him; he knew the necessary tricks and gaps that always existed. That was how he would get out of the mess, for politics was always a dirty business – the great man in Weimar had been right. He had been right in many things and it was not up to him to pass judgement on the great man. He was a merchant who did as much as he could for his firm; his merchandise was glass. Perhaps it would be better if the world were made of glass, Father might have thought. Then everybody would have had to be careful and considerate so that the world would not break.

The Lauritsch grandparents had come to Lynette's birthday too. Grandfather was unsteady on his feet. Lynette and Mutti were glad when he had sat down in the end; at least he would not fall then. Lynette wondered how old he was. He did not know his exact age himself but if you had lived as long as he had, a few years more or less did not really matter. His hand trembled when he stroked her hair, announcing that she would not need to worry about her dowry. Grandmother had a chest full of porcelain and baskets full of linen that were still from the old Präger Farm. Old Präger had ruled on the Präger Farm. Grandmother kept talking about him. He had his children clean their shoes and boots themselves. Old Präger was hard on everyone. He showed compassion only towards his pigs; when they grunted, he said 'Gad uk de Schwan wos', which meant something like: Feed the pigs. He ate his semolina only with salt, so his wife, his children and all the maids and servants had to eat it with salt as well. But the great-grandmother sprinkled salt on his semolina while she secretly put sugar on the semolina of all the others. In this way everyone was content, for he thought of course that his wife obeyed him, but women had to be cunning sometimes. During mealtimes passages from the *Odyssey* were recited in melodious Greek. Old Präger's rule was not that much different from the rule of an Odysseus or Agamemnon, after all. Whenever Lynette tried to imagine the Präger Farm, it was veiled by the mists of ancient times.

The freesias withered and Fräulein Pechwitz threw them away. That was how it was: everything withered. It snowed outside; a blurred sun hung still in the sky and seemed to dissolve in the milky white. A winter sun, thought Lynette, who looked forward to spring when she would go to Dresden with her family.

Mutti held out the tickets to a man who wore a sailor's cap as if they were not going up the Elbe for a leisurely trip but out on the high seas. It was warm, so they sat outside under the awning; even Mutti did not object to that. But she did not like to see them at the rails though it was very interesting there, especially at the back where the ship ploughed a trail into the water, with shrieking seagulls circling over it. There the flag flapped, sooty from the smoke that rose from the ship's chimney. Fruit trees blossomed on the shore and Lynette thought that the blossoms looked like snow. She would remember that to record it in her chronicle.

Father folded the newspaper. He smiled; he looked much

more approachable, relaxed, and the reason for this was probably that he was on this ship, leaving his office and all his worries behind him. He gazed at the waves that bobbed up and down under the glistening sun, asking Lynette and Heinz whether they knew the Bila. Mutti said that the Bila was the river that flowed into the Elbe down at the station. Father had jumped from ice floe to ice floe in those days when he was a scamp. Lynette imagined him wearing mittens, a woollen hat and a scarf. He slid on an ice floe wanting to hold on to it. But the current pushed him under water. The water poured into him. This was a pleasant feeling and he did not struggle against it; he let this roaring and thundering in till he was full of it. He felt giddy. He almost felt cosy in the gleaming darkness that was the realm of the wild Waterman who desired the beautiful Lilofee. The Waterman would have kept him in his castle if some people had not accidentally seen the boy and had fished him out of the water with poles. But perhaps he would have dived to the surface with him; his tail would have immediately turned into two legs. He would have put the boy over his mighty shoulder and stamped off in the direction of Augiessl while cap, scarf and mittens drifted towards the sea. Baba stood in the doorframe, arms akimbo. She took his burden off the Waterman, dried the boy and put him into his Sunday best. Then the boy was brought down to the Türmitz churchyard. There he lay between flowers which withered together with the fresh skin. You did not need to be afraid of death, Lynette thought, but you had to come to grips with life; life could be tough, especially if you were not all that robust and thick-skinned. But it was still beautiful, she thought, observing how a castle rose slowly out of the landscape. Its name was Pilnitz. The water splashed along broad stairs. On curved roofs pagoda turrets hovered in the silvery mist. Lynette had the impression that she had not only gone to the old Reich but straight to China. A gentleman soon reminded her that she was in Saxony since he referred to the weather as *driebedimpflich* which was Saxon dialect and meant 'dull and miserable'. There was a light drizzle when the steamer docked at the Brühl terrace. They had travelled from the sun into the rain: that was the North for you, it always rained in the North.

'Well, well... the ladies and gentlemen come from Aussig,' said the waiter in the café; his hair was plastered down, which was probably meant to look elegant. 'Who would have thought that, one day, you would be able to travel from Bohemia to Saxony while never leaving Germany?'

There were precious cakes in the shape of turrets, and the Zwinger Palace looked so light and lucid as if it had not been hewn in stone but was made of pastry too, covered with icing sugar by a pastry-cook. The old town was full of corners with houses that had tilted roofs, which reminded Lynette of Prague. The dome of the Church of Our Lady rose up like a giant bell, and some postcards in the souvenir shops gave the impression that the city's sole purpose was to carry this bell. The guide pointed out the cracks in the dome; but none of the travellers would need to worry since the whole of the miraculous building would soon be refurbished so that it would last for the next two hundred years. And the guide began to explain the details of the work that would soon be undertaken.

'Dresden is also called the Florence on the river Elbe,' Mutti explained when they were back on the steamer again, this time inside, since the benches were wet from the rain. Florence was a city in Italy. Herr del Vesco came from Italy.

Father and Mutti had gone to Venice for their honeymoon; well, Venice, Venice was a dream. 'As long as you're on your guard,' Father remarked dryly. 'There are quite a few thieves down there.'

Father knew Italy. As a young man he had lived there for almost two years, representing his firm. He had played chess in a café near Milan Cathedral and had drunk a bottle of Orvieto with his lunch in Perugia. People waved their arms and shouted at each other across the streets. They were loud and passionate. Mutti always thought that they were about to have a go at each other. Don't worry, Father said, they're only having a little chat. When he had travelled from inn to inn on his own, Father had always leaned a chair against the door handle of his room. One night he was woken up by a loud racket. The landlord had probably unlocked the door with his key and was trying to push it open. Yes, there were quite a few thieves down there but, of course, you could find thieves anywhere. Later, when the war was over, they would all go to Padua which was where Herr del Vesco came from. In the meantime he had to march around under the hot African sun and Father was once again glad that he had one short leg. That was why he could stay here in Aussig where his home was now. He turned to the side and, through the window, looked up at the Schreckenstein which Lynette had been waiting for for quite a while.

Now at last the Schreckenstein had appeared in the distance behind a bend in the river. The castle lay crouched above the steep rock. A tower rose up; decayed walls and vaults, with swallows nesting in the corners. Hundreds of years ago the halls, which the wind had uncovered, had been full of life. Banquets had been held there but something had driven the inhabitants away from the Schreckenstein. Since then the castle had been decaying until a restaurant for holidaymakers was opened there; Lynette, too, had been up there, eating sausages with crunchy straw potatoes.

'It's nice to be home again,' Mutti said when the sailors moored the ship to the shore. The people queued on a bridge made of wooden planks, jostling each other to get on land. Lynette took a deep breath; there was an earthy smell and the odour of lilac.

# 8

Lilac bushes blossomed behind the house. That was where the plots of land were; each flat had a plot. Mutti sowed kitchen herbs and Lynette kneeled in her plot that was a corner of Mutti's plot; she sank the sunflower seeds she had from Herr Filip deep into the moist soil. She noted down this date in her chronicle, drawing sunflowers on the same page: those giant majestic plants whose heads followed the course of the sun in a leisurely way. The yellow blossoms looked like flames blazing. They blazed like the flames in Freudenthal. Perhaps the smoke from the flames numbed any feeling just as water did, Lynette thought, and Lili and Irmchen had probably not suffered all that much.

Uncle Franz wrote frequently. Mutti opened his letters, read them to herself first, then she read them aloud. Franz wrote about the lady in whose flat he lived. She was an educated lady and he had interesting conversations with her.

She spoke German fluently since she came from Alsace. In the evenings she got the liqueur and cognac ready and he stretched out his legs while the night veiled the city of lights outside, though it had ceased to be a city of lights since streets and squares were blacked out because of the war. The lady seemed to like Uncle. Lynette thought of the picture of him in the family album, which showed him as a neat cadet, holding white gloves in one hand while the other hand hung down nonchalantly with the thumb hooked inside the pocket of the long coat. Then he had still been in the old Austrian army but now there was not all that much left of its old elegance; these days the soldiers wore heavy boots and peaked caps. He had several times tried to call on Jacques, Uncle wrote. But each time the concierge had told him that unfortunately Monsieur Rivet had gone out. As strange as it sounded, though Uncle was in Paris he longed to be back home; only duty held him there.

Lynette also did her duty, if you could call it that, by competing on the school's sports ground. When running she saw Gerda's plaits tossing in front of her; Gerda was far ahead and the boys (there were always some boys there, gawping) laughed. Lynette laughed with them; she couldn't do anything else really. But if it had been up to her she would have changed into her blouse and dress and walked towards the hills where the wood anemones blossomed between tree trunks. There she could have dreamt of the wild Waterman. Was it really surprising that Mutti thought that she was not like other girls? It seemed to Lynette that Mutti would have been happier if she had had a daughter like Gerda.

Gerda stepped in front of the assembled pupils and teachers when the new school year began and the flag was hoisted; she recited Körner's poem about the Schreckenstein but started stuttering and, red in the face, had to be prompted by Fräulein Lämmert. But nobody teased her because of that. She was forgiven for everything since she was a bright, blonde girl. But Lynette was dark-haired and much too plump, which was down to too much chocolate; the other girls made fun of her because she was plump and that made her sad so that she ate more chocolate. That was how it went on and on... She recalled the anthem of the Czech republic that she had had to sing in Prague every morning before school lessons began. *Kde domov můj*? Yes, where was her home? If it was anywhere at all, it was most likely to be in the park or with Anne. The redcurrants had ripened at Anne's house once again. Piano music wafted into the road outside; its sound was hesitating, muted... somebody was not playing for others but for himself. Lynette wondered whether Herbert really did anything apart from playing the piano. Oh yes, said Anne, he read poetry.

'Poetry? What kind of poetry?'

'By Rilke.'

Then they played ball. Lynette put her foot down clumsily and slipped. She fell backwards; Anne shook with laughter. But when she saw that Lynette did not join in, she walked over and helped her to get up. She stood there facing Lynette for a while, with her arms around her shoulders. Lynette felt the warmth exuding from the other body through her blouse; Anne gave Lynette a short hug and she felt Anne's soft and gentle chest. Then Anne turned round and walked towards her house. They were both sweating from the ball game but also from the heat. It was as hot and sultry as a greenhouse; the sky was covered with dark clouds and a thunderstorm rumbled in the distance. They were thirsty and went down to the cellar. It smelled musty, water dripped somewhere, heaps of junk lay all over the place... if Mutti had been here, she would have rolled her sleeves up straight away and started clearing up. There were bottles of lemonade in a wooden box. They took one bottle, fetched three glasses from the kitchen and poured the foaming lemonade into them. The third glass was for Herbert who put it on his piano without letting himself be distracted by them from his improvisations. The piano sounds were like occasional, clear drops of glass that solidified; blending in with them from upstairs was the muffled beat of American dance music. At one point Lynette heard a shrill scream and she could not tell whether somebody had screamed with pleasure or pain. Well, well, Lynette thought... Frau Domansky, the wife of a high-up civil servant in Berlin, played American dance music on her gramophone; the record must have still been from the times of the Czech republic, for you couldn't get anything like that any more. As if from far away, she heard Anne say: 'It's a pity about the nice redcurrants; we should have picked them but you wanted to play ball...'

The storm shook the redcurrant bushes. The sky was a bilious green. Hail came drumming down onto the greenhouse; it broke the cracked glass, so that pieces of glass fell into the poppies. Frau Domansky came running barefoot in her far-eastern dressing gown; she was about to open the garden door but changed her mind and went upstairs, swearing.

'Poor Mama,' remarked Herbert, closing the piano.

When Frau Domansky came downstairs again, she was accompanied by the young man from the Savings Bank. She seemed to have calmed down; she was almost a bit too blasé. She put her legs on the young man's lap and, looking into the garden where the hailstorm had caused havoc, she began to talk about tempests and catastrophes. They were mostly harmless in Europe if you compared them to the vast continent of Asia where a single giant wave or a volcanic eruption could wipe out the whole population of large areas. After some time, other people moved into those areas, taking possession of what was left. It was strange to think of cooking on stoves belonging to people who had perished or had been driven out. Frau Domansky laughed distractedly and wrote something in the air with her pointed finger. She promised them mallow tea. Lynette waited politely. Frau Domansky put the tie around the neck of her lover and it looked like a noose; she laughed. Lynette wondered whether she still remembered about the mallow tea? Lynette wanted to say good-bye but Frau Domansky said that she could go with Rudi if she waited for a moment; Rudi had to go home since he had to get his beauty sleep. Rudi giggled. But Lynette wanted to be on her own; that was why she said something about her mother who had expected her back some time ago and she began to walk home.

Torn off branches and twigs lay everywhere. The storm had been particularly bad for the roses: their countless petals had been scattered across the ground and the depetalled stalks jutted up, bare and stark. Rübezahl would have a lot of work to do cutting back the roses. Herr Filip said that he had not seen such a storm for a long time. But now the air had been cleansed and felt like velvet. Yes, yes, a good storm from time to time could only be beneficial, said Herr Filip, winking. If he had been looking for an assistant she would have applied immediately. Then she would have become a shop assistant, who was looked down upon by Latin pupils like her brother. But that would not have bothered her much; the shop would have saved her from school which was the main thing. When she walked to school in the mornings her stomach felt queasy like the 'lift feeling' in Prague. It became stronger when she saw the square blocks of the school building emerging behind the bushes, which was like the lift going up; and when Anne said 'hello' with a smile, it felt to Lynette as if the lift came to a halt. But the doors still remained closed; they only opened at noon when the rattling school bell set her free.

The afternoons were hers. She drifted along, listening to Fräulein Pechwitz, who dreamt up tales about old times, or strolled around the park. Heinz had begun to listen to the special broadcasts from the Front. They reverberated through the whole flat but it seemed that he still could not stand close enough to the wireless. The broadcasts reported the tremendous victories of the German army which was forcing its way deeper and deeper into the endless lands of Russia. The fields stretched so far that they dissolved into the horizon. Birch trees grew in marshy ground and people lived in cottages that often did not have a first floor. But the Ukrainian towns with their baroque churches and municipal buildings from the time of the Old Austria often looked like back home. Uncle Franz wrote all that in a letter. There was no second letter from him and Uncle Karl did not write at all. Only once had he hurriedly scribbled on a postcard that he was fine but he could not stand the sight of caviar any more. Karl seemed to take things calmly. Or was it gallows humour? Heinz had put a map on the wall, pinning little flags on it stretching further and further east. He could sit in front of this map for a long time losing himself in gazing at it; the moss-green volumes stood on the shelf, abandoned. When the days became colder and shorter, the flags remained more or less where they had been and, around Christmas time, her brother even had to take some of them back. He did it quietly and stopped showing off with the special broadcasts, since there were not that many any more.

Mutti donated her old coat to the winter relief collection for the Front. At least she was doing something so that the soldiers did not freeze to death: after all, her two brothers were in Russia. Her little Heinz could have been there as well if he had only been a few years older. They were taking on very young men by now; perhaps they preferred the young ones since they joined up full of enthusiasm. When you had lived a while you had seen too much already and settled down in life.

Mutti also sent a coat from Father who was annoyed about it, for he had been fond of this coat. 'When the war is over, you can buy yourself as many coats as you wish,' Mutti consoled him.

Father nodded: yes, the so-called final victory. Lynette would get a horse then, a beautiful riding horse, and so would Heinz, of course. They would live like royals as befitted the victors. Until then Father had to come to terms with only having one coat and Heinz and Lynette had to carry on going on foot. Lynette did not mind, for she could not really imagine herself sitting high up on a horse. She smiled and Father smiled too; he did not seem to have meant it too seriously when he had talked about getting riding horses.

Father sat at the table, looking through a magnifying glass. Men jumped from the skies with parachutes above their heads. Tanks rattled past a smashed house; only one wall was left standing. A ship burnt while a submarine surfaced in the foreground. 'Yes, the war,' Father sighed, putting the stamps in the album.

Lynette hoped that the war would be over soon. After the war Heinz was to have the beautiful Bisiach violin that Father had seen in the music shop at Market Square. Father had looked at the music shop's message board but in vain. A lot had been going on before the war started. The great Burmester and the singer Leo Slezak had performed in the public library. Now it had all gone quiet; that was because of the war. 'When the war is over you can wish for whatever you want,' Father told her, 'it doesn't have to be a riding horse.'

Perhaps she should have wished to have a grand piano, Lynette thought, as she lay awake in bed. Then she could have been her brother's accomplished accompanist when he played the song of the wild Waterman on his Bisiach. Sinking deeper and deeper on her piano stool, there was nowhere to hold onto. She heard water roaring... and as she opened her eyes, staring into the darkness, she realised that somebody had flushed the lavatory. Something prosaic had been turned into a dream by her imagination, her brain or whatever it was that her skull contained. That was strange, she thought, and soon afterwards she was riding on a horse. Fields stretched on almost endlessly and a house burnt in the distance. This had to be Russia. Wanting to get out of Russia, she pressed her knees into the horse's flanks so that it would trot faster. She began to feel a pain in the pit of her stomach and she found that her nightshirt was soiled with blood when she woke up. This thing happened to women, said Mutti, putting the nightshirt with the dirty laundry. Mutti did not say more. But Lynette knew already from Anne about these things.

The blood circulated through the body and as long as the blood kept circulating, everything was fine. Your body, however, seemed to have a life of its own, following its own laws, and people were deceived if they believed that they were masters over their bodies. It was exactly the other way round, thought Lynette, stepping out onto the road with her brother; at every step she felt the wound that had opened up overnight. They came to a stop and Heinz took his different path. He was carrying the violin that he had borrowed from his school. He would have liked to have hidden it under his cardigan if that had been possible. But as it was not, he kept close to the houses so that he could quickly dip into an entrance should his group leader appear. He could not be allowed to see him with a violin in his hand.

Lynette saw a man with a black patch over one eye sitting in the park; only a stump was left of his right arm. He was in uniform; from his chest dangled a medal that was probably supposed to make up for his arm and his eye. He was still very young but life would not be the same for him any more. She saw herself helping him to undress and carefully removing the patch from his eye. Imagining this, she had a strange feeling inside her and did not know what to make of it. She liked the man in the park much better than the man who resembled a perfect-looking actor in Gerda's little picture, which she showed to almost everybody in her class. But no, this was not an actor who had been chosen for the role of Reichsprotektor; it was the Reichsprotektor himself. He looked so perfect that he seemed like an actor playing himself. Proud and young, he sparkled in his smart uniform. They said that he was a good violin player... but others said that he played the cello. So, what did he play: the violin or the cello? But perhaps this was not really important, for he probably did not have a lot of time left to play either instrument. He seemed to be constantly going around in his big, black limousine; he held banquets and ruled high up in the castle at Prague. One day a bomb put an end to this splendour, tearing this body apart, despite its youthfulness and vigour. London was behind it all, of course... but nobody was able to get at London. Therefore the assassins were made responsible for it. It was said that they took refuge in a small village: a village called Lidice. His dramatic decease had drastically increased the Reichsprotektor's value, with Gerda being able to receive no fewer than five pictures of actors in return for his picture; the men looked all very much alike and it was easy to mix them up with the Reichsprotektor.

Today Heinz had gone out to do something with the other boys from the Party's youth organisation. Mutti was shopping with Fräulein Pechwitz, a lengthy undertaking, for Mutti not only wanted to have the food to which she was entitled by the ration-cards but also some cream and butter. Lynette was alone in the flat, which she liked since she could laze around without being disturbed by anyone. She unwrapped a bar of chocolate from its silver foil. She wanted to bite into it but held herself back, for she did not really know when she would get some chocolate again. It was a miracle that Herr Filip was still able to get chocolate for her. It certainly meant a lot of effort for him and it would not have surprised her if he had spent much more money on it than he asked off her. She knew what she wanted when the war was over: a whole cupboard stuffed with chocolate. She strolled down the corridor past Uncle Karl's room, the door of which was ajar. Uncle was in Russia but this was still his room. His shaving brush stood in the bathroom; it had a spicy smell. He had taken smaller, handier shaving things to the Front; they were the same ones he had taken to the Tatra Mountains. The lid was loosely screwed onto the box that contained the shaving soap. Broken into pieces, an alabaster styptic pencil lay next to it: things men used, unfamiliar and alluring at the same time. Even Fräulein Pechwitz did not tidy up these things because Uncle would not stand for it. That was why these things lay around, waiting for Uncle till he came home from the Front for Christmas or perhaps New Year.

Lynette stopped at the door that was ajar. She pushed it gently open, slipping into the room. There was a smell of leather, probably from the shoes and boots that had been carelessly lined up in the wardrobe. She held the handle of the top desk drawer, hesitating. Then she jerked the drawer open. Pens lay in it, jumbled up. The wood at the side was stained black and Lynette suspected that an inkpot that stood there with its lid on had tipped over. The next drawer was littered with letters; there was no string to hold them together. The letters' addresses had been carefully written in a beautiful, neat hand that would not have been out of place on a calligraphic print. Lynette opened one of the letters, which smelled of hyacinths. The writer of the letters had definitely been a woman; Lynette found it hard to imagine that a man could have had such pernickety writing. Had Uncle not liked the gloves she had knitted for him, the writer asked, for he never wore them though she had used best quality wool. By the way, she had baked coconut macaroons; a whole plate full was ready for him when he came next time. Did he want to remain a bachelor for all eternity, she wrote in another letter and beneath it she had written: With love, Yours, Dagmar. Now Lynette realised who the lady was, whose writing had appeared familiar to her from the beginning. It was the needlework teacher who always put herself down as 'Dr. Plötzl' in the class register. This 'Dr.' to which she shortened Dagmar revealed ambitions that would come true if she succeeded in marrying Uncle, for then everybody would address her as 'Frau Doktor'. But that was hardly likely, Lynette thought, shutting the drawer.

Something fell when she opened the bottom drawer. It was a bottle of cognac that had been standing next to a bottle of red wine. A cork stood out from the red wine bottle; its contents had become cloudy. Lynette felt some unevenness under the flower-patterned drawer liner. She got out the envelope that lay under the paper. In it were brown tinged photographs of naked bodies that were female and blessed with voluptuous curves. This was young skin, which looked taut and healthy. Complacently, a girl gazed at the velvety fruit of her bottom in a mirror. In another picture a girl had to do penance by being chastised by two companions: one of them held her while the other one lashed out with a long-stemmed rose. This too was something to do with love. If Mutti had known about it, Lynette thought, pushing the envelope back under the flower-patterned drawer liner. For Mutti, something like this was sin. But what was sin? Maybe you had to be strict with yourself, but being strict did not appeal to her nor even to Mutti who kept on reading her novels and enthused about operas. Though it was a bad time for operas.

# 9

Fewer and fewer operas were being performed in the Town Theatre since the Front kept devouring the tenors and stage workers. And there were rumours that all the theatres would close down soon. For New Year at least there would be some pleasant change; Mutti held a card and a letter in her hand: her two brothers had written that they were coming home. Only Wenka could not come. He was a *muschig*; it was more difficult for him to get away. But Wenka would never rise any higher; he was much too melancholic for somebody who was supposed to give orders. Had there ever been a poet who had made a good soldier? Rilke had been put into the administration during the last war but even there he had soon been dismissed.

Mutti was almost always in town now. She wanted the food to be the same over the holidays as it had been before the war and it was not easy to get all the ingredients. Uncle

Karl brought sparkling wine from the Crimea. He had changed; Lynette did not recognise him at first in his uniform. His youthful face that had always reminded Lynette of a schoolboy had become furrowed, especially above the nose; something broody had got into his features. He seemed distracted when playing rummy; once he even discarded the wrong cards. Again and again he poured some cognac from the bottom drawer of the cupboard into his glass; he had never drunk cognac before when playing cards with them.

But whereas Uncle Karl seemed aged, Franz had been rejuvenated by the war. His back had straightened, and he strutted around attending to the light switches. Champagne he had not brought but he had produced a bar of chocolate for Lynette and Heinz, which probably came from his special Christmas ration. At the table, he was surprised at the rich dishes and later at the salami on the canapés that were served with the Hungarian wine. 'Heavens,' he shouted, 'you are well-provided for; we don't have such luxuries at the Front.' Mutti bit her tongue rather than say anything about the supreme effort the shopping had cost her.

Father said: 'The salami is from Hungary; genuine Hungarian salami.' Then he talked about his trips that had taken him as far as Turkey. Turkey bought much of their glass now after the overseas trade with South America and the Far East had become too unsafe. When on a trip he always brought plenty of goods back with him. His suitcase was always full of salami and wine. The customs officer knew him already and said smiling: Yes, of course, I know, this is your food and drink for the journey; you need a lot of sustenance when you travel, don't you? It was nice, Father said, to see the Hungarian landscape gliding past, those far-reaching plains with rows of poplar trees on the horizon. In the villages, the high poles of the wells rose above the flat roofs. The houses had only a ground floor, the roofs were wavy; yellow maize was stored in open barns. The conductor for the sleeper carriage got the bed ready for the night. The bed was quite luxurious with its white sheets and you soon fell asleep since a lullaby was hummed by the turning of the wheels and the wind that was caused by the train's speedy advance. The conductor brought him breakfast in the morning, a sumptuous breakfast as befitted a man on his travels. Didn't the conductor remind him of somebody...? Yes, of the Stifter scholar whom he had known when he was at Prague University. Father had read law until Heinz was born; he had also gone to lectures on music and German literature. He had even heard the great Sauer give a lecture. The Stifter scholar was called Alfred Stier. The walls of his room had been covered with engravings from early editions of the writer's work and the cactus *Cereus peruvianus* stood in front of the window; it was the same cactus that played such an important role in the last chapter of *Der Nachsommer*, after the main character tells the narrator about his thwarted love affair which has come to a late blossoming. Perhaps because his name did not seem aesthetic enough to him or just to try to get closer to his idol, he only put his initials, 'A. St.', on his lecture handouts. Stier gave his lectures slowly, hesitating again and again: a tall burly man like the conductor who ruminated for a while before passing on some information in his solemn, dignified way; the conductor hesitated in the middle of a sentence, began again... and that was exactly what Stier had done. The conductor was called Stier too, at least in Father's mind. When he had travelled on business to

Hamburg who opened the carriage door for him but Stier. Father smiled at him and Stier made a slight bow. Father liked going to Hamburg. Brahms had come from there and one of his works achieved something like a marriage of the stern Hansa city with the fiery Magyars. The people of Hamburg with their polite discretion and solid ways appealed to Father. He was not even put off by the continuous drizzle. That had been in spring when Hamburg still existed. The waiter had brought Father a cheese board after an excellent meal. When Father wanted to cut off a piece, he noticed that the cheese was alive. The waiter explained to him that the cheese was supposed to be like that. Gourmets ate cheese only with maggots; they were the proof that the cheese was really ripe.

'Well, Madame,' said Karl when he had some cheese, 'where are the maggots? A gourmet like myself eats cheese only with maggots.'

Mutti turned away. The things Karl got up to. Even now he had not changed. Mutti was horrified by maggots, especially in cheese. She tried to change the subject by asking her other brother how he had liked his time in Paris.

'It was magnificent,' said Uncle Franz, 'the parade first of all. Something like that only happens once in your life; never again.' Saying this he looked at his brother above whom the picture of the great Rühr hung. Rühr had let Karl down once and Lynette had to smile at the thought that he was sitting under his picture now. This seemed an additional burden to him though he was already very quiet and worried.

'We were lucky with the weather,' said Uncle Franz, 'blue sky as if it had been especially arranged for us. *Kaiserwetter* as an officer from the Reich said. I always knew the Arc de Triomphe was big but I never imagined it was that huge. I felt tiny under it, though I was on horseback. It was a great feeling riding under the Arc de Triomphe. There was something elevating about it...'

Mutti nodded. Perhaps she was thinking of the columns of dashing soldiers, similar to the ones marching into Prague. But Lynette got the impression that her nodding expressed worry as well as approval. After all, things could not be going that well since food had to be rationed and the news from Russia was not good.

'Ach, Russia,' said Karl, 'Russia is so enormous; it's endless. I like the Russian peasants. They don't give us the feeling that we come as conquerors. They let us sleep in their huts; they sleep near the oven where it's nice and warm. They put their slaughtered chickens in the same oven. The oven isn't hot at all but they leave the chicken in it all night and half a day. By then the meat is wonderfully tender and it comes off the bone almost by itself.'

'Russia must be so beautiful,' said Mutti, 'just think of the magnificent churches, of Tchaikovsky...'

'Yes yes, but that's not the Russia we fight in; we're in the Russia of the Soviets, full of commissaries and tanks. And I have to do lots of paperwork just as I have to do here. The only difference is that I'm an officer for the court martial now and should be signing death sentences but so far I've refused.' Mutti sighed. No doubt they would come for Uncle and arrest him one day. Then he would be put on trial and the officer who dealt with his case would not be so stupid: he would not hesitate to put his signature under the sentence.

'By the way,' Uncle Karl said, 'I've begun to learn English.'

'English,' replied Franz, 'why would you want to learn English? It will only spoil your German. And anyway, who will be speaking English when the war is over? German will be the language of the world then... and French *naturellement*,' he added, looking at Madame.

Later on Lynette had some champagne; her palate had outgrown childhood and she enjoyed the fizzy sensation that felt so gentle and smooth. But her brother still preferred the sweet Tokay. She was also allowed to stay up longer. She listened to both uncles who began to sing; they had their glasses in their hands and their legs over the chairs' armrests. They seemed like the best of friends now and all the tension had disappeared. They had united as two brothers against their sister, which probably reminded them of their childhood days. Their sister was such a refined lady who only sipped real champagne; and even then not more than half a glass of it. Yes, their sister who would still have been able to recite from memory all the aristocratic families of Prague without leaving out a single one, perhaps even all the noble houses of the whole Old Austria. The highest duty of an officer from bygone Austrian times was not making war but being charming towards the ladies. But Lynette wondered whether Mutti would really have felt at ease in the company of officers; she seemed too scared for that, lacking in *joie de vivre*. It was different in novels where she could mix with officers without being hurt by an unforeseen impetuosity... only in opera the rudeness of this world was transformed into beauty and melodious harmony.

'Ach, dieses Atems wonniges Wehen! Süßes Vergehen, seliges Grauen,' sang Uncle Karl, who held his hand to his lethal wound while gliding down from his chair onto the carpet. He took his time dying, repeating the lines again and again, for in operas even death had to be enjoyed to the full. Karl applauded, laughing, while Mutti shook her head, quite rightly so, Lynette thought; men were like children, especially when they had drunk too much.

She soon went to bed but was unable to sleep. Whenever she was about to close her eyes, she saw Auntie Lili's freckly face smiling at her. The party had been sad without Lili and Irmchen, without Uncle Wenka and Auntie Bertha. Fräulein Plötzl would have loved to have come but Uncle had told Mutti to tell her that he would not be there. She had given red roses to Mutti. They stood in a vase in his room; he had hardly looked at them because he did not like roses. But the inside of Lynette's eyelids were reddish like rose petals when she looked up at the ceiling light with her eyes closed. Then she turned the light off again. Somehow she must have fallen asleep after all, for when she opened her eyes the room was full of daylight.

The two uncles were still sleeping. Franz was snoring on the carpet; Karl lay with his legs pulled up on the sofa and had his back turned to Lynette. She opened the window because of the stale cigarette smoke, for Franz had been smoking continuously, of course. Fräulein Pechwitz, who was strong, grabbed him under his shoulders; Mutti picked up his legs. That was how they carried Uncle out of the room, putting him on Karl's bed where he kept on snoring. They put Karl to lie down next to him. Then they collected the empty bottles and discarded the cigarette ash, which was checked by Mutti first in case it was still glowing. When Monsieur appeared, the *Palace* looked more or less tidy. He leaned back in the armchair, turning on the radio, from which the sounds of the New Year Concert began to flow...

It was a year like every other year. It began in a leisurely way but its days passed by ever more quickly after a while. The park was covered by a deep white blanket that melted again. Lynette did not get freesias for her birthday in February this year but primroses which came in a flowerpot since their short stems made them unsuitable for a vase. The door to Uncle Karl's room was ajar; Lynette was sure that Uncle longed to be back in this room from the vastness of Russia. Franz too was fighting in Russia now and Lynette did not doubt that he missed the lady from Alsace as well as her cognac. Both brothers were fighting in the same country but so far apart that proud Germany would have fitted in the area between them several times over.

Mutti cleaned, cooked, tidied up as conscientiously as ever with the help of Fräulein Pechwitz. Father was the first one to leave the flat every morning, coming back when everybody else had arrived. He had Fräulein Pechwitz help him out of his coat. Today he did not say a word at mealtime whereas usually he at least inquired how things had gone at school. After supper he retired immediately. He did not even touch the newspaper, for the violin could be heard straight away. He chased the scales up and down, making the bow jump though he usually preferred to play quiet, melodious pieces.

Lynette would have loved to go into the *Palace* where her chronicle was. Through the opaque glass, she saw the violin bow that never rested growing out of Father's silhouette before submerging into it again... till all eternity. But this was an eternity that ended when Father got ready for his chess evening. His keys jangled as he walked up and down the corridor, a process which Mutti called 'antechambering', though Father was about to go out and was not waiting outside a chamber. As soon as the front door had been shut Mutti began to chatter, her words tripping out of her mouth like the ringing of small bells: 'I can't talk my man out of anything. He has definitely been there today. But he doesn't say anything... only when it's too late. What times we live in! I had to put up with quite a lot when we were under the Czechs but now they're taking it a bit too far. You have to be careful... there's not a lot else you can do. But Mani... it's absolutely unnecessary that he puts himself out on a limb like that. His friend Otto won't be able to help him all the time either. He's not that high up on the ladder... ticking his name off for Mani when he didn't attend the Party meetings is one thing but to help him with what he's got himself into now is something quite different....'

Fräulein Pechwitz had listened patiently while she washed the dishes left from the evening meal. Now she remarked that the picture Madame painted was probably a bit too black on the whole. She was sure that nothing would happen to Herr Taussig. There was no mugging and murdering in the streets any more; now order ruled and even a woman was able to go to the parks in Prague in the evening. Lynette thought it strange that Fräulein Pechwitz should say something like that, for she could not remember her ever going to any of the parks.

What had happened to Father today, Lynette wondered. Mutti hesitated at first but then she began to tell Lynette in her light and quick way, so that Lynette could see everything clearly in front of her. Yes, she saw him walking down Bismarck Street. There he visited the Villa Weinmann. That was what Lynette and her family still called that grand house, though the Weinmanns had not lived there for many years. The garden with its lilac bushes was bare now. Barbed wire had been put on top of the wall and flag posts rose up behind it. Guards stood at the gate, motionless, their chins pushed forward as if hewn in marble. Father passed them, limping slightly. He looked indifferent as if he were on his way to work early in the morning or to one of his chess evenings. Everything was in turmoil inside him but Father kept up appearances. He briefly took off his hat in the high vestibule, stretching his hand up for the required salute but not in a brisk, forceful manner; he did it more like someone who wanted to wipe a cobweb out of the air. The officer on duty examined Father's passport. Then he asked the guard to accompany Father, who was expected. Lynette imagined the furniture as being luxurious, for the Weinmanns could not have taken a lot with them. Precious paintings hung on the wall and Persian rugs covered the floor, softening Father's step. A man who looked weary despite his youth sat behind a massive desk, the only piece of furniture that had been added to the room. He got up and walked towards Father. He looked delicate, fragile. He would probably not have lasted one day in the winter cold of Russia but seemed quite comfortable here in the warm room behind the desk. Father was allowed to take a seat on one of the sofas. Very politely the civil servant asked whether Father wanted a coffee. Father drank his coffee black and with sugar. Black as Night, hot as Hell and sweet as Love, Father joked because he felt dejected inside.

'I see, Mandel is his name,' the civil servant said, 'he's the brother of your secretary, her half-brother... but you're happy with your secretary, aren't you? You may keep her; after all, her work is important. Our soldiers need bottles and glasses, beer and schnapps are important for morale... don't you drink?'

The civil servant poured Father a glass of sticky sweetish liqueur which he had got out of his massive desk. An orderly brought the file. The civil servant nodded, leafing through it: Adolf Mandel. He expressed his regret. He would do whatever he could. Then he asked about Otto Dewald.

'I see, I see... an old school friend of yours; he thinks highly of you. Please pass on my best regards when you see him next time.'

Father left through the gate taking a deep breath. The notorious secret police had turned out to be nice and obliging, completely different from their reputation. But he had not got anywhere. They had been evasive, hiding behind a shield of politeness. He was powerless. That was how he felt when he came home in the evening. By playing the violin, he seemed to want to prove to himself that he was after all in control.

A few weeks later Adolf Mandel was released. He lived with his half-sister who looked after him, for he could not live on his own any more since he wet the bed, started up screaming in the middle of the night and had developed other disturbing habits. That was what Mutti said and Mutti was bound to know it from Father who had been told by Fräulein Mandel. But something else that Mutti said made Lynette forget all about Adolf Mandel. Mutti said that Fräulein Pechwitz would have to leave them, though Lynette could not believe it since Fräulein Pechwitz had been with her family as long as she could remember.

# 10

Fräulein Pechwitz stood in the corridor one morning. She was not wearing her usual work clothes but a costume that she had only so far worn when attending Party meetings. She had packed her suitcase which contained virtually all her belongings; she did not own much else. After all, what was the sense of gathering riches if you could lose everything anyway? That was what had happened to her father... hadn't it? She had cleaned Lynette's shoes yesterday evening for the last time; they gleamed now as she was leaving. The *knödliges Fräulein* and Heinz... they were her children too; she had seen them grow up and had looked after them. Herr and Frau Taussig... they were good people. Tears bowled down her cheeks. She just let them fall since she was holding the suitcase in one hand and waving with the other. Then she disappeared round the corner where the trams stopped.

Today Lynette kept thinking about Fräulein Pechwitz; she

kept getting in between Lynette and the things that were happening at school. She saw her standing in the factory; the factory would be Fräulein Pechwitz's home from now on. She was standing in a vast hall at an assembly line; there was always a draught there so that she had to tie her headscarf tight. At midday a siren blared and she walked over to the canteen where she had her meal, crowded together with many other women. On her way back she walked past piled-up boxes of ammunition. Then she stood at the assembly line again till the siren blared for the night meal. That was how it went, day after day. Imagining this, Lynette did not find it very surprising that tears had rolled down Fräulein Pechwitz's cheeks when she was saying goodbye. But now everybody had to stick together, that was important, preached Fräulein Lämmert at school. Yes, indeed, that was important, thought Lynette, since the cart had to be pulled out of the mess into which the man in the picture frame above the teacher's desk had got it. He would have loved to have hypnotised the whole world with his gaze but even Fräulein Lämmert was probably doubtful by now that this man knew the answer to everything, though she was unable to admit it since, apart from this certainty, there was only emptiness.

Each of us has to contribute in our own way to the overall effort, Fräulein Lämmert said. She did it by teaching, Fräulein Pechwitz by helping in the ammunition factory and Auntie Bertha by cleaning Baba's staircase every fortnight. Baba had made sure that Auntie Bertha did not have to go to a factory. Wiping down stairs was bad enough for her since she could not stand dirt and work in general. She had not even been prepared to do some office work for her husband, Wenka. She would not have had much to do there anyway, for most of his folders were likely to be filled with material that was not really work-related, namely drafts for future literary works. 'Yes, Auntie Bertha,' Mutti said, 'she has done nothing in her life but sit at home and look after herself; she's bound to get very old because she's had an easy life. Her hands are always well-kept, not coarse like the hands of the likes of us who have to wash the dishes for the whole family every day.'

Mutti began to feel the burden now that Fräulein Pechwitz had left. She got up even earlier to boil Father's shirts, then starch them; she dusted or polished shoes in the evenings, so there wasn't much time left for reading her novels. She did not have the time to play the piano either, so that it was unlikely that she would accompany Father next Christmas. Some fruit and bread would have been enough for her lunch; it was for Lynette and her brother that she cooked simple meals like *himmel und erde*, heaven and earth, a dish that combined apples which hung from branches high up in the sky with potatoes that grew deep in the soil. She was able to get potatoes and apples with no difficulty but not much else. Baba, though, still had everything and she only lived a few streets away. Baba was a practical and robust woman; she always helped out when Mutti asked her and Mutti was not shy about asking her.

'There you are at last,' Baba said. 'I thought you'd never come; the food has been ready for a long time.'

Lynette had waited in front of the house. But her brother didn't come. Then he sneaked round the corner; when he was standing beside her she pressed the downstairs doorbell. They saw the flat door standing open when they walked up the stairs, Baba's gross figure filling the doorframe almost completely.

Inside the flat there was a stale smell of onions and garlic which had seeped into the upholstery over the years. This was not a pleasant smell but Lynette got used to it after a while. It belonged to Baba, along with the many old things that surrounded her like layers; every layer held a deposit of Baba's life. And some things came from a time when even Baba had not been alive. The coffee mugs that were called *dipfel* in Bohemian dialect, for instance, had been handed down from Baba's grandmother. Then it had not been all that long ago that the great Napoleon had been defeated (the memorial near Arbesau still reminded of it) and the barges had to be pulled up the Elbe with horses since there were no steam ships. The mugs' gold-plated rims had become pale but some of the flowers' blue and green colour still looked fresh. These mugs stood behind glass; Baba did not use them any more, they were just there as decoration.

The dining table was round and rested on a single leg which ended in a lion's paw. The chair Lynette sat on looked strangely old-fashioned with its curved back; she sat higher than usual. The chair seemed like a throne to Lynette. Baba brought the goose to the table and then put some of it on their plates, first on Lynette's, then on Heinz's. She herself took the crisp skin that dripped with fat; it was the skin she liked best. Hot dumplings steamed in a bowl; there were other bowls on the table filled with cabbage, to which Baba had added some *speck*, and diced swede that had been sautéed in goose fat. Baba poured some Moravian wine to accompany the meal. Lynette and Heinz had to drink some wine too for whoever ate rich food was in need of wine or beer and Baba would not have any argument about it. Her brother picked at his meat, trying to force it down.

'Leave it, you don't have to eat it,' Baba said.

Her brother did not like poultry ever since he had seen a chicken with its head cut off; the chicken was still very much alive, running away with blood gushing out of its neck. But it was different with Lynette: she liked the food and held out her empty plate.

'At least one of you seems to like my food,' Baba remarked, nodding. She sat there, a broad, matronly figure, eating. She had plaited her hair into a bun. Her arms and face looked plump and her eyes seemed small, but penetrating. There was nothing vague in the way she looked at you, as if she were pinning you down, and Heinz, who did not like her way of gazing at him, looked mostly to one side. Not a beautiful woman, grandmother maybe, but strong and earthy. 'The dessert is in the kitchen,' Baba said. 'Go and get it for us, there's a good boy.'

Heinz pulled a face but Baba did not see it since she had turned to Lynette. He returned with a bowl full of apricot dumplings and Baba put a generous helping on each plate; the dumplings were eaten with sugar and cinnamon. Heinz had a second helping, stilling his hunger with the dessert after he had hardly eaten any goose. Then he fidgeted on his chair looking at Lynette, who avoided his gaze. He pushed back his left sleeve pointing at his watch, which Baba noticed. 'What's the matter with you, boy?' she asked.

'I think I must be going now.'

'Well, go then,' Baba said, 'you could have gone long ago.' He left and it did not even occur to Baba to walk him to the door. He would complain to Mutti about Baba's rough way and Mutti would agree with him since Baba was not her mother but Father's. Lynette could be touchy too but got on

**151**

well with Baba, which Baba noticed, and since Lynette did not hurt her feelings she had no reason to be rough to her. Baba got some chocolate out of a tin; it already tasted a bit old but Lynette ate it without telling Baba that it tasted old.

They walked over to the living room. Baba had a small box on a shelf; she asked Lynette to bring it to her. She had received the box for her Holy Communion. A ship was carved into the dark wood, parting the waves under full sail; its low bows made it appear Scandinavian. A Viking ship as a present for a little girl... that was strange, Lynette thought. But perhaps it was meant to be symbolic. The priest always spoke about the sea and ships when he meant life. Storms alternated with tranquillity and the water carried the ship gently along but also tossed it against the high crests of the waves.

Buttons rolled around in the small box: glimmering buttons made out of mother-of-pearl. Baba pulled out an envelope of photographs from under the buttons. She asked Lynette who the gentleman with the proud, twirled-up moustache was. His gaze was firm and very clear as if water shone through his eyes. His stiff, stand-up wing collar was open in the front. But who was this gentleman? Well, he was Baba's husband, Lynette's grandfather, who was not called Taussig like Father and Baba but Maresch. Lynette knew Maresch, for Mutti sometimes talked about him during her endless kitchen chores. Maresch never married Baba. It had not been possible since Baba was already married and had Uncle Adalbert from her first husband. Baba and Maresch were both adulterers, which sounded grim, like something out of the Bible. To make things worse he was a civil servant; that was why they had to conceal it since such conduct did not befit a civil servant. Only after his death an application was handed in so that it could be officially confirmed that he was father to Mani and Auntie Bertha. Maresch's death had been mysterious. He had always been conscientious when on duty and knew exactly what he was doing but despite this he was caught by a fast train, and it was passed off as an accident. Mutti did not believe it. Maresch had always gone to see specialist consultants in Prague, even as far as Vienna. He became convinced that some tumour was growing inside him and the doctors tried in vain to talk him out of it. The more the doctors argued against it, the more certain he became. He lay awake at night listening to the rumbling of his stomach, and once when he called with Baba for coffee, he was pale and sweat ran down his forehead. Maresch became more and more a tormented, persecuted man. You could not do anything against such an enemy. It may well have been that he just imagined it all but that did not mean that it was less real for poor Maresch. He was hounded by this enemy who crouched deep inside him, slowly and maliciously gnawing away his nerves. That was why a fast-approaching train must have been something like a salvation for him, Maresch, her grandfather, Lynette thought as she looked into those eyes that were so firm and clear.

The next photo which Baba put on the table was a sepia picture showing a young gentleman with a kind of floppy hat in his hand. A hint of a moustache like down lined his upper lip and with a certain playfulness he held a cane in his other hand. His hair was short and curly; a broad silk tie that resembled a shawl streamed down his front. He had an enigmatic smile with some arrogance blended into it. This dandy was bound to be brother Karli, Lynette thought. Sometimes Auntie Bertha talked about him. Money had been saved for him so that he could go to the gymnasium and from there to university later. He was the oldest son and therefore entitled to it. But he also had to go to war and was killed by a Serb sniper, taking all his Greek and Latin to the grave.

Now it was Father's turn: there was no doubt in Lynette's mind that he was the man in the next photo, holding his head up high and thrusting his chest out. He had probably just passed his entrance exam for university as an external student when this photo was taken. He seemed ready for any challenge since he knew that he could do the things he meant to do. His very posture showed this confidence. Baba laughed: 'This is Karli, not your father; you know, Karli who was killed in the last war.'

The dandy, on the other hand, was not Karli but Lynette's father, which surprised her. It seemed to her that she had two fathers: the one who looked like a dandy had died before her birth.

At least she did not have any doubts when she looked at the next picture: this was Auntie Bertha. No longer did she look so endearingly, with large, velvety eyes, across her shoulders, if indeed she had ever done so since this posture had only been for the photographer. The languishing gaze was meant for anybody who would be looking at the picture, including Lynette. Perhaps many people who had not even been born yet would one day admire this picture of a beauty with a sailor's collar and high Slavic cheekbones. Time had made the velvety eyes of this beauty cloudy and had furrowed her skin. But in the picture Auntie Bertha would always stay young. By now her face had changed, turning her into somebody else, thought Lynette, who wondered whether she would have recognised Auntie Bertha in the photo if it had not been among her brothers' and parents' pictures.

'That's me,' Baba said looking at the last picture, 'that's what I looked like once, not as a young woman any more but still quite a bit younger than I am now. Keep the photo; I don't need it because I know what I looked like.'

Baba had not changed a lot. Her hair had turned grey but it was still dense and plaited into a bun as in the picture. The clothes that were stretched in some places made you already suspect a certain stoutness. Her hands grasped the back of a chair while her right hand held some flowers. Her mouth and nose were broad; there was something challenging in her gaze as if she was saying: how much longer do I have to pose here; I've got better things to do. That was just like Baba. She did not exactly mince her words, hurting people's feelings, as had happened with Heinz. But she was not aware of it and when somebody asked her for help she gave them a hand straight away. She did not do it in a ladylike way with two delicate fingers only but used both her hands and with her sleeves rolled up. If she had not been able to get down to things she would hardly have got on in her job for her job was hands-on work. 'Go over to my wardrobe, Lini; you'll find a paper roll behind the clothes there; if you could bring me that roll...'

Between lines of print *Elisabeth Taussig* was written in large letters with ink. Lynette was hardly able to read the name since it was embellished with such an abundance of flourishes. Even the printed words had some decorations that were worthy of the occasion. A stamp with the Double Eagle shone forth resplendent on the side. Directors and professors had made a display of their glorious signatures; they tried to outdo each other by their signatures' boldness and originality. They testified that Baba had undergone the 'cours' properly and correctly and had taken therewith a most rigorous examination with satisfactory success. The word 'satisfactory' had been put in firm and angular writing in the gap that had been left for it; Baba was a practical woman who had not done more than was necessary.

'You know, it all began like this...' said Baba looking towards the window as if her past lay out there. Life kept on sliding into the past but during days like this one when everything seemed wide and bright you could survey it all as if from the top of a hill. Since Lynette happened to be with Baba she could participate; her mind began to colour in Baba's words with images.

Clouds were drifting across a high blue sky. Under this sky Baba stood in a billowing dress that had been fashionable around nineteen hundred. She wore a hat, though hats did not suit her. But she was going to Prague today and therefore it was better for her to have a hat on. A young man stood next to her, looking after her luggage. He would stay behind on the platform after having put the luggage in the compartment and receiving his farthings from Baba. Baba went on her trip without a male escort. Maresch, who was not her spouse (at least not as far as the church and the public registry were concerned), had gone to work as he did every day. Her children were at school and a girl from the neighbourhood would look after them in the afternoon. Maresch would put them to bed since the girl went home in the evening. But Baba was in Prague. She had taken it into her head to go to Prague. You could not talk her out of things she had taken into her head. Perhaps Maresch had been against her going to Prague since women were supposed to stay at home and not become itinerant busybodies but soon he had given in. The gossip in Augiessl did not really matter to Maresch. That was probably why Baba had taken to Maresch, since he always gave in in the end and she got away with doing the things she wanted to do. Now she wanted to go to Prague.

The station was still deserted. Baba had arrived much too early. That was how it was with people who came from small towns and hamlets; they always arrived much too early. Slowly several gentlemen began to appear, wearing stiff hats and carrying walking sticks *comme il faut*. Some of them were accompanied by ladies, arm in arm as if they had grown into each other. The stationmaster ran out of his cabin, full of excitement, which probably meant that it would not be long before the fast train arrived. Sure enough, soon after the stationmaster ran out of his cabin, the huge engine steamed, hissing and pounding, into the station.

Unintentionally Baba took a step backwards. Her luggage carrier stretched out his arm to help her up into the carriage. She was lucky to have him. Without his help she would have found it difficult to get on the train because of her long dress and the heels of her high, laced up boots. The iron steps were just too far apart; it was much easier for a man to climb up these steps, since he would be able to stride out using the full, unrestricted length of his legs. A gentleman who kept lowering his newspaper to gaze at her was sitting in the same compartment. Whenever she looked at him he pretended to be absorbed in the paper as if he had done nothing else but read. Perhaps he was considering whether he should offer her his help since she was a woman travelling all on her own. Outside, the river Elbe shimmered in a silvery haze; it was hemmed in by meadows and trees. Could there be anything more beautiful than the Elbe, Baba thought before getting out one of her *speck*-filled rolls that she had brought as food for the journey.

When she arrived in Prague, Baba took a coach that brought her to the Institute. Lynette imagined the Institute to be a grand building with wide staircases and columns since everything had been grand at the turn of the century. The rooms had high, whitewashed walls. In those rooms women whose bodies were pushed open from the inside stared at the ceiling with maddened eyes. They all suffered the same torments and there was no difference whether they had conceived with lust or the yearlong routine of a married woman. Here the daughters of officers and high civil servants bawled just as loudly as prostitutes; their pain made them all equal. Out of their bodies came eventually a wrinkled-up, crab-red Something, a homunculus that was another link in the long chain that stretched from the past into an uncertain future. Baba wore a white apron, helping women, calming them but also sitting in lectures where a professor with a long beard and a stick that was just as long as his beard pointed at a diagram of the uterus. It was the same professor who had handed Baba the diploma that she had shown Lynette, and while Baba had told her about her time in Prague it had been lying rolled up on the table.

'I've never regretted that I left for Prague so suddenly,' Baba said. 'You need to build something up for yourself... you'll find out the same, I'm sure. Don't worry about the men, they will come and if not, then it's no great loss. You must believe in yourself, that's the main thing; everything will work out fine then.'

Yes, Baba was a woman who had a firm grasp on life, Lynette thought and perhaps she envied Baba for that since she herself felt the dark desire in her to duck out of everything. But Baba had had to learn too and perhaps

**158**

Lynette could be like Baba one day.

'When you've got to meet people often, things change,' Baba said, 'you're not worried so easily any more. Believe me, you'll lose your shyness then. People are not all that different from each other; you have to talk to them, that's the most important thing. I've got to know many people, yes, by God, many many people. They are grateful to me and bring me presents even now. I always went to the christenings, that's the custom: me and the priest. Everybody used to sit down then, eating and laughing a lot; you need to join in so that nobody gets offended. I liked it best with Czechs; it was often quite a bit livelier then.'

She had been invited by fairly poor people once. That had been over there in Karbowitz and Baba indicated the direction by a movement of her hand. The child's father was a woodcutter who was just working in the Bohemian Forest then; they had a small house which his wife had inherited from her parents in Karbowitz. That was where the wife lived, separated from her husband for most of the time. He was hoping to get work in the Erzgebirge or perhaps even in the nearby forests that belonged to the town of Aussig. In their narrow garden sweet peas blossomed between herb beds stretching from the front door to the road. The house was really only one room that had a big tiled stove. The neighbours brought their own tables and chairs. Many people came. It was almost always like that: there were always more guests with poor people than with the rich. How they all fitted into the small house was almost a miracle. They were all cheerful, happy. It was almost as if they had gathered for a meal after a funeral; people were always at their most cheerful after a funeral, at least that's how it had been at the funerals that Baba had been to during the course of her life; everybody rejoiced then that they were still able to indulge in eating and drinking. The cot with the child who had been the cause for the commotion this time stood near the tiled stove. When the baby cried the mother opened her blouse. But when she had cleaned the baby and he would still not stop screaming she hung a cotton ball that was filled with poppies in the cot. Sucking it, the baby fell asleep. The celebration went on: shouting, laughter, cheering. It was always very lively with poor people. There was foaming beer drawn from a barrel. A dark-haired man whose moustache ends pointed downwards played the fiddle. He played with such carefree, artistic lightness that it seemed understandable why the term *Bohemian* had been adopted throughout the world. There certainly had been gypsies among his ancestors, for any violin player who was any good had some gypsy blood in him. Baba sat down to eat. She sat on the left side of the child's parents while the priest sat on their right. There was cabbage, dumplings and excellent meat which surprised Baba since the people were poor. The meat was not pork. Herr Wenzel, the woodcutter, insisted that the two dignitaries, namely the priest and Baba, shared the last piece among themselves. What kind of meat was it, Baba wanted to know, for it really tasted excellent. The woman grinned and asked her to wait till after the meal. When the meal had finished, the woman began to bark and the man barked and then the whole table joined in. Now Baba knew what kind of meat she had eaten.

'Yes, those were Czechs,' Baba said, straightening her bun, 'I can't imagine Germans doing something like that; they always make a big fuss of animals.'

Of course, Lynette did not tell Mutti this story. Mutti was

**160**

very sensitive in this regard and who knew whether she would have eaten any meat at all after hearing such a story. Instead, Lynette told her about the goose and the apricot dumplings. Baba still had whatever she wanted to eat since people kept giving her victuals. Next week Lynette was again expected by Baba for the midday meal; Heinz was invited too if he wanted to come. Mutti gave a sigh of relief, for her pantry was empty. The food ration-cards did not get you a lot and Father had a blessed appetite.

Mutti got a box of nails ready to take to the collection. Father could not do a lot with them anyway; he was quite ham-fisted. Many years before, when he still harboured do-it-yourself ambitions, he had ventured as far as to attempt knocking in a nail. The result had been disappointing, to say the least. After hammering away for some time, he stepped back from the wall, only to find that both the nail and a substantial piece of the wall remained grasped in his hand. Since then he had always got somebody to come in to do such jobs.

The flower-beds around the Wagner memorial were all well-kept, which made Lynette notice the emptiness on the plinth even more. The Master's head had been made out of iron; that was why it had been taken away to be melted down, together with old saucepans and buckled rails. Now the plinth was empty and it would have been possible to put almost any cast-iron head on it. The window display of the Café Falk looked very tidy and clean but the former magic had disappeared. The chocolate boxes had been replaced by paper samples of food ration-cards and explanations of how many of them could buy you a cup of coffee that had no coffee in it anyway. The Market Square itself was deserted. Lynette could not see a single car in its middle where Wenka always used to park his car. The flag poles rose up and looked desolate in their unremitting straightness. There was nobody to be seen in front of the swanky Municipal Savings Bank. It was quite likely that it was closed and perhaps even the friend of Frau Domansky, the young blonde man, had been called up by now and was lying somewhere in Russia's swamps, rather than in a warm woman's bed. A poster had been glued to an advertising column showing a goat; on it you could read in narrow, angular writing: 'Do not bleat!'

A soldier was limping around a corner. Lynette, who had her eyes fixed on the book shop, failed to notice him and they collided. If Mutti had not grabbed him he would have fallen down headlong on the paving-stones. The soldier swore till his swearing dissolved into sobbing. But Lynette's thoughts were mainly on the book that she wanted now. The shop girl fetched a ladder and climbed up to the shelf that held the large, expensive books. At least you could still buy books without ration-cards. The books may have been expensive but Mutti did not worry about it; money hardly bought you anything any more. Lynette chose the largest and most expensive book which was so heavy that she had to keep changing the hand she carried it with on their way home.

She pored over it in her room. You could unfold coloured tables that depicted everything in great detail. Not even the tiniest bone was missing. An almost endless number of pages initiated the seeker of knowledge into the dark, mysterious world of the internal organs. She was particularly drawn to the diagrams of the brain, where the apparently endless ramifications of the nerves came together. The brain looked like the top of a tree. Nerves and arteries branched out from it in all directions. The eye was a round chamber. In it the outside world was caught and, just like the sounds in the ear, flowed to the brain. There images and words came into being. It was magnificent how everything was connected with everything else, working together; only once in a while something was not quite right. Those were the faults, illnesses. They had Latin names that were printed in italics to draw the reader's attention. Lynette read them with the same reverence that she felt when listening to the Latin prayers in church. While repeating the words like a litany, she saw herself standing on the station platform waiting for the train to Prague. That was what Baba had done and what Baba had done was right for her too. She would go to Prague University. Then she would open her own practice. She saw herself sitting in the surgery. Its windows looked onto the backyard where the light was always muted. Pigeons were cooing; they nested between the corners and wavy roofs of the old houses. She would be sitting in her practice and she would not mind if it were quiet and nobody came. Perhaps an artist lived in the flat above her practice; artists lived within old walls since the rent was cheaper there. They were also sensitive and were drawn to anything that was beautiful and decaying. The artist would play Schumann in the flat above and, once or twice perhaps, the song of the wild Waterman. She thought of the white-haired gentleman who had begun to teach them English after their teacher had had to go to Russia like so many others. This gentleman was said to have lived in Ireland for several years and from there he had brought a verse which the whole class had learnt by heart. Lynette was almost drowning in this verse that sounded so melodious and beautiful; she had to grab her own hair to pull herself out. Even in her chronicle she had written the lines:

**163**

*The last rose of summer left blooming alone*
*All her lovely companions have faded and gone.*

But Lynette was not quite as lonely as the rose. There was Anne. She spent a lot of time with Anne when they had to do their harvesting duty outside town.

Little old women with headscarves bent down, picking the potatoes from the field and throwing them into baskets. One of the most industrious potato pickers was a spindly young man who had a hopping gait and an idiotic smile whenever some of the female pupils called out his name, which they did at every opportunity. The potato leaves and stem had to be thrown onto one heap that would be put on fire in the evening. But it was still a good while until then and Lynette was sweating in the scorching, dusty heat. The pots of buttermilk were all empty already. She carried on picking, making her eyes small so that she was able to see the brown potatoes in the brown soil.

Heinz picked potatoes too; together with his peers from the gymnasium, he picked in a different field and girls were not tolerated there. He would have loved to leave the school bench behind to take his place as a man alongside his fighting uncles. But then he could be extremely sensitive as well since he was unable to bear it when Baba was rough with him. It all seemed very strange to Lynette. Perhaps Heinz was picking potatoes near Herbert while she was picking them close to his sister. Lynette was sure that Herbert did not like this kind of work much either; he was a shade-loving plant himself, thriving in sheltered rooms. His glasses were probably encrusted by sweat and would keep slipping down his nose since he had to bend down.

Gerda had filled yet another basket of potatoes. She and Heidi, who had to be called Adelheid according to Fräulein Lämmert, carried it to the wagon in front of which two sturdy horses were waiting patiently. There a sprightly old man helped them to empty the potatoes into the wagon. Gerda ran straight back; the sun had turned her pale skin bright red. She began to fill her basket once again, humming a melody to herself. It was alright for Gerda, Lynette thought, since she was always part of everything and did not seem to know what it was like if you always felt that you stood outside of it all. It was easier for Gerda since she let herself be carried by the flow of the stream rather than swim against it.

Lynette always felt out of place. This feeling became stronger when everybody held each others' hands, dancing around the crackling fire while singing *Die blauen Dragoner*, The Blue Dragoons. It had become dark and the sparks that flew up looked like stars mixing with the stars in the sky. Up there were stars that were lonely and by themselves but other stars formed such a dense crowd that their individuality was extinguished in a foggy broth. Everybody was singing on cheerfully when Lynette was grasped by one hand and pulled away. It was Anne. Lynette followed her into the darkness where it became cooler.

The wood creaked in the shed when they climbed up a ladder. The moon gave them light; it was a glistening silver light. The light peeled Anne's figure out of the dark. Lynette felt comforted being with her and soon the straw's stinging on the naked skin felt more or less like a pleasant tingle. They kept quiet when a torch approached the shed. It was held by the sprightly old man. They could hear him underneath, putting things in a basket; then his light disappeared outside again, moving towards the fire. Lynette and Anne felt relieved, cuddling closely up to each other. It was so nice lying with Anne like this. Perhaps Lynette had found herself through being together with Anne.

The fire in the distance had already burnt down; it was only smouldering. Anne was the first to notice and they put on their skirts and blouses hastily before running out of the shed. It had got dark around the fire and nobody saw them joining up again. Lynette was lucky; her name was called out. But Anne whose name came earlier in the alphabet had come too late. She reported to the old man when he called out her name once again at the end of his roll call. Lynette feared that she would need to explain where she had been. But the old man seemed relieved that none of his charges had got lost and did not ask. So they all walked towards home singing, following the horses and the full wagon. Anne walked next to Lynette, the two of them holding hands.

# 11

Herr Havelka himself was waiting for them in front of the station. His servant had been called up for the army and soon got killed... that was how it went sometimes. Havelka had to sacrifice his beautiful burly horses for the army or the so-called final victory too since he did not have a farm, only a Pension. The horses were wasted for just fetching guests from the station; better use could be made of them at the Front. It was a slow ride with an old nag pulling, though they were not in a hurry since the summer holidays had begun. But they were not real summer holidays since the summer was over already. The tree tops rose up sparse and the sun's golden light was caught by the withering leaves. Only where the fir trees stood had the forest remained dense and dark as it always had been.

The forest floor looked strangely bare as if it had been wiped clean. An elderly couple pulled a hand-cart full of fallen twigs and branches along the road. When picking berries Lynette and her family were not on their own this year; others swarmed all over the forest. Most of them did not come from the nearby crofts and hamlets but were town people too. Lynette's basket was filling up quickly, for she picked blackberries and not wild strawberries that had ripened earlier in the year. She would be able to return soon to sit under the elm trees. The coffee tasted bitter but the cake that Havelka made with the picked berries was excellent, as always. Sadly it was cake, not a gateau. Afterwards Father played a few pieces. Herr Stelzig had not come with them this time. He had kept the few days at All Saints completely free for composing before he would have to carry on with his teaching. It was his last year since he was going to retire in the next one. Then he would have enough time for both his hobbies: walking and composing. But composing was much more than a hobby for him: he had felt a call to write music from early on even though the necessity of earning his daily bread had kept him from it. Mutti was here too; Mutti could have accompanied Father. However, the piano that stood in a corner under a pair of antlers was out of tune; Lynette thought that she heard Mutti give a muffled sigh of relief when she found out. In the end, Father played outside on his own till it got dark and he was unable to read the music even if he looked at it from very close.

Lynette settled down under her warm downy duvet. Outside, the treetops were gently rustling and an owl screeched. In the morning she was still in bed when the sun had already been shining through the curtains for a long time, dipping the room in clear light. She indulged in that state between waking and sleeping that Mutti called *sammern*.

There would be school when she was home again and she would need to get up early.

Now Lynette did not part from her brother any more when they left the flat in the morning. They both went to the Town Gymnasium. Lynette's school had been turned into a hospital and it seemed to Lynette that the barren building had been built for that purpose from the beginning. Though soldiers kept being discharged as healed, the war made sure that the wards were always full.

She walked down Bismarck Street with Heinz. Here was where the rich Jews like Miss Feilchenfeld used to live. Briefly a pair of watery blue eyes appeared before Lynette; the passing of time had made them even paler so that they almost dissolved against the light background of Lynette's memory. Now the villas housed the offices of the police. It was not so long ago that Father had come here to make his request. A bush covered with white berries stood near the Protestant church and her brother picked one of them, bursting it between thumb and index finger as they walked on. Her brother was also one of those who would have loved to exchange the school bench for the anti-aircraft gun since that was more exciting. Meanwhile he sat in his room pulling the last little flags out of the Russian bear's body. Perhaps he thought that he could put an end to the decline with his child fists. Her brother had to be strong since he was a boy. Or at least he had to pretend that he was strong.

Lynette scrutinised the green façade of the Town Gymnasium. The windows were high and flooded with light; pillars framed each window, carrying a pediment. At the corner a copula rose up and Lynette discovered more and more decorative detail and playfulness all over the building. That was how it should be, for anything that was merely there for its functional purpose was repulsive. At least that was the way Lynette felt; it seemed to her as if the august façade also raised her own self-worth.

Inside she was received by broad staircases as befitted a gymnasium where Latin was taught. A boy glared at her with hostility; another one evaded her gaze with some confusion when she walked past him. On the stairs she walked into Herbert, who did not seem to notice her. Completely wrapped in his own world he left her behind, holding his schoolbag close to him. She hesitated, wondering whether she should call him. But he was probably too far away in his thoughts and would not hear her. His eyes had a blank, empty gaze. And his glasses, she thought, were they not like a shield rather than a window – a window through which she could make contact with him?

That was the only time she met him that day. The girls' classrooms were in a separate wing where they had to stay during the breaks as well. Lynette's classroom was larger than in her old school. Nevertheless, there was less space since two classes had been put together in one room. Everybody had to move closer together so that boys and girls could be accommodated in the venerable gymnasium. Anne and Lynette sat far back, removed from the sweat zones of ambition. Lynette had insisted on having the bench near the window so that she could see the sky and the clouds. That was where she could cast her eyes to and lose herself when time became sticky and did not run. But now the others propped themselves up on the windowsills, stretching forward with their jiggling feet that banged against Lynette's desk.

Behind them a row of curious onlookers stood on tiptoe. There was a lot of giggling and calling. Plaits flew around girls' heads in excitement. From the other side, the voices of boys responded and some of them already had a dark timbre.

Lynette straightened her back, beginning to lecture Anne about the heart amidst all this tumult; generally the view was held that it was the seat of very special feelings but really it was not much more than a common muscle. She acted the precocious, experienced one.

'Professor,' Anne said laughing, 'you've forgotten your glasses again today.'

Glasses! Glasses, no, she did not wear glasses. She preferred making her eyes small. Without glasses faces and colours around her merged soothingly into each other, which was not bad at all. It was some kind of protection if you did not notice everything that went on around you in full detail. And professor... well, she was certainly not a professor. They all looked so thin, the woman professors. This came from all the sacrifices they had to make. They also looked strict. They probably had to be much more strict and forbidding than their male colleagues so that they were accepted in those high altitude spheres where the air was thin. If she could be a doctor one day, sitting in a practice with muted light and cooing pigeons, then that would be enough for her. Meanwhile, she had sown sunflowers in her small plot of land, adding some fertiliser so that two flowers by now proudly raised their sun heads. The flowers' round plate-like core that was surrounded by a blazing circle of petals held the seeds. She had put a handful of them in a tin for next year. The rest of them turned brown, then black before they decayed on the narrow compost heap. Lynette hoed the soil so that it would be loose for the new seeds.

'Stay outside with your shoes,' Mutti called, taking Lynette's slippers to the front door. Thick lumps of earth stuck to the soles and Mutti had just cleaned and swept. She handed over a brush and a cloth to Lynette. While scraping the shoe soles, Lynette thought of Fräulein Pechwitz who had always held out the freshly polished shoes to her with a 'there you are, *knödliges Fräulein*'. That was a long time ago. She took it for granted then that her shoes had always been clean. Mutti, however, got up long before her, boiling Father's shirts in the large washing pot. She was still dusting when Lynette had gone to bed again. By now Mutti only made contact with the piano when dusting. When she and Father had played together for the last time (it had been a few days after the holidays), he had been impatiently tapping the rhythm on the piano with his bow. Mutti banged the piano lid shut as a response. What on earth did he expect of her? She was supposed to cook, to clean, to shop and, on top of it all, to practise the piano for hours on end...

'Yes, Fräulein Pechwitz,' Mutti sighed. She missed Fräulein Pechwitz and there was little doubt that Fräulein Pechwitz would have preferred to be here where her children were, that is Lynette and her brother. She had had to exchange her cosy attic room for barracks. It was much easier for somebody like Auntie Bertha of course, even though she had never been a member of the Party, whereas Fräulein Pechwitz had joined it as soon as it had become possible after the invasion. Before that she went to church where she was rapt in listening to the priest when he talked about paradise and now she was just as engrossed in listening to one of the spokesmen in the Party meetings. But despite all this she slept in some barracks, whereas Auntie Bertha was allowed to remain in her own flat.

There she twiddled her thumbs or kept herself occupied with other people's business; that was why she emerged regularly at Mutti's, striding from room to room with her hands folded behind her back.

'They're like two peas in a pod,' said Mutti, meaning Auntie Bertha and Wenka. Yes, Wenka always pretended to be busy but it was all make-believe. If you had opened the multitude of folders in his office all bearing elaborate signatures on their backs you would have held poetic outpourings instead of important documents and contracts in your hand. The folders were nothing more than sham. If it hadn't been for Baba... but since there was a Baba and she was the way she was they could get away with a swanky lifestyle. *Naturellement*, his Lord and his Ladyship had to drive around in their own car. Uncle always behind the steering wheel. For Auntie the town's best tailor was just about good enough. Her spouse, this elegant gentleman, always wore a bow-tie which made him appear so respectable that the Grand Hotel Puck would have employed him straight away as head waiter.

That was how Mutti was talking, quite sharp really but that was the way she could be at times. She did not mean it like that; she just enjoyed mocking others and getting rid of some of the anger she felt when the kitchen was flooded with dirty plates once again. Lynette joined in laughing about poor Uncle who was a common soldier, a *muschig*, now. There was a kind of complicity between her and Mutti and it seemed to Lynette that she was getting on better with her than before. They did not bear any ill will against Uncle, whose visit Auntie Bertha had announced for the night of Saint Sylvester. Fräulein Pechwitz came too. One day she was standing before the front door with her suitcase. She got her attic room ready herself. Though she had come as a guest and not as a housekeeper, old habits prevailed and she took off her elegant clothes that looked strangely stiff on her, changing into her work outfit.

She put up the Christmas tree which for the first time did not reach up to the ceiling. The tree looked meagre. The impression was exacerbated by the dearth of candles on it. They were mostly stubs from last year, for it was not that easy to get wax any more. What about the figures of Saint Nicholas, the sledges, the shimmering parcels that had hung so luxuriously from the trees of bygone years? Lynette and her family owed the single chocolate angel to Herr Filip. He had taken it out of the drawer under the counter with a smile; winking, he presented it to Lynette. This was perhaps her nicest Christmas present: Herr Filip's chocolate angel. Heinz got the Bisiach violin from Father, who had bought it in the music shop in the end, putting it up with all the other presents. But this particular present was hugely valuable; Father had always been a generous man. Heinz unwrapped the other colourful presents first before he opened the dark violin case. There was the Bisiach resting on velvet lining. Her brother smiled a smile that was supposed to express joy but appeared merely strained to Lynette. She sat down at the piano and together they played the wild Waterman. Heinz played with firm determination; he executed his bow strokes as if with a rapier. Perhaps he did not relish standing like this in front of Father. That was why he wanted to appear strong and unwavering. But for her there was a lot of sorrow in the tale of the wild Waterman; the song should have sounded muted and sad. It was all about loss and regret, for Lilofee had not been able to resist the courting of the Waterman and had followed him into the lake. But then she longs to be back in the castle again where she has grown up. Slowly she realises that she must abandon leaves and green grass and has to stay in the blue watery sphere that will remain alien to her as long as she lives… poor, wretched Lilofee. Father gave a short nod when they had finished before wiping the rosin off the violin case with a cloth.

Mutti had baked traditional Christmas biscuits that were in the shape of a half-moon. There was real butter in them. She had hoped to keep some of them back for New Year's Eve. But Heinz stuffed them into his mouth and Lynette did not hold back either. Mutti shrugged her shoulders; her brothers were not coming anyway. Yes, that was how it was. Lynette was disappointed that Karl had not come. They could have played rummy. He and Lynette were joined together by a secret he did not know; she thought of the envelope under the flower-patterned drawer liner. Perhaps a love affair prevented him from coming: possibly a Russian girl who was less conventional than Fräulein Plötzl. In his letter from the Front he had simply written that he had been unable to get any leave this time. Uncle Franz also stayed at the Front. He probably would not even have come if he had got leave. He had to hold his own as a man, which was especially important now since things were beginning to crumble. There was no Irmchen or Lili any more and he had nobody else. He preferred to stay at the Front; besides, getting home was not without its dangers either. But Wenka got home; he arrived promptly on New Year's Eve, so that he had just enough time to bathe and change his clothes. He had intended to come three days earlier. But the train stopped on open track and nobody knew why. He had enough time to gaze across the snow-clad plains of East

Prussia; he might have thought of poems, sad ones that he noted down. He was supposed to change trains at a station of a small town but there was no station any more. So he had to continue his journey by Shanks' pony. Having been in Russia, Uncle was used to marching on foot. He only went in one direction there: backwards in retreat.

He had become thin, Uncle Wenka. Not that he had ever been fat but now his suit hung loosely from him. The bow-tie had slipped out of place since his neck was so thin that it did not hold the ribbon tight any more. Auntie Bertha, on the other hand, had kept well and it looked strange how little, shrunken Wenka sat at the side of his imposing spouse.

Perhaps Wenka would put on a bit of weight now. Mutti had got hold of as much food as she possibly could. Baba had sent the goose; she always had a good supply of geese. The goose was nice and fat, as if it were a goose left over from peace time. There was even cream with the dessert. Wenka drank water. He had just recovered from jaundice; now, as he said this, his skin seemed yellow to Lynette. For the first time, Fräulein Pechwitz sat at the family table. She had been reluctant but Mutti had insisted on it. She was a visitor, after all, and apart from that she was the daughter of an industrialist. Therefore, she knew how to behave and was admitted to sit at the festive dinner table. She had a good appetite but, like Mutti, she never put on any weight: she was just too busy all the time. Father was quiet, ate and drank thoughtfully. Wenka talked about the theatre at the Front. This in turn made Mutti talk about Eleonora Duse. Mutti always spoke of Eleonora Duse but she had never really seen her in person. Perhaps that was not really important; it was for the very reason that she had never seen her that her name sounded like magic to her. Eleonora Duse was imbued with legendary greatness and Lynette always imagined her face as looking like an antique mask.

'We don't want to be outdone, we're gifted actors and actresses too,' said Wenka who had got up from his seat. 'We will have the audience decide whether it's a comedy or a tragedy. The play's title is *The Bitter End*; it was conceived by myself and I am also one of the lead actors, apart from Heinz and Lynette.'

How large his eyes were. They seemed to have got even larger, probably because his face had become thinner. He took an apple from the fruit bowl before all three of them left the room.

'Who knows... he may have rewritten *Wilhelm Tell*,' Auntie Bertha suggested.

Uncle opened the door and walked into the room again; Heinz followed him. Lynette held the apple in her hand and bit into it heartily. They marched around the table, once, twice...

'This looks like a very modern play to me,' Mutti said, 'yes, one of those political plays that used to be staged in the Town Theatre where they talked all the time but you, you're not even talking.'

Now they walked round the table for a third time with Lynette following as the last one of the three. While eating the apple she screwed up her face as if she was not biting into the apple's juicy flesh but its bitter core. Fräulein Pechwitz was the first to understand what it was all about, giving an interpretation of the play; Mutti and Aunti Bertha laughed but father shook his head. The worn-out troupe of actors was allowed to sit down at last.

177

'You wouldn't believe the things this man gets into his head, dear me,' Auntie Bertha boomed. 'Though I'm a bit annoyed with him since there's nothing bitter about Lynette – she's a fine young lass.'

At midnight Wenka opened the window. Everything was quiet, dead silent. The bells had been recast into something more useful long ago and it was said that the Russians were already approaching Przemysl. Lynette had walked up to Wenka who stood at the window and heard him say under his breath: 'Yes, that's it: the bitter end.'

# 12

That New Year's Eve would stand out. It was followed by days that slowly dissolved; running into each other, they became memory. The paths in the park stayed covered in snow since there was nobody left any more to clear them. Lynette had not seen Rübezahl for quite a while but this time he did not turn up again and remained missing. Dark pillars of smoke drilled themselves into the grey winter sky on the other side of the bare treetops where there were old houses that had not been connected to the district heating system. Hardly any time had passed at all when Lynette received her primroses, replacing the freesias because of the war. This was another day that left its mark in the monotonous flow of time. Lynette wondered whether she could stop this incessant flow by writing her chronicle. Well, she wasn't too sure about that really but at least she was able to record some events, like Aunt Gudrun's arrival.

It happened sometime between Saint Sylvester and Lynette's birthday. It was a beautiful, cold day. The coldness bit into Lynette's face when she was waiting with Mutti at the tram stop. There were no taxis any more because of the petrol shortage. The train was coming from Berlin, taking the route via Dresden. It was late; nobody really knew when it would arrive. They sat down in the waiting room which was not heated but at least warmer than the draughty platform.

Mutti had worried a lot about how to recognise Aunt Gudrun. But as was often the case, she should not have worried. Apart from a few elderly couples, it was mainly bandaged, limping men who got off the train. A solidly built woman who kept putting down her suitcase was approaching from far down the platform. It had to be Aunt Gudrun. Her thick coat did not quite close over her bulging belly; judging from this, Uncle Franz had not been idle. Neither Mutti nor Lynette knew for how long he had had Aunt Gudrun on the side. Only now had the family found out about her since it would be safer for her in Aussig than in Berlin. Lynette couldn't help thinking of Lili, who had been so delicate and gracious. Aunt Gudrun, in contrast, looked heavy, stout, almost gross. Wiping the sweat from her gold-rimmed glasses, she handed her suitcase over to a porter who was so old that carrying it was even harder for him than for her. She was surprised that everything was still standing. For a long time she had not seen a town where the houses still had their roofs on. She was very enthusiastic about the Riunionehaus when they passed it. It was an austere building with an equally austere tower at its corner. Such a modern building! They had plenty of them in Berlin, of course, but here in Aussig... after all people here were very much on the periphery. Berlin was the centre where all the intellectual life was, as well as the great political ideas. How strangely harsh and grating Aunt Gudrun sounded when she spoke, Lynette thought.

Aunt Gudrun came from Mecklenburg, explained Mutti when Aunt had withdrawn to her room for a while. There people did not talk like you and me but spoke as if they had a plum in their mouths. That was well-put, Lynette thought, since everything Aunt said sounded so very important even if she were only asking for a slice of bread at the table.

Father got up briefly at the table to welcome her. When Father had sat down, Aunt rose up. She pulled a piece of paper out of the bodice of her dress, unfolding it with some awkwardness. Dear Mani, she said, dear Antschi, dear Lynette, dear Heinz. She straightened her gold-rimmed glasses and cleared her throat; she waited a while before she began. She read sentence by sentence and after each sentence she looked around. She began with the Thirty Years War that had originated here in Europe's heart, Bohemia, or to be more precise, in its capital, Prague. Once again mankind was undertaking a titanic struggle. But this struggle was not rooted in religious dispute any more for the world had turned its back on transcendental ideas ever since Nietzsche. Men and women were to be turned into better, more refined and noble beings and such a sublime aim justified the greatest sacrifices; thus, she had left her beloved homeland. But the family of her husband whose proud member she had become made sacrifices too, she was well aware of it; it was not exactly child's play to take in another hungry person, no, two persons really, in the middle of a war. Finally, she bowed and sat down slowly but still kept holding the piece of paper in her hand. Father remained quiet and Mutti too did not seem to know what to make of it. There we are... this is Aunt Gudrun, Lynette thought, wondering whether Aunt had already become a refined and noble being. She was brainy without doubt but would cut a poor figure on the sports field. The teacher would probably not hold it against her since she approached people openly, not trying to avoid them. Besides, Aunt Gudrun was a grown-up woman so there was no need for her to endure being chased around the athletics track. For this, Lynette envied her.

The next day was a Sunday and Lynette went to town with Mutti and Aunt Gudrun. Heinz stayed with Father; it was beneath his dignity to be seen with all those women. Again Aunt Gudrun was surprised that all the buildings were still standing; not even a windowpane was broken. Yet Berlin had been laid waste; most people lived only in cellars there by now. She was impressed by the Town Theatre, a grand building from the turn of the century, but it was the Riunionehaus that sent her into raptures today once again. Being from Berlin, she had probably thought that people still lived in huts here in the Balkans and now she had found that there were not only grand buildings but also audacious examples of modern architecture. And then the Café Falk! There was not a lot left of its former luxury. The multitude of gateaux and cakes behind the glass counter had gone, including the chocolate gateau that Lynette always remembered first. There was only an apple cake with *streusel* topping. But Aunt Gudrun felt so enthusiastic about it that she made sure of a second piece for herself. 'I could never make something so delicious,' she said, 'I can only admire anyone who can.'

She herself was ham-fisted. She did not like cooking and once she had left a roast in the oven for so long that it had turned into charcoal when she got it out. No, she had been made for the world of books, for reading, learning, teaching. Aunt Gudrun was a gymnasium professor. Uncle had met her for the first time at a seminar held by the Party. And Uncle had made a speech; he was a superb speaker. His speech was extemporé; he did not need any notes. He accompanied his words with expansive gestures. He raised his voice beseechingly only to quieten down again. She did not really know what his speech was about. Afterwards she simply accosted him. They went to the Wannsee together; sitting outside, they ate and drank under the trees. That had been wonderful... yes, Berlin had been wonderful then. That was how it had all begun with Uncle and her and then his first wife had had this terrible accident. But at times she could hardly believe that she was expecting a child by Franz since everything had happened so quickly.

Lynette went with Mutti to the hospital. Aussig had a hospital to be proud of. It was an almost brand new building and the labour ward was on the fifth floor.

The corridors were endless; they all smelled of cleaning fluid. The many windows were flooded with light which made the walls' clean whiteness shine forth even more pitilessly; the bed frames' chrome sparkled. Mutti did not have any flowers; there were no flowers to be had unless you had your own garden. Instead, she brought a volume of Hölderlin, since Aunt had a weakness for him. Lynette looked down at the treetops when Aunt read aloud the passage raving against Germans from Hölderlin's Hyperion; laughing, she said that the Germans weren't as bad as all that. Lynette could not see the buds on the bare branches since her eyes were not good enough but she could sense them, knowing that they were there. Soon the leaves would pierce through the buds, downy and creased. That was not much different from a child whose head forced its way out of the mother's belly. Now the nurse brought Aunt Gudrun's child with her creased, red skin, her flat nose and her slanting forehead. Mutti hugged the baby. Such a little sweetheart, Mutti said, and she looks just like her Papa. Lynette had to hold little Erika too; holding her, Lynette smiled. But the baby began to cry and Aunt Gudrun waved to the nurse who took little Erika away. All that still lay in store for Lynette: having a child. A tiny Something pierced through the flesh between your legs, which had to be terribly painful. Aunt looked so relaxed lying in her bed while Mutti kept on smiling as if she still had little Erika in her arms. Both of them seemed to be in conspiracy, for neither Mutti nor Aunt Gudrun mentioned anything about the pain of childbirth. Perhaps it was not as bad as Lynette imagined; perhaps she would feel more for a child when it was her own.

But all that was still far ahead. She was just a schoolgirl for the time being and who knew what the future held? There was this war. Aunt Gudrun said there was no doubt that things were improving. You noticed it with the food, for the food was always so plentiful and good. She looked expectantly at Mutti, who nodded. What else could she have done? She did not want to contradict and a joke would have been out of place; Aunt Gudrun would not have understood it. She took everything much too seriously; she lacked the nonchalance of the South Germans, Austrians and Bohemians, which worked like a buffer.

Yes, the war: the war was coming closer and closer. A few days ago the sky had been blood-red. It could not have been the glow of the descending sun since it was in the north and the sun had already set. Lynette ran to her parents. Father, standing at the window in his nightgown, looked at the blood-red sky. He shrugged his shoulders: he had never seen anything like it. Mutti crossed herself. Lynette was sure that if Fräulein Pechwitz had been here, they would have convinced each other that it was a sign of God. When Lynette had settled down in her bed again she noticed to her surprise that she was trembling slightly. A guardian angel was sitting on your forehead and one on each of your shoulders – that was something Mutti had always said when Lynette prayed as a small girl before turning in. She began imagining the guardian angels and while she tried to figure out what they might look like she became calmer.

At school she was told that the burning Dresden had cast that glow like a nightly sunset against the sky. Fräulein Lämmert said it; her voice sounded hesitant, hoarse. So many people had perished that they had to be piled up in the streets since there would not have been enough space if you had laid them side by side. Nobody would ever know how many had died. Lynette saw herself on the steamer again, going along the river Elbe; for a moment she saw the huge dome in front of her, hovering above the city like a bell. As she closed her eyes briefly, this picture evaporated against the red backdrop of her eyelids.

'I'm very grateful to you both that you've come to see me on the ward,' Aunt Gudrun said. 'Please give my regards to Mani and Heinz.'

Outside, the weather was mild. The forest looked brown on the surrounding hills that were still speckled by the leftovers of snow. Freed from any snow, the Elbe streamed speedily northwards. If the wild Waterman's wife, Lilofee, wanted to forget her longing, she would have been able to travel along the Elbe to see the rubble that was once Dresden, and if she had not been satisfied and carried on swimming she would have got close to the sea where she would have had a view of decimated Hamburg. Only in Aussig had every stone been left standing.

Once again crocuses peeped out between the trees in the Town Park. It did not matter to flowers whether they were tended by the directing hand of a gardener or not; they were pulled up by invisible strings that the sun was spinning. Then the flowers opened their cups to collect the light. A blackbird rustled in the undergrowth and Lynette took deep breaths of the air which was full of the scent of spring.

The air was clear and pure. The bluish smoke that was left behind by motorcars had been absent for a long time; the old houses at the other side of the park were not heated any more since it was already quite warm during the day and any coal had to be saved. Lynette nibbled at a very small chocolate bar. She let each piece melt slowly and reverently on her tongue. Wherever did Herr Filip get the chocolate from, she wondered. It was the real thing, no substitute; she could taste that.

Herr Filip rejoiced at the reports from the Front. He often spoke in Czech to her. She still understood Czech but could not speak it any more. She had forgotten it during the last years. As things looked now, she would soon have the chance to learn Czech once again. Then everything would be as it had been in the Republic, Lynette thought, as if there had never been a war in between.

She walked past the pavilion; it had been a long time since a band had played there last. Under the pavilion's roof, leaning against a pillar, stood Herbert, reading a book. She walked up the stairs, giving him enough time to put the book quickly in his coat pocket. He seemed embarrassed and looked sideways. His embarrassment spread to her and she regretted now that she had walked up to him at all. But now, standing in front of him, she could not just run away.

'We're going to the same school now,' she said, 'the Realgymnasium has been shut down.'

'Yes, I know,' he replied and she clearly noticed how his face became tinged with a pale redness. It was strange that he got red so quickly but she took it as encouragement.

'What's the book you're reading?'

'The book... oh, yes... it's Rilke's *Larenopfer*,' he said. He smiled apologetically as if he thought that she must find it strange that he was reading this book. Perhaps he thought that it did not mean a lot to her and that she was not interested in reading.

'I love poems,' she said, 'I could recite some poems to myself for hours, a verse of an Irishman, for example, who's called Thomas Moore. But I'm interested in medicine, too. I know a lot about the heart. And the skeleton. There's no need to be afraid of the skeleton, you know, since it's only a kind of frame and without it our bodies would collapse into a lump.' She couldn't help laughing since she imagined herself and Herbert as two lumps that had to hold on to each other so that they would not roll down the stairs.

'It's good that you study such things,' said Herbert. 'But what about other questions, questions about the soul? That's much more interesting really; you can dissect the heart but the soul and our ideas about it... I think I prefer that since it gives you some room for your imagination. Sometimes I

**187**

wonder whether our soul and music aren't the same thing and what else are poems than music that's frozen in words....'

All this sounded confusing to her; she smiled, insecure. He carried on speaking to her, unperturbed, and she did not doubt that he was the cleverer one of the two of them: the Latin pupil from a higher form. As he spoke so learnedly, he seemed to have regained his self-confidence. At least he did not look askance any more and glared at her instead, expecting her to contradict. But she did not contradict. She only said that she would like to know all the other things he was interested in.

'Come to my place then,' he said a bit abruptly and she followed him, though she was not really sure whether she would have preferred to walk through the park on her own.

Anne opened the door. The corners of her mouth trembled slightly when she saw Lynette with Herbert; Lynette noticed it clearly. Then she just disappeared, though in the morning they had been sitting next to each other at school and Anne had let Lynette copy her maths homework. Lynette would have preferred it if all three of them had gone into the windowless room. To be precise, there was a narrow window but a tree grew right in front of it, keeping it shadowy, and the room was a bit like a cave. A lamp diffused some yellowish light from the ceiling; it was not enough for the room so that its corners were almost completely veiled in darkness. On the floor several carpets lay on top of each other. Lynette did not see any chairs. There was no need for chairs, Herbert said, when you had such soft carpets. A pair of elephants, as well as two dark, carved wooden birds dipping their heads between their tall legs, propped up the books. Three monkeys sat side by side; the first monkey cupped his hands over his mouth, the next one over his ears and the third one over his eyes. That's how one should be, like these monkeys, Herbert said, life would be easier then. He took a dagger from the wall and unsheathed it; the dagger seemed to Lynette like a flaming zigzag. Herbert called it a 'kris'. It was handed down from father to son, with the son being endowed with the father's strength. Herbert smiled while telling her that and pushing the dagger back into its sheath. Lynette was slightly taken aback by it all. She had thought that his room would be more or less like Heinz's, perhaps without toy soldiers and moss-green volumes but still suitably furnished with a table, chairs and a bed with a blue cover like any boy's room. Lynette wondered where he had got all these exotic things from? Maybe from his father, Herr Domansky, who was a high-up civil servant presently residing in the capital Berlin?

'Oh no, not from him,' said Herbert laughing, 'he's never got further than Lake Balaton. But my great uncle, Gitti's uncle, was an explorer. He got several commissions from different academies. He specialised in Asia, South East Asia, and from there he brought all this stuff. He had no children of his own; that's why Gitti got it.'

Lynette had to get used to Herbert calling his mother by a nickname, for Gitti was none other than Frau Domansky. Herbert had not only got the furniture from her but also almost all his books and music; the music piled up in the camphorwood chest with its Arabic writing, piled up so high that the chest did not quite close any more.

Several art books stood on the shelf. One of these books showed pictures by a painter who interwove voluptuous bodies with gold. To Lynette such sultry pictures seemed to fit in with

**189**

this dusky room. In another book all the pictures were clear and feather-light; they could be so light since they were not weighed down by any cumbersome concreteness; the very essence of things and people seemed to be distilled in colours and configurations. Nowhere could you see such pictures any more and Lynette was amazed that Herbert had books with this kind of art that was generally considered to be 'decadent', and that was the least disparaging expression. Of course, he had these books from Gitti too, that is Frau Domansky. He could take anything from her; he did not even have to ask. The things that belonged to her were his too. It was not the same with Anne; she did not get on with Gitti that well. Herbert didn't know why. Lynette pulled out a book on psychology from the shelf. The human psyche was dominated by drives but these drives were not like the organs and the blood that truly existed. Drives grew in the dusky world of the imagination; they were slippery and you could not grasp them. Here, love was called 'libido'. When Lynette got up she felt the blood that filled her muscles like nettle stings. She looked at a watercolour painting that hung on the wall; it probably had also been handed down by this great uncle, the explorer: a goddess bent her knees so that her feet pointed outwards while a troop of monkeys danced around her.

'Can you play chess?' asked Herbert.

Of course she could. She was the daughter of Father who went to the chess club almost weekly. Chess had always been around her. But she did not find it very easy, for she kept thinking of other things during the game. The castles of Herbert's chess set were in the shape of elephants and all the other chess pieces had far-eastern features too. He seemed to take the game very seriously. He stared at the chessboard for a long time before he made any move; he seemed not to notice anything else as he was completely immersed in the game. Yet Lynette watched Herbert and also surveyed the exotic surroundings of his room. So, it was hardly surprising that something was brewing around her queen. She was aware of it but did not feel like disentangling the complicated constellation of the chess pieces. Frau Domansky saved the queen and Lynette by inviting them to have some mallow tea.

This time she had really made some tea which she poured into delicate cups. The crumbs from the last meal were still on the table. She offered Lynette cake, only to find that the cake tin was filled with Russian tea. She had bluish bags under her eyes; she looked worn-out, aged. Perhaps she was worried since her Rudi was at the Front by now too. It had taken long enough, for Rudi was young and healthy; a clerk at the counter of the Municipal Savings Bank was surely dispensable. Now it had become quiet in the house: no American dance records, no laughter or giggling. And what about her husband, the civil servant in Berlin? They did not get on with each other and that was quite sad really. The same thing would not happen to her should she marry and have a husband; she came to that decision while waiting for Anne. What had happened to Anne? Well, Anne wasn't coming, said Frau Domansky, she had an upset stomach.

'Be a gentleman for a change,' said Frau Domansky to her son, who obediently put on his coat. 'Be nice to the girl; boys your age always think that they have to be rough.'

It was dark outside. There were no streetlamps any more; some house walls had been covered with dark paint. Trenches had been dug in the park where you were supposed to hide should the enemy bombers come. But this was doubtful since

Aussig was not Dresden but a small, unimportant, little town. It was true that there was some industry and here and there a beautiful church with the moon shining above. This looked idyllic, as if copied from a picture by Spitzweg. Not far away the war raged.

She stood beside Herbert in the entrance of the house where her flat was. She thought of the pictures that were interwoven with gold. In one of them two lovers embraced, melting into each other. If he were to try to give her a kiss now she would turn away of course. But he did not even think of it. His hands in his coat pockets, he wished her good night very curtly and left. It did not feel right to her that he just abandoned her like that. If she had had a bar of chocolate, she would have put it in her mouth.

# 13

'Where have you been all this time?' Mutti asked. 'We've all been waiting for you. Come in, Father has something important to tell you.'

Lynette stepped into the living room. Father was sitting in his armchair looking towards her with his head raised. Her brother was curled up on the sofa with an air of slight boredom about him. Mutti withdrew to her seat under the standard lamp where she bent over a doily. Her glasses sat on the tip of her nose and Lynette was surprised that they did not slide off.

'What would you say if we were to emigrate?' Father said, pausing a while so that she could take in his words. 'Heinz doesn't seem to mind and Mutti also thinks that it may be for the best, considering how things are going at the moment.' Probably it would still be possible only from Hamburg now, Lynette thought. Father knew Hamburg, of course. But the ships of the English and Americans were lurking everywhere and whoever wanted to slip through the Channel's narrow neck needed a lot of luck. It all sounded like an adventure, almost as if it had come out of the moss-green volumes which she used to read to Heinz. But Father could be stubborn at times, once he had got something into his head....

A business friend from Argentina had offered Father his help; this friend would be expecting Father and his family. They could stay with him until Father had found a job. It would not be very difficult, for hard-working people were sought after in Argentina too. Besides, they would not be the only Germans there.

'We'll need to come to a decision soon,' Father said. 'He wants to know what's happening after all and it is a very generous offer.'

Lynette lay awake thinking about Argentina. Argentina had a long, ocean-washed coast and was not wedged in, in the middle of a continent. The ocean gave you a feeling of space, perhaps even freedom. She saw herself sitting on a veranda with a straw hat on, swaying back and forth in a rocking chair. She would have a horse there of course since the distances were so large. In the mornings she would ride to school across wide plains with high grass where cattle grazed. They would have tortillas instead of dumplings for the midday meal and the meat would be fried, not boiled. A parrot would be perched in a shadowy corner calling 'bon appetit, bon appetit', in Spanish of course. She would learn Spanish quickly; Father would make sure of that. She thought of Herbert and his face got mixed up with all these colourful pictures which caused a stirring of wistfulness in her. When she fell asleep at last, she dreamt of a snow-white house on fire and somewhere a baby crying.

The baby turned out to be little Erika. She was hungry and Aunt Gudrun fed her. Lynette found it strange that her aunt was still getting fatter since she would have thought that this hungry Something that was always attached to her would have sucked her dry by now. But of course, Aunt Gudrun was on an increased food ration as a new mother. Today was Sunday and there was more on the breakfast table than usual. There was even an egg for each of them. They had to thank the Lauritsch grandmother for that; she had come visiting a few days before, bringing with her a full basket. She also brought a holy picture in memory of grandfather. Nobody knew exactly how old he had got, but this was not really surprising since he had not known himself. He had left all those beautiful things that were still from the Präger Farm to Lynette as a dowry. Yes, Lynette was lucky since she would get everything from her grandfather and would not have to buy anything when she married. And these were not just any old things... they were things that had been handed down from generation to generation and therefore were not dead but had their own lives and stories. Old Lauritsch had always wanted to talk about these things and their history if only it had not been for his poor 'G'merk', as they called the memory in the Egerland where he came from.... Yes, his memory left him in the lurch.

Sundays stretched out endlessly since Karl was not there any more. Lynette shut the medical book; closing her eyes, she thought of Argentina. Father sat at the table writing Spanish words in an exercise book. He left the flat only on weekdays now, when he went to work. What was there to go out for, after all? Herr del Vesco was fighting far away and the chess club had adjourned its meetings until further notice since there weren't enough members any more. Herr Stelzig, however, was ill; he had caught a light chill by sitting, bent over his music, deep into the night. There wasn't enough fuel; that was why it had been cold in the room. No, Father would not go to visit Herr Stelzig; he did not have a lot of patience with people who were ill anyway. Things had to get really bad before Father would himself accept that he was ill.

Lynette sat down with Mutti in the kitchen and helped her to peel the potatoes. Mealtimes were something like the skeleton of a day, holding the many hours together. You hung on from meal to meal and felt that you were supported somehow. If she thought about it carefully, it was quite cosy in the kitchen really and she would not have wanted to do anything else. Mutti chopped the onions, had a good cry and then the food was almost ready.

Mutti sent her to call her brother for the midday meal. She knocked lightly at his room door and as there was no answer she opened it. Heinz was lying on his bed and quickly pulled his duvet over him. She saw Uncle Karl's envelope next to the brown tinged photographs on the pillow. Carefully, she closed the door again. She felt ashamed that she had become the witness of a secret he had never wanted her to see. Good that Mutti didn't know about it, for she had a thing about sin. Lynette pondered on Heinz liking to look at pictures of naked women. Then she remembered Herbert's psychology book. Yes, it was all down to this strange thing called libido. It woke your interest in your own body and the bodies of others; it made you seek closeness and intimacy. But closeness could also mean pain and suffering... she thought of Herbert. Things had not worked out all that well between them. And now she would be going away, leaving him behind. Mutti wanted to know what things were best to pack for Argentina. The fast train was to leave the day after tomorrow and they would need to hurry anyway if they still wanted to get out of here.

Five suitcases were too much luggage really. But it would work out alright if Lynette and her brother would help with the carrying; after all, they were big enough. Mutti had stacked half a dozen white, well-starched shirts into one of the suitcases as carefully as possible. The card game had to come with them, of course; Mutti tried to make Heinz and Lynette abandon it to save some space, but they were so insistent that she finally gave in. But as far as the medical book was concerned, Mutti put her foot down: it was simply too heavy and had to stay here. Father took a few especially valuable stamps out of the album and put them into his wallet. Then he opened the violin case; folding back the velvet cover he looked at his violin for a long time.

'Do you know that Brahms was Dvořák's protégé?' Father said after he had sat down in his armchair again. 'Yes, they were friends, the two of them. It didn't matter to Brahms that Dvořák was Czech and Brahms happened to be a German from Hamburg who lived in Vienna. No, it didn't bother them because they had their music in common.'

Lynette wondered how Father would get on in Argentina, for it seemed to her that he could not live away from Middle Europe, though it had become old and hunched. In its sadness it had succumbed to the rat catcher but it still had some breath of magic, if only in its music.

'By the way your grandmother, Baba, has bought a plot of land,' Father said. 'It's over in Hotowitz; there the hills begin and you've got a beautiful view over Aussig and the Elbe valley. After the war, she wants to build a house there. The garden's quite big and there would definitely be room for a riding horse. I'm sure Baba is going to plant apple trees and you could help her with the harvest. Fresh apples are wonderful and Mutti could use them for cooking.'

Meanwhile, Mutti showed Aunt Gudrun how to do a few basic things in the kitchen. Aunt Gudrun would stay on, alone for the moment until Franz came back from the war. Anne was sad that Lynette was going away. If she had known earlier, she would have given her something as a keepsake. But it was too late now. Anne did not explain what had been the matter with her when Lynette had visited Herbert. In any case, she seemed to have forgotten about it since she gave Lynette her hand when saying goodbye. Then Anne walked away without turning round.

Now Lynette, Heinz and Mutti sat next to their suitcases, waiting. They were expecting Father to come at any moment; he had only quickly gone to the office in the morning to tidy things up. He also wanted to make sure that nothing would happen to Fräulein Mandel in his absence, as far as possible. He should have been here by now... Mutti was almost continuously looking at the clock. It was not so easy to get tickets for a train that went westwards. This time it had worked out, thanks to Father's old school friend, Dewald. But he wouldn't do it again. Where on earth had Father got to? He was always on time. Something must have happened; that was the only answer. Mutti was in a constant worry anyway. And now this came on top of it. They waited till it got dark in the room and then Father arrived, properly dressed with a hat and stiff collar as always. The train, of course, had left a long time ago and Lynette was sure that Father was aware of it. He put his briefcase down, apologising to Mutti that he had not been able to get away from work earlier. Then he withdrew to play the violin.

Next morning Anne was glad that Lynette was still here. Anne told Lynette what she had heard on the wireless: last night's train, packed with fugitives, had been attacked by enemy planes and had been left burning beside the track. If anybody had got out of the train alive he or she had been truly lucky. Lynette thought it strange that she was sitting next to Anne once again. It seemed to her that she was watching herself while she sat there. And in the afternoon it was as if she accompanied herself back to her flat via the Town Park. Father returned early from work, taking an envelope of stamps out of his wallet; these were not the stamps he had taken out of the album for Argentina but a new batch.

Men thrusting forward their bayoneted rifles stood bent under the wings of an enormous eagle. This was the stamp in honour of the mobilisation of the last reserves but Father had managed to get out of it. In October he had had an invitation for the medical examination though he had one leg shorter than the other. Lynette found it difficult to imagine Father fighting a war; he was a man of trade and commerce, used to quiet offices, who jumped even when a door banged.

In the evening he told them about his medical examination with the impish smile which he sometimes wore. He cupped his hand behind his ear; that was how he had done it in front of the commission. Once again his name was called out and once again he bent forward, visibly eager to catch whatever had been said. You're hard of hearing as well, the chairman said and turned him down. But Herr Stelzig had not been so lucky; though ill – what was wrong with him? – he had been called up.

He looked thin, Herr Stelzig, thin and pale; his face seemed hardly strong enough to keep the delicate glasses up. The same Herr Stelzig who had been Father's duet partner for many years had to march to Karpitz station while a band played uplifting marches. Poor Herr Stelzig... Lynette could just imagine how he kept up with the column, more dragged along than walking of his own free will; yes, she saw it clearly before her, though she relied on what Father was telling her since she had not been there herself. As the column marched on, it moved more and more slowly till the men's boots were treading on almost the same spot. Further on, carriages blocked the road. These carriages were mostly simple carts pulled by horses, oxen, donkeys. Weighed down by clothes and furniture, they moved very slowly. The folk, mostly women with headscarves, drove on the emaciated-looking animals. A pig escaped, sniffing at the boots of the standard-bearer until its mistress came, driving it back. This was the solemn march past of the last reserves in Karbitz.

The folk were Silesians who were fleeing from the Russians, trekking in long caravans across the mountains towards Bavaria. Some stayed to rest or because they believed they were already in safety. Lynette and her family did not have to take anybody in; they already had Aunt Gudrun and her child living with them and their flat was not that big after all. Frau Domansky was spared any unwanted arrival too, which was probably down to her husband; a blind eye was turned to the Domanskys, for the family of such a high-up civil servant could not be expected to put up any fugitives.

Every day Lynette could not help noticing that the war was coming closer. The chaotic stream of fugitives flowed almost continuously down the street that had once been named after Petschek, Masaryk and Goethe. In February the sirens had blared for the first time. But nothing happened; the attack had been aimed at Brüx, which was an industrial town. Whenever Mutti had a lot of dirty dishes in the kitchen and dreaded the washing up, she would say, shaking her fist: 'I wish for a bomb to drop.'

That was what Lynette was thinking about when she sat in the school and the sirens began to blare. The sun shone through the tall windows. It was a beautiful, clear spring day. Clouds as light as down moved across the sky. Fräulein Lämmert had the class file out in twos. She did not enthuse about the ancient Germanic tribes any more but kept reminding the class that the German word *Aussig* was derived from the Slavic 'Vsty'. They walked down the stairs quietly as if a single loud word could betray them to the planes of the enemy. There was a hold-up in front of the cellar door: classes from the boys' wing were joining them... it was a mixed crowd. Some of the boys laughed and cheered each other in an attempt to show that they had not been intimidated at all by the alarm. Lynette saw her brother but he turned away and began to talk to another boy. Herbert was on his own; they had not sought each other out but were pushed towards each other by the jostling crowd. It just happened and it seemed to Lynette that it had to happen.

A musty smell wafted towards Lynette when the cellar door was opened; the cellar was an ancient vault that had never been aired. Herbert sat down next to her in a corner. An elderly woman cowered down not far from them. Lynette recognised her: it was the cleaning lady. The ceiling lamp began to sway when the first bombs fell. The swaying lamp made the faces appear blotchy. 'Let us live a little bit longer,' whimpered the woman, clasping her hands as if she were praying with a rosary. What was the matter with this old woman? Lynette thought. The cleaning lady kept repeating her 'Let us live a little bit longer'. Lynette was surprised at herself that she stayed so calm though she had more reason to whimper than the old woman, for her life was still ahead of her. But perhaps the old woman clung to life so much since she had got used to it over the years.

Her 'Let us live a little bit longer' accompanied the dropping of the bombs as if it was part of the ritual. Then there was a terrifically loud bang and the light went out. Now it was completely dark; even after Lynette's pupils had expanded she was not able to see much more than Herbert's shadowy silhouette. Outside it kept on raging and thundering and he moved closer, cuddling up to her. She stroked his hair. Had her brother not told her once that they had found lovers in Pompeii (or had it been Herculaneum?), whom the ashes had preserved for thousands of years? Lynette and Herbert were sitting close to each other and she felt a great calm inside her while outside destruction raged. It was strange that it should be just now that she felt so much at peace with herself and the world. He began to unbutton her blouse and touched her with his cold hand. Her very soul lay bare under her nipples; at least that was how it seemed to her. She started back, moved away. She had not minded Anne touching her, for Anne had been more tender. Now she suddenly shuddered with each bang: the shield protecting her had been cracked open and the outside began to penetrate her without mercy. All she saw of Herbert were the dark outlines of his figure and she began to feel hot, though the cellar was cold and musty.

There was a bang, accompanied by a terrifying shattering noise of crushed glass as if the whole world had broken apart. The vault trembled, dust came floating down. The cleaning lady coughed before carrying on with her litany. The bombing went on and on and Lynette noticed that she was shaking. At long last the inferno ceased. When the cellar door was opened, the door frame was filled with light. That was how Lynette wanted to imagine heaven from now on if there was something like heaven: as a gateway of light after a long darkness.

You had to be careful upstairs since there was shattered glass everywhere. The windows were all broken but apart from that the building was still standing, which surprised Lynette. She ran out of the building without looking for Herbert, Anne, Heinz; she was glad that she could be by herself again.

She crossed the road where the corner house had still been standing that morning. Lynette remembered a woman putting a flower pot on the balcony when she walked past. But now there was only a heap of rubble; nothing else. Clouds of smoke drifted across the sky with the chimneys of the Schicht Works looming up behind them. Beyond the drifts of smoke lay the forested hills that had a shimmer of fresh green. The destruction had not bothered the hills and forests: they just remained the same. Lynette found the Materniplatz ploughed up: two large craters had been blasted into the pavement. Perhaps that was not too bad, Lynette thought, for they could clear the pavement slabs after the war to lay out flower beds and plant trees once again and also rebuild the dreamy Elbe Fountain. The tower of the Town Church had been left standing but it looked dangerously lopsided. It seemed likely that it would collapse soon.

Lynette walked past the music shop. The house had been hit; the glass had broken and the air pressure had blown some sheet music as well as a few instruments out onto the street. She picked up a violin's neck that had been severed from its body. And while she was holding it she saw the master violin maker at his work. The furrows on his forehead were an expression of his effort and care. It had taken him many years before he could build a violin at all. And even now the building of each instrument was a challenge to him; that was why he was fond of every instrument. He needed solitude and seclusion to be able to listen to the secrets of the wood and the veneer. Perhaps it was no accident that all the great masters of violin-making had lived in centuries past when there was no engine noise. Lynette let the violin neck drop and turned into the former Goethe Street.

She pondered whether she should walk across the Materniplatz once again. But she only had to walk down the street now to be home. She did not know then how lucky she was that she had decided on the direct way home, for she would hardly have found shelter as quickly in the middle of the empty square. Now she just slipped into a house entrance when the low-flying fighter planes appeared. They probably thought they could get easy prey since everybody believed that the attack was over and old people, women and children were creeping out of their cellars in relief. Again and again shots thundered through the streets. It had been quiet for a long time before Lynette dared to come out again to continue her walk home.

The corner house on Weiss Street stood unscathed. Not even a window had been damaged. She ran up the stairs where the door to her flat was slightly ajar. The cot was empty; the dirty dishes from the midday meal were piled up next to the washing up basin. Lynette realised that they might have run out onto the street since they had known as little as herself that enemy planes lay in wait for them. She shouted. No answer. She knocked next door. The door remained shut. There was nobody on the next floor. Nor on the ground floor either. And in the cellar...

...in the cellar they were all camping with their baskets and blankets. Surprised, they looked up at Lynette who stood in the doorway. Why were they all still down here, Lynette thought and looked over to Mutti, beside whom Aunt Gudrun sat holding the sleeping Erika.

'What are you doing here?' Mutti said crossly to Lynette, 'can't it be dangerous enough for you!'

'But the all-clear sounded ages ago,' Lynette explained.

Lynette did not have to go to school for the foreseeable future. By the time the broken glass had been cleared away and new windows put in... by that time there might be peace already. Meanwhile, Lynette helped Mutti with her domestic chores or Aunt Gudrun who was ham-fisted, as she kept reminding everybody. Indeed it seemed to Lynette that Erika did not scream as much when she changed her nappy as when her mother did. But her favourite occupation was sitting in the *Palace* room, from where she was able to look out at the wide road. There was quite a lot going on out there. German soldiers moved past. They just abandoned their vehicles and tanks when they had run out of petrol. These trucks were soon surrounded by folk who climbed up to help themselves to boxes of food, blankets, bandages. There were frequent fights and once two fuming women went away with a box between them; each of them pulled at the box from one side and neither considered letting go. They would have been at each other's throats if the box had not been in between.

Lynette was able to laugh about this scene since she was not part of it. And the stream of soldiers did not cease. They did not march in formation but stumbled on in a chaotic mess; some were limping. All of them were unshaven and looked thin, emaciated; their coats were torn. The proud eagles that still shone forth from caps and uniforms looked out of place now. It seemed to Lynette that their talons were about to let go of the sun symbol so that it would be smashed to smithereens far below them. Lynette was reminded of the soldiers who marched into Prague: how their dashing step had pounded the pavement and how shiny their polished boots had been.

Uncle Karl, who was always sceptical, had been right in the end. And Uncle Franz would soon find something else to give his life meaning and a certain grandeur. As far as Lynette was concerned, she was glad that she would probably never have to stand around in the track and field ground for hours on end any more; physical education would become a subject among others again and nobody would turn up their noses at her for being plump and thin-skinned. And Mutti too was hoping for peace every day. Peace would bring Fräulein Pechwitz back, since nobody would need ammunition then. They would have *tafelspitz* on Sundays once again and Father would have a fresh shirt that had been carefully starched and ironed. He hated having to go to the office with a collar that was not really stiff. But at the moment he did not have to worry about that since he stayed at home. The works in Teplitz had been liquidated. Father was not a *glosblutzer* any more. Instead, he played the violin from morning to night.

He came out briefly at mealtimes. He played on his own. Mutti did not have any time and Herr Stelzig lay far away in the East under heavy soil through which the water of the melting snow was seeping. He had left a lot of paper behind, covered with music; Frau Stelzig would safeguard it till it became yellow and decayed. And Father played the violin: he played and played. He said that he could earn their living by playing the violin if he could not do anything else. But perhaps he just said that to justify his withdrawal. The chaos around him was kept at bay by the music.

When Lynette opened the window, faraway artillery thunder wafted in with the warm spring air. Lynette quickly laid out forks and knives on the table and was about to hurry out to get the plates when Aunt Gudrun called her back; Lynette had put down the cutlery lopsided and Aunt Gudrun straightened it up. That was important now, she explained, to keep up appearances, since everything was falling apart. It was probably quite true what Aunt Gudrun said, thought Lynette, and Father came to her mind: yes, keeping up appearances gave you a certain feeling of security.

The music on the wireless was interrupted. They stopped eating, listened. The wireless crackled. It crackled once again. Then a slow but firm voice announced that the Leader had been killed fighting for the Fatherland. When Aunt Gudrun heard this announcement, she lost her composure. Although she had ensured that the table had been laid in an exemplary manner, she started to sob uncontrollably. Her breast heaved up and down and it seemed to Lynette that she had grown even grosser and more matron-like. Aunt Gudrun, a grown-up woman, a gymnasium professor and a mother, was sobbing. The sobbing had come over her, had taken hold of her; keeping up appearances could not help her now. Would she have sobbed like this if Uncle Franz had been killed in action? On the newsreels Lynette had seen women who had been beside themselves screaming and cheering when HE moved past. And in Lynette's memory they all looked like Aunt Gudrun: respectable and plump with gold-rimmed glasses on their reddened noses. HE had had his reasons why he never married. From a distance HE remained grand and desirable. A husband, on the other hand, crowded his wife every day and was unable to hide his weaknesses and bad habits; so, not even the most magnificent man could escape unscathed. Aunt Gudrun continued sobbing, though Mutti stroked her back soothingly. 'What will become of us?' she muttered and: 'This is the end.' Little Erika began to scream. Aunt Gudrun forced herself up from her seat. When she came back from Erika her eyes were dry; she sat down at the table once again, picking up her knife and fork.

Out in the street were people who had still kept some hope. They dug ditches with spades and pickaxes; sand and stones were heaped up to form barricades which were supposed to stop tanks. Lynette watched the hustle and bustle out there thinking that she would go to Prague one day when she had finished school. Then the Czechs would rule again and Czech would be spoken in all public offices. These few years had only been a brief intermezzo that would soon be forgotten. Mutti removed the traces of those years as far as they had left their tangible mark in the flat. She walked around with a bucket throwing into it Father's Party badge that he had hardly worn, followed by the thick, important book written by HIM; it was presented to Father when the patriotic party to which he had belonged was automatically taken over, though Father had never been asked for his consent. He had not read this book since he preferred Stifter or books that were written in other languages. Heinz's cravat went into the bucket, as did a certificate that he had won at some sport competition. But Mutti felt pity for the flag; it was made out of excellent material after all and nobody knew when you'd be able to buy decent clothes again. Mutti was a good seamstress. So she sat down with her sewing machine, turned the material over so that its treacherous symbol disappeared and made a red skirt out of it. There was nothing dangerous in this since the Russians would not object to red, Mutti joked. The bucket was full now but who was to take it away? Father was playing the violin, Mutti was of a nervous disposition anyway and Aunt Gudrun's face went completely white when Mutti wanted to hand the bucket over to her. The Russians could be here at any moment, she said, and told Mutti that she should have got the bucket ready much earlier. Heinz was strangely subdued, hiding away in his room. There was only Lynette. Again she was surprised at herself: how calm she was, walking to the park with the bucket in her hand.

Crows rose up from the treetops that had a green shimmer this year once again. The roses bore rose-hips; they were brownish and had shrivelled over the winter. Lynette felt like sitting down on one of the benches, which she used to do on her way to school. But she put it off since she had to get rid of the stuff in the bucket first. She heard something murmuring; of course, that was the Kleische stream. She was sure that the wild Waterman would not mind her passing on the bucket's contents to his realm. The thick book would probably remain lying on the bottom of the stream. Yet the Party badge at least would wander to

**209**

the Elbe and from there to the sea.

When she got back, she took up her observation post at the window again. Before long, more soldiers appeared down below. Good that she had not dawdled before since these soldiers' uniforms weren't the woodruff green colour of the Germans. Some soldiers had their peaked caps pushed backwards with a quiff of hair protruding; quite a few soldiers were whistling. They all appeared fresh somehow, though they must have marched a long way to get here. Bicycles were piled up on trucks. This seemed to be an easy-going army that conquered other countries by bicycle. Father appeared, Mutti and Heinz; they did not walk up to the window but looked out from further back in the room. Father sat down in his armchair again staring down in front of him. She had never seen Father like this; usually he was someone who had to be doing something all the time.

Two tanks remained on the Zappe Meadow. From there it was not far to Herr Filip's corner shop. With their arms full of spirits, soldiers came out of the shop; one bottle fell and burst. It seemed to matter little to them that the spirits belonged to Herr Filip; after all, showing a bit of a rough edge was part of being a victor. A soldier put his arm around Herr Filip's shoulder. He had been standing on the side watching; now he went with them, more pushed along than walking of his own free will. He sat on the Zappe Meadow in the shadow of a tank, wretched in between the brawny bodies of two soldiers. They were singing, bawling; one of them slapped Herr Filip amicably on the back. Now he also put the bottle to his mouth. *Na shledanou*, little man, thought Lynette, as she drew the curtains.

She dreamt about Herr Filip. It seemed as if his face was

reflected by a convex mirror since his nose looked very big and his mouth too. He opened his mouth as Lynette woke up. Somebody was screaming outside; the screaming was dreadful and went right through Lynette. She pressed her ears closed with her fingers but the screaming did not cease. It sounded desperate. She had never heard screaming that had sounded so desperate; it was shrill and piercing – the screaming of a woman. Lynette was relieved when the screaming stopped; it was quiet once again.

Father was just sitting down in his armchair after breakfast when there was a knock at the front door. He got up and as he walked towards the door there was another much louder knock and somebody shouted something that sounded like a curse. Mutti did not move and held her hands in the pockets of her apron. Aunt Gudrun had come out of her room and Heinz too. They and Lynette stood together in the corridor looking at Father who was at the door. Lynette had never seen him behaving as he did now: he was bubbly, laughed loudly and put his arm round the shoulder of one soldier while carrying on speaking Czech. Lynette had to remind herself that this man was her father, who had always been so careful to keep his distance. Even with Herr del Vesco a handshake had to suffice. And now he embraced this soldier as if he had found a long-lost brother. The soldier seemed to like it; he laughed and the other two soldiers laughed too at this misunderstanding. They waved their caps to say goodbye and when Father closed the door they knocked at the neighbours'.

Father sat down in his armchair and Lynette noticed that his hands were shaking. He was German after all and that was why he had not pinned a Czech flag on the door, which would have kept away any danger. All Germans had to wear white armbands from now on. Why did they have to be white, Lynette wondered, putting her armband on. Her socks that had angered Herr Novák in Prague had been white too... but that was a long time ago. Did Czechs always think of the colour white when it came to Germans? This nonsense would soon stop anyway, Mutti said; they could not carry on insisting forever that almost a whole town always put on an· armband before leaving their homes. But for now it was wise to keep doing it; otherwise you disappeared into a camp. The camps had stayed, only their occupants had changed. By keeping the old camps, the new authorities got away with not having to build new watchtowers and safe barracks where they could take any unwanted man or woman.

Mutti was sure that Fräulein Pechwitz was in such a camp if she were still alive. Fräulein Pechwitz would have come to Aussig straight away, to her 'family', since she did not have a family of her own. The Russians had taken over the factory and there had been no escape for Fräulein Pechwitz. She had been a believer and by believing she had become guilty. What she had believed in had not been much good but you could forgive Fräulein Pechwitz for that since many others had been led astray too. Now Mutti missed Fräulein Pechwitz who would have put on her working clothes straight away and done the shopping.

Shopping had become an exhausting exercise that wore you down. Mutti often stayed away for half a day. Everywhere people were standing in long queues and when a Czech came they all had to step back. That was how it was now but it would also pass, as everything did. You could not get a lot for the food-ration cards that had 'German' printed on them anyway. Mutti took the picture by the painter Rühr from the wall, returning with some sugar and a piece of butter on the same day. One by one her carefully crocheted doilies disappeared and Father contributed a few stamps from his album.

He listened to the wireless a lot. Everything was said to be changing for the better. He had heard that before. Only the roles had changed: now the victors condemned the previous masters. Father had his mother, Baba, to thank that there was still a wireless at all. Baba had gone to the authorities to whom Mutti had obediently taken the wireless. Baba put her arms on her hips giving those civil servants hell so that they let her have the wireless back straight away.

Standing at the window, Lynette heard the radio in the background. Mutti did not want her to go out on the road since she was young and a girl. But Lynette did not feel like staying up here in the flat forever; she felt like a prisoner. She persuaded Father to fetch a box of old clothes from the cellar for her. Rummaging through the box, she found a pair of Father's trousers that she turned up and put on. The trousers were big and hung around her like a sack. The next thing she put on was a checked shirt and a pair of braces. There was a *tschepitse*, a cap that was flat and looked like a workman's. Lynette wondered who had worn it. Perhaps Father, before he did his entrance exam for university? Whatever... the cap was ideal for Lynette's purposes since she could stuff her brown hair under it. Father got some coal dust for her from a neighbour in the house next door and Lynette rubbed the dust into her face. When she looked in the mirror she found herself staring at the face of a street urchin; only her eyes had stayed the same.

It felt strange to be able to stroll through the streets once again. Her sense of regained freedom bordered on intoxication. She had her hands in both trouser pockets, passing men and women who wore a white armband like herself. They were knocking dust and mortar from the bricks which they got from a smashed house. A guard was watching them. Here and there a wall was going up already but many houses' ceilings were still the sky. Swifts and swallows nested in sooty nooks and crannies. At Materniplatz the torn-up craters had been filled with gravel and huge beams propped up the leaning tower of the Town Church. Once Lynette tripped over a street sign; picking it up, she noticed that the street name on it was in German. Only now did she notice that the street signs were missing everywhere. It would probably take a while before the Czechs agreed on new street names; and then the writing on the signs needed to be done too. Sign-writing was a profitable job; as a sign-writer you were never short of work in times like these. There would be no physical education class up on the track and field ground for a long time since it was studded with vehicles. One car body stood next to the other and each had been totally disembowelled. Even the seats were missing so that a metal skeleton was all that was left. Behind all this the hills rose, softly and in full green.

She wanted to call in on Anne quickly. Just to see how she was. It was not far from here. She knocked, called. Nobody answered. Lynette feared the worst. It would not have been all that surprising because of Anne's father who had been something high-up. But Lynette could not really believe that they had arrested the whole family because of that either. Then it seemed to her as if something had darted away from one of the windows. She was probably mistaken; it must have been the reflection of a bird or a branch that moved in the gentle wind. She shrugged her shoulders and decided to make her way back slowly through the Town Park.

Near her old school, the Realgymnasium for girls, Lynette saw Fräulein Lämmert. But no, this woman could not be Fräulein Lämmert, for she had pinned a Czech flag on her blouse. Lynette called out her name: yes, the woman was Fräulein Lämmert after all. She asked how Lynette was and then she began to talk about the greatness of the Russian soul. Lynette should read Gorky, everything was contained in Gorky.

At home, she searched the bookcase but did not find Gorky. There was a volume by Tolstoy; he was a Russian writer too and might just do. She liked the small book since it contained a picture of a violin player leaning over a lady who wore a glittering diamond necklace. Yes, this was Russia: a land with lavish banquets that lasted forever. She would have loved to learn some Russian. But Czech was more important now. After all, she would need to be able to speak Czech when she got on the train to Prague to study medicine. And who knew whether there would still be a university where they taught you in German? But by then the hatred might have died down, and German too would be tolerated again as it had been in the days of the Republic.

Lynette's enthusiasm rubbed off on Aunt Gudrun. She was cut out for learning and studying, as she had said herself, and she was willing to take on any challenge. Lynette wrote down the numbers in Czech and Aunt Gudrun began to memorise them. Each time she got stuck with the number four. The number four was quite a tough one and you had to have an agile tongue to tackle it.

'There, you see what a mess I make of it,' said Aunt Gudrun, 'though I'm a teacher; but this seems to be far too difficult for me. By the way, I think you would make an excellent teacher.

And you'd look good in glasses... why is it that you young girls always have to be so vain? Well, I'll carry on till I can master pronouncing four in Czech. It would be ridiculous if I couldn't learn it. Uncle and I will come to live here soon and I need to know my numbers when I go shopping.'

But things turned out differently. She got a letter from Uncle, who was a prisoner of war with the English, somewhere near the Rhine. He was well looked after; there was no need for her to worry. He was treated with respect. The English knew what they owed to officers. The land around here was beautiful; the broad waters of the Rhine streamed past and France was near. He wanted to live here when he was free again, here inside the borders of what had been the old Reich, and he asked Aunt Gudrun to come and join him; a lot had been destroyed but the English would get her a place to stay.

'He has no idea,' said Mutti, 'as if there weren't any dangers. And with little Erika too.'

Aunt Gudrun did not seem to hear her. She looked through Mutti with glassy eyes and Lynette was sure that her thoughts were already with Uncle Franz. Though she tried to appear to be an intellectual and in control, her emotions got the better of her. She did not show her emotions, kept them locked up; only sometimes they erupted as had happened with the news on the wireless.

Now Baba swung into action since she had to get the necessary papers. Two days later Aunt Gudrun was on the move, a heavy bag in one hand, little Erika cradled in her other arm. *Ahoy*, Aunt Gudrun, thought Lynette. *Ahoy* was what sailors said but in Czech it was another way of saying goodbye and Lynette wondered whether it was true after all that Bohemia was beside the sea. But no, the sea was far away. Lynette was sure of it since she and her family had gone there before the war had started. It had been the Baltic Sea. She had collected starfish and shells while her parents had sat in wicker beach chairs that had a hood to protect them against the sun and Heinz had built sand castles. She had kept the shells; taking one out of the jar, she held it to her ear. There was a roaring sound; this was the sound of the waves that had been caught by the sea shell's spirals. She remembered the wide, empty beaches and the waves that dissolved and returned, dissolved and returned, coming into being and passing away endlessly... yes, she even thought she could smell the seaweed when Mutti called.

There was a visitor for her. It was Herbert. She had almost forgotten about him. But no: that was not quite right. He was always somewhere in her mind though she had tried to push him into the background. He seemed embarrassed, did not really know what to say. Perhaps he regretted now that he had come, especially since Mutti had announced him as 'your young suitor' at the top of her voice. He did not seem to like it much that he was seen in this light. Lynette said that she had come to see him and Anne but nobody had been at home.

'Really?' he said. 'That's strange since we don't go out; there's always at least one of us in the house. We don't open the door for everybody; Gitti is suspicious, but we would have opened it for you.'

Lynette told him when exactly she had come and that she had seen something moving behind one of the upstairs windows.

'That's right: I always look out from behind the curtain to check who's there. But if I had seen you, I would remember it. There haven't been many knocking at our door anyway.

Last time it was a boy who looked quite grubby. Gitti thought that we'd better keep our door shut.'

Lynette could not help smiling. She excused herself, disappearing into her own room, where she slipped into Father's baggy trousers; she stuffed her hair under the cap and did not forget to rub some coal dust on her face either. When Lynette returned they both laughed.

'That was you,' Herbert said and after a while: 'Very pretty... you've got yourself ready to go out, isn't that what women do? But they usually don't use coal dust for it. Well, you might as well come with me now.'

That was how he was: he did not want to make her think that he was asking her to come with him. Everything had to appear as if it happened by chance, as if he did not really care about anything. So he had hidden his invitation in a fair amount of roughness.

Heat engulfed them in the street. A lot of dust was whirled up when a military vehicle carrying Russian soldiers roared past. Of course: summer was coming. Why should this year be an exception?

# 14

Lynette sat down to write her chronicle. The sun was just setting. Though it was only ten, it was time for her, as a bearer of a white armband, to have to be back. She had had to hurry since she had not been aware how time had passed when she had been with the Domanskys. It had been a beautiful day, full of shimmering butterflies that she pinned down with words now, for memories were butterflies.

Frau Domansky had opened the door. She was barefoot and looked unkempt with her hair uncombed and dirt under her fingernails. For the first time Lynette noticed a streak of grey in her hair. She seemed to be the same age as Mutti but acted as if she were much younger. Anne was there too; she did not avoid Lynette this time. She sat down at the table with everybody else and when nobody said anything Frau Domansky suggested that Herbert should play something. Herbert disappeared, returning with some sheet music.

'Ach, no, not that kind of music, not something old-fashioned,' Frau Domansky said loudly, 'all that's just a lie.' He put the sheet music to one side, closed his eyes and played. It sounded incoherent, fragmented. It was music that had no foundation, everything was loose and swaying.

'That's more to my liking,' said Frau Domansky, puffing out the smoke of a cigarillo that she smoked as she lay back. She turned to Lynette and said: 'Has he told you that he wants to be a composer, a great composer who'll go down in musical history? He's already working on his first symphony... isn't that true Herbert?'

Herbert turned red in the face and glared at his mother or 'Gitti' and said nothing. At length he asked Lynette hesitatingly whether she wanted to go out with him to pick currants; they had to be picked while they were still fresh. Frau Domansky smirked. Lynette wanted Anne to come too but Anne stayed in the house. So Lynette came to be alone with Herbert who bent the shoots towards him so that they could pick the berries more easily. They did not put all the berries in the basket; many went straight into their mouths. She liked the red berries best. The light coloured berries tasted slightly bland and the blackcurrants had a strangely musty taste.

'And what about me?' Herbert asked.

Well, he only had to open his mouth. And when he did so, she put a red berry into it. But he wanted more, the greedy boy. And then he wanted a kiss which she pressed on his lips in the end. But it was still not enough for him and she got to taste his tongue. They were standing behind the bushes but Lynette worried that Anne or Frau Domansky could see them. She was also surprised that he was not hesitant or clumsy at all as she would have had expected.

'Come on, there are so many berries still,' she said, and he began to bend the shoots towards her once again.

'You never told me that you wanted to be a composer.'

'I'll write a Redcurrant Waltz which I'll dedicate to you,' he said, laughing, and she did not know whether he meant it seriously or as a joke so that he could hide behind it a little.

'Gitti doesn't like the old composers but I like them; I also like folk songs. She thinks that's all much too dreamy. She only likes Rilke's later poetry and I like his early poems; can I recite you a stanza which I'm especially fond of?'

Then he had recited the verses which Lynette now recalled while writing them down. The verses were imbued with a deep melodious flow to which Lynette could not help succumbing as night was filling the outside world and she would have loved to be with Herbert. She listened to his voice reciting the stanza slowly and a bit monotonously; it was almost as if he wrote through her:

*Mich rührt so sehr*
*böhmischen Volkes Weise,*
*schließt sie ins Herz sich leise,*
*macht sie es schwer...*

It touches my heart
Bohemia's melody
making it quietly
wistful and sad...

She read the stanza once again before closing the chronicle. She took a few redcurrants out of the basket that stood on her chest of drawers. There was no sugar on them; she put them in her mouth and their taste was sweet to her. Then she took off her clothes, stood in front of the tall wardrobe mirror. It seemed to her as if she had become desirable all of a sudden. But perhaps that was only down to her not wearing glasses and therefore not being able to see herself very clearly.

When she had gone to bed she went through the past day slowly, step by step. In her imagination she indulgently lingered on some moments, again and again reliving those moments that had been especially beautiful to her; it was just like reading a very special poem or listening to a beautiful piece of music that she would have liked endlessly repeated. I'll take the basket back tomorrow, she thought before falling asleep.

She was woken by a knock. It was still very early; the light still had a dim and sleepy quality to it. The days were getting longer and it would soon be the longest day. There was again a knock, only much more forceful, and a woman's voice shouted: 'Open the door please.' Lynette was not sure what happened then. But somebody must have opened the door as she heard quick steps and then suddenly a young unshaven man with a gun stood in her room. What was going on? She pulled her duvet up to her chin as if it were some kind of protective shield. At first the man with the gun did not take any notice of her but looked in the corner behind the wardrobe as if he thought somebody was hiding there, possibly a lover. He brandished his gun, visibly proud that he was still allowed to play war though there was no enemy. But perhaps he took Lynette for his enemy since there was nobody else in the room. Get out of my room, Lynette wanted to scream, but her throat had clogged up. Her voice was numbed by fear; the man had turned round and was now pointing the gun straight at her. He shouted something in Czech. She had learned Czech and was able to understand it. But at this moment she could not remember any of it. She was only able to make out some threatening hissing sounds, failing to put them together. The man stepped forward, shouting at her even louder. What did he want from her? She felt like screaming. Screaming for Father, for Mutti, for her brother. Where were they? She was all on her own with this man and his gun. But then a woman commissar appeared and said something to the partisan guard. The man lowered his gun and stepped out into the corridor. The woman smiled and said in German that Lynette should get dressed; justice was to be done at last and Lynette and her family would need to leave their flat at once. She advised Lynette to put on as many clothes as possible; it would be a hot day but that did not matter. 'Everything else has to stay here, you understand, don't take anything; it all belongs to the Czech people now.'

How could that be? How could everything which was hers belong to the Czech people now? Her autograph book, her dollies, her old biology exercise book into which she had carefully copied a human heart. And who were these Czech people... this young man with his gun and this woman who forced their way into people's houses and flats? Lynette was furious. She folded back her duvet and found herself banging her fists against the woman's chest. How dared she...! But the woman only laughed. She grabbed Lynette's wrists and pushed her back onto her bed. 'Pomalu, pomalu, my little Němka,' she said, 'I would be very sorry to do it but I would need to call him in again if you don't calm down.' The woman seemed to be quite a motherly type who wanted the best for Lynette as far as it was in her power. 'What about Mutti, Father, my brother?' Lynette shouted. 'They're getting ready to leave too, just like you,' the woman said. 'I'll let you get on with it, little Němka, you see, I'll trust you. But I warn you, you'll regret it if you abuse my trust.' The commissar stepped out of her room and Lynette, swearing under her breath, began to follow the woman's advice: she put on vest after vest, blouse after blouse and a cardigan on top so that her body volume had almost grown to that of the commissar's. Then she opened a drawer and took out Baba's picture. This was quite dangerous really since the picture too belonged to the Czech people now. If the commissar or the partisan guard had found out... she did not even try to imagine what would have happened. But she could not leave without a picture of Baba since she would forget what Baba looked like. And who knew what was going to happen to Lynette and her family? She slipped the picture down her front and could feel it coldly touching her stomach. It was held in place by her skirt which was tight around her waist. There was a ring in the same drawer. It was the wedding ring of old Lauritsch that grandmother had brought when she visited last, probably as a first instalment of Lynette's promised dowry. Where was she going to hide it? Slipping it down her front was no good since the commissar would have found it too if she had found the picture. Her armpits? – but what if she was asked to raise her arms? She remembered Heinz telling her once that the ancient Greeks put a coin under the tongues of those who travelled across the river Styx to the world beyond. Wasn't she getting ready for a journey something like that too? It made sense to slip the ring under her tongue; she would not be needing her tongue since there was no point in saying anything, for things seemed to be taking their course without her say so. It had all become unreal by

**224**

now as if she was watching herself on a cinema screen or was reading about a girl to whom this was happening.

She walked out of her room and saw that there was another guard in the living room and yet another guard who had taken up his post in front of Heinz's room. All in all there were three armed partisans in their flat. The commissar had gone to the bathroom with Mutti. She probably wanted to make sure that Mutti was not carrying any hidden jewellery or anything else that was valuable and had become the possession of the Czech people now. As if Mutti, who was nervous even without the presence of partisans in her flat, would have done such a thing! No, it was Lynette who had a gold ring and a photograph; thinking about it, Lynette felt a satisfying sense of triumph. She saw Father standing in the corner of the living room glancing over at the stamp albums. But the guard never took his eyes off him and Father was unable to do anything about it. Leaving would have been so much easier if he had had some valuable stamps with him. On one of the living room shelves next to the sideboard with the tokay and other spirits lay Father's violin and the Bisiach. Lynette knew how much his violin meant to Father. But soon it would be a Czech enthusiast who would be playing it. And for a moment Lynette once again had that queasy feeling deep down in her stomach, a feeling that reminded her of the lift in Prague: the 'lift feeling'.

They all had to line up in the corridor where they were searched. The commissar took care of Lynette and Mutti. Lynette went rigid with fear, for she thought that the motherly woman would find the photo and the ring. But she only looked into the pockets of Lynette's cardigan and slid her hands down her sides. Father was less lucky. He slumped against the wall

225

after his face was punched by the fist of one of the guards. The guard pointed at the army watch which Father had probably forgotten to take off since it was not very valuable. The man ripped it off Father's wrist and put it in his pocket. Lynette shuddered: if Father was treated like that for the sake of an unimportant watch what would have happened to her if they had discovered the ring? It was a ring of high-carat gold, for in the time when Lynette's grandparents married you didn't try to save money when it came to things like wedding rings.

It was cold outside; Lynette could feel the chill even through her many layers. The sun was still behind the roofs. But when the sun rose, it would be hot: another hot summer's day. They waited with their guards near the tramway stop as the other inhabitants who had been cleared out of their flats were led up, family by family. It wasn't just the house with the mighty arches that Lynette once thought had been lived in by titans from the Giant Mountains that was being cleared but all the houses right down to the corner house on the other side of the street. Quite a crowd had assembled by the time they were told to start marching.

The town seemed empty since it was still early morning. Only here and there an early riser looked down on this train that was escorted by partisans. Again and again they had to stop to accommodate more people. It seemed like a river to Lynette, a river that kept on absorbing tributaries; and this river ended in the Materniplatz.

Other deportees were already here, waiting, surrounded by guards. There didn't seem to be any hurry: whatever was happening was slow in its beginnings. Lynette had a lot of time to look at the façade of the Town Theatre that seemed unfamiliar to her all of a sudden since a huge banner, announcing BENEŠ-STALIN-DIVADLO written in enormous letters hung resplendent on this turn-of-the-century building. Mutti saw it too but did not say anything. She did not seem to have taken in what had happened and just stood there silently, her lips pursed. Poor Mutti, thought Lynette, and tried to distract her mind by figuring out what had once been written on the oval ornamental shield above the theatre's entrance. She had never noticed it properly; only now did she become aware of it because, suddenly, it was empty. Beside the theatre was the empty plinth which, she remembered, had once served as the base for a bust of Wagner.

Lynette hummed the song of the wild Waterman. Her anger had subsided into sadness and her humming was slow and subdued. She felt the sun caressing her neck and tried to convince herself that she was lucky really since the sun was shining; after all, it could have been raining. They all squatted down. Only father was still standing. New troops kept coming, bringing more and more people. Lynette could only make out a fluid mingling of colours and shapes at first; it was only when the troops came closer that the people became disentangled, gaining their own individual outlines.

Hours later, the guards shouted at them that they had to get up. They were marched down Teplitz Street and to the station. The first group of people were counted and one of them was taken aside by the guards, who talked to him. Then he too followed the others to the open coal wagons waiting at the platform; they all had to get into the first wagon. Lynette and her family waited till it was their turn, which took a long time for there were many people. Lynette's knees felt weak; it was only now she realised that she had not had any breakfast.

After they had been separated from the others one of the guards took Father aside. Father was promoted to the position of wagon leader. It had to be a man, of course, since it was a man who counted them and it was all men and no women in the governments and high-up posts. But there were other men apart from Father in their group. So why Father? Lynette wondered: was it true, as Mutti sometimes said, that he had a kind of aura which made everyone respect him, even strangers who didn't know him? But Lynette was not so sure. Perhaps it was all down to the clothes he was wearing. Just like every morning he had put on a white shirt with a stiff collar and a tie as if whatever expected him was only an unimportant detour on his way to work, to which, of course, he had not been for months. He held his head up high; it seemed to Lynette that it was important to him to hold his head up as high as possible. Mutti ducked behind his back. She had such a misplaced sense of pride, Mutti had; it had all been terrible to her since she had felt ashamed to be led along the streets like a criminal. But criminals were human beings too; and sometimes they were better than the others who had an air of respectability about them. Heinz had tears in his eyes. He should have remembered Old Shatterhand, Lynette thought. Sadness groped for her too but she tried to escape it; by telling herself that things could have been even worse, she kept her composure. At times she felt almost serene; her head was filled with a strange lightness that was unreal and somewhat alien to her.

Father had to step forward and report how many women, men and children were in his wagon. A partisan woman wrote all this down on a list. There was just enough room in the wagon for everybody to sit down. Lynette hesitated but when she actually had sat down it did not matter any more since her clothes had been dirtied by the coal dust. Even Father sat down. Nobody in the wagon said anything. It was as if everybody was numb and had to wake up from their numbness first. They were dozing, waiting; time went quickly if you dozed, if you did not think of minutes or hours. Slowly the sun was approaching the zenith as it did every day.

The iron of the wagon heated up. There was no breeze and the heat was trapped in the wagon. A child screamed. The mother held it out of the wagon so that it would get some cool air; it did not help, however, and the child kept on screaming. In the distance the façades of buildings rose up, with staring black holes; holes that had once been windows. Now you could see the Town Church tower that tilted to one side even from here, since many of the roofs and walls in between were missing and everything had become open and transparent. The Market Square did not hide behind tall rows of houses any more. The town centre was not much more than a landscape of ruins; if you looked at it in moonlight, the town centre would have reminded you of one of those landscapes painted by Caspar David Friedrich, who had come to Bohemia many times to paint... at least that was what Fräulein Plötzl once said. On the other side, towards the outskirts of the town, the chimneys of the industrial works still ascended into the blue sky with the Ferdinand Rise in the background.

The woman partisan who had made the list was sitting down on the steps of the station building; with her rifle on her knees and a glass of beer in front of her, she had her midday break. She swore when the guard beckoned her to come over. She took her rifle and her list and quickly emptied her beer, leaving the glass on the steps. When she returned she was accompanied by Baba. The woman partisan laughed as Baba talked to her. After they had arrived at the wagon that held Lynette and her family the partisan got herself some more beer and settled down on the steps again.

Baba put down a large saucepan and next to it the bag that she had slid down from her arm. She said that she had gone straight to the authorities when she heard what had happened. But authorities and civil servants... they knew themselves how long everything took. To get them moving you had to make fire and Baba said 'under their arses' which was not all that refined but that was Baba all over. Once when a millionaire, who was well known in the whole town, won another million in the lottery, Baba's simple comment was: 'The devil always shits on the same heap.'

Now she got an official paper out from under her clothes and tried to hand it over to Father. But he wasn't willing to take it since he had coal dust on his hands; Father, correct as he was, did not want to dirty the document. So Baba held it up so that Father could read it. Everything was written in Czech which did not pose any difficulties for Father. He shook his head in the end and said in German: 'No, we will not do this; we will stay where we are.'

'But Mani, don't be a fool, you can have everything back; it was a mistake, nothing more. Nobody knows what they'll do to you.'

'It doesn't matter,' Father said, holding his head up even higher, 'we are not Czechs, we are Germans.'

Mutti sighed. Father decided on important matters; that was how it had always been. But usually Father had asked for her advice at least. Mutti would have probably liked to have gone back. After all, it was her town where she was born and grew up; even the few years in Prague had not been much to her liking. Mani, on the other hand, could have passed as a Czech if he chose to but not Mutti who could hardly say a word in Czech. How would things turn out for her if she stayed: for her, the only German for miles around? It was not so bad with children who could quickly get used to any change. What kind of town would it be? Who would move into the empty shells of the houses? Whatever was going to happen, this town would not be the town she knew; everything would change and the town would be different too.

Baba heaved the saucepan up and then the heavy bag. There was sauerkraut in the saucepan; mixed into it were pieces of salty, smoked pork and goose giblets: a rich and nourishing meal. They had not had such an opulent meal for months. But Baba had not forgotten about the need to digest the meal, for in her bag were a regional schnapps called 'Karlsbader Wasser', beer and Moravian wine. They could indulge themselves once more, have a feast. Heinz and Lynette drank some of the wine, beer, even the Karlsbader Wasser; otherwise the fatty food would not have agreed with them after all these weeks of fasting. Baba was more than generous when it came to food. She cooked big portions so that nobody would go away hungry. There was still something left for the mother whose crying child had become quiet; nobody knew whether it was quiet because it felt better or whether it was just exhausted.

Baba took the empty saucepan, the dirty dishes and cutlery off them, slid the bag over her arm and went away. She did not turn round again, not even when she disappeared behind the partisan with her rifle and her beer sitting on the steps of the station building. Baba was an unsentimental woman. She

231

gave a hand where it was needed but where she could not help any more she withdrew. Lynette was sure that she had witnessed many sorrows in her work; her experience had probably taught her to accept things as they were.

Lynette began to feel better. It was so much better when your belly was not empty. And the heat had become less intense; the sun was already approaching the chimneys and hills in the west. The wagons had still not moved. 'Maybe they'll let us go back after all,' Mutti said. 'Otherwise they would have moved us by now.'

Just then a train arrived and people in uniforms and other folk stepped out of it. Everybody spoke Czech; all of a sudden there were only Czechs. A young man with his arm around a girl laughed.

A light wind got up, which was pleasant. Slowly Lynette put on the layers that she had discarded in the midday heat. The sound of iron scraping on iron made a shrill screeching noise that seemed to jar each single nerve ending. Lynette held her hands over her ears. When the train had gained a comfortable speed, the terrible screeching stopped.

They were moving at last. The draught caused by the train's speed merged with the evening wind and blew any numbness away. All of a sudden there were conversations going on. Father was joined by a man whom he knew from the chess club. He was small and agile and his eyes seemed to glisten with good-natured happiness even now. He bent forward to Mutti, assuring her that there was no need for her to worry; they would be carted off to Bavaria into the American zone where their lives would be much happier since there would be no Czechs and so no permanent wrangling. But a woman with a sinewy neck insisted that they were all being taken to Russia, perhaps even Siberia, who knew? Then, for the last time, they saw the Schreckenstein. It was just a ruin, like the town itself.

They followed the Elbe. Everything looked much milder now because it was evening and the stream was veiled by a soft silvery haze, framed by wooded hills. The water still kept playfully sweeping along the stairs of Pilnitz Castle as it had when Lynette passed it for the first time, though not in a coal wagon but on a steamer.

They stopped in Dresden. Here, the huge dome of the Church of Our Lady was missing; without it, the sky looked empty and unfamiliar. Dresden had come to look similar to Aussig now, for there was not much difference between one ruined town and another. But in Dresden almost every house was destroyed. In the end Mutti found a house whose ground floor was still intact and knocked at the door. A woman opened and looked suspiciously at Lynette and Mutti.

'Who's there?' asked a male voice in the background.

'Refugees,' said the woman.

'We aren't refugees; we were driven out of our home, we were forced to leave,' Mutti said.

The woman shrugged her shoulders as if to say that it made no difference: whether they were refugees or not, they all wanted the same thing. She returned with a jug of water and some bread that tasted mouldy; they had hardly any bread themselves. Lynette promised to bring the jug back after Father and Heinz had had some water.

It was easy to find the way back to the station; there were no rows of houses that would have obstructed the view and made it difficult for them to see where they were. At a corner they saw a man being stopped by Russian soldiers.

He did not have any papers and they arrested him. Before they pushed him into the car he turned round to look at Mutti as if she were able to help him. This was not something that could have happened to Mutti and Lynette. They were in safety for the time being; they had their wagon and their names were on the woman partisan's list. The wagons had become something like their home which they had to hang on to. Their guards must have been well aware of this; they let them swarm out while the train waited at the station since they knew for certain that they would return. The wagons were the only fixed point amidst all the destruction, all the chaos.

Lynette would never have thought that she would be overjoyed one day to be able to return to a coal wagon. The interior of the wagon had changed for the better by now as far as the sanitary facilities were concerned. Some energetic people had discovered a barrel which did not seem to be owned by anybody near the railway tracks. They fetched it and put it in a corner of the wagon. Somebody donated an old rag that could be stretched over its top. So they were now equipped with a state-of-the-art toilet.

The train moved on. The air was getting very chilly indeed. Lynette put on her cardigan. With her many blouses and vests she was like an onion. And once again tomorrow when it got hot she would be shedding her many skins.

The wagons stopped. There was nothing for miles. Only darkness and silence. The child still whimpered, though; it had probably been whimpering all the time but Lynette had been unable to hear it when the train was moving. At long last the child fell silent and the stars sparkled in the firmament which also held a pale, indifferent moon.

Lynette sat leaning against the wagon wall; she had her legs propped up. Mutti sat next to her on one side, her brother on her other side: their physical closeness kept her warm. Her stomach rumbled. Now she remembered that she had stuffed some redcurrants in her bundle this morning. She ate a few, grimacing: they had not tasted so sour yesterday. She thought of Herbert and her mind went over the last day once again; she had lost count of how many times she had recalled yesterday in the minutest detail. But it only made her sad and so she tried to think of other things: of Pilnitz Castle for instance and of the white clouds she had used to gaze at and which you could find everywhere in the world.

Ratatata, ratatata... this was the wheels' rhythm that had sounded harsh in the beginning but grew softer, almost comforting, as she got used to it. She dozed off easily. When she woke up she could already see the red fireball of the sun that was still a bit hazy and around it some orange-tinged clouds. The dew had moistened the meadows overnight. Between fruit trees and farms morning mists wove their delicate ethereal fabrics, which looked beautiful. Lynette had never seen an early morning landscape; she had always preferred to stay in bed, *sammern* as Mutti called it.

Loud, agitated talking startled her out of her contemplation. It came from the other side of the wagon where the man from the chess club kept on and on talking to the mother who pressed her child firmly to her breast, shrinking back from him. At last the man went to Father and explained that the child had died and that the dead body needed to be removed. Of course, the man was right; it was dangerous because of possible diseases, not to mention the heat. But maybe it was better for a woman to go and talk to her, Father suggested.

Mutti agreed to do it. She could be patient and she was still talking to the woman when the train had been moving for a long time. But she did not have any success either.

And they moved on and on through rural landscapes. On both sides were fields of wheat and potatoes. In the middle of these fields were farms just like the Präger Farm had been: large and spacious with a tall gate. Farmers and farm workers raked and hoed; carts and strong horses stood in front of them, waiting patiently. Scythes sliced through tall grass, which Lynette imagined to be almost silent, just a whizzing sound followed by the grass blades' snapping. That was how it had always been and that was how it was today. Nothing reminded you that there had been a war. The hay had to be brought in, that was important; the wheat and potatoes were harvested later. People were in need of food and this thought made Lynette feel her own hunger. It bit her from the inside: hunger was an animal with sharp teeth, gnawing many holes.

The further they got the more clouds came up. They were going eastwards, towards Siberia, as the woman with the sinewy neck kept reminding everybody. They would be put in a camp there and would never return. It was quiet in the wagon. This woman's talk darkened even the mood of the lively little man from the chess club. He did not mention Bavaria and the Americans any more. Again and again Lynette looked up to the clouds that were not white but dark and heavy, though the hot weather still lasted and there was no rain.

It was already afternoon when the wagons stopped in Cottbus. It was only a short stop and nobody was allowed to leave the train. When the train started again it went back the same way they had just come. So the human freight was carted through the land and Lynette was able to indulge in a sightseeing trip of Middle Germany not once but twice. Things could be worse, she tried to convince herself. If only she had not been so hungry....

Then the train arrived in a landscape of ruins that seemed to be endless. The hollow houses looked ghostlike against the background of a gloomy sky. To Lynette the clouds appeared to be giant mushrooms thriving sumptuously on this decay. The city the train was slowly and solemnly coming into was Berlin. This was the proud capital of the former Reich; Aunt Gudrun had talked so much about it. Nothing was left of its glamour. Aunt Gudrun, however, was surely with the English by now and was well looked after.

It began to rain soon after they had come to a halt at the station. The rain pattered down into the wagons. Lynette began to feel the wetness; even her many layers could not protect her, the rain just seeped through. Father had to make a report to the two guards who went from wagon to wagon; he had no choice. The guards climbed into the wagon and then the mother was left crouched in a corner, pressing her empty arms against her body when they left.

Mutti had bartered the grandparents' golden wedding ring which Lynette had saved for a loaf of bread. Mutti cut a slice off for each one of them. She kept the rest, for who knew how long this odyssey was going to last. The worst hunger was stilled and Lynette would have been ready to sleep if there had been no rain. But it was a good idea to keep awake in this wetness, stamping your feet or moving your arms to keep warm.

Next morning a Russian soldier stormed the wagons, firing shots. He did not seem to have had enough of the war and carried on playing some sort of private war game, taking civilians for his enemy targets, Lynette thought, ducking down behind the iron wall. There was a shot that had a different sound to it; then it was all quiet. Lynette saw an officer putting his gun back in his belt when she emerged from her cover. The soldier, however, still lay there next morning. There was no hurry to carry him away; people had got used to the sight of the dead. Somebody had died in the wagon too; he was an elderly man who had become feverish during the night.

After that night they moved on. The wagons trundled slowly; a good sprinter would have probably kept abreast of them, Lynette thought. The rain eased off and she peeled herself out of most of her layers which she then dried in the sun. Another night on the open track... and that night was followed by another day and then things began to flow into each other, day and night, and in the end Lynette could not be certain any more for how long they had been on the move. They had run out of bread and her hunger returned; she had got used to the hunger as far as possible.

She almost got sick in Löwenberg. A Russian soldier, meaning well, held up a cigarette to her. She had never smoked and was about to shake her head when Father nudged her with his elbow. There was no doubt that he was right: it was wise not to reject this cigarette. She therefore took it, blew the smoke away and tried to smile. The soldier seemed happy and said goodbye. Then her stomach contracted but she could not vomit since her stomach was empty. Lynette was surprised how well Mutti was getting on. She had always been thin: a worrier. But now she showed astonishing strength, though she was very quiet as if she had still not quite understood what was happening.

The train stopped once more in Wittenberge. Here a pastor rode past on his bicycle, followed by his two daughters who were also riding bicycles. In the wagon the woman with the sinewy neck stretched so far forward that she almost cricked her neck to get a good glimpse of the three bicycle riders, perhaps because she'd never seen Lutherans before. But she had not been right with her announcement that they would be taken to Siberia; after Cottbus the train had been going westwards. The man from the chess club was laughing up his sleeve. Had he betted he would have easily won a pair of old shoes, he joked when the wagons came to a halt. One wagon after the other was opened by the guards and their occupants were escorted to a big hall.

The land was flat; stretched out wide and open to the horizon, extending deep into Russia. There were no hills that would have given you a certain comforting feeling and Lynette also missed the presence of a river, its running water connecting towns and villages. Potatoes grew in the fields. This land here was the Mark Brandenburg; the soil was sandy and good for potatoes. Aunt Gudrun would have been surprised if she had known that Lynette and her family had ended up in her homeland now. Lynette would never have thought that she would end up in the Mark Brandenburg. But that was where she was now and, as things looked, where she would be forever... how strangely things had turned out. Mutti, who had a good memory, remembered Uncle Franz's address; she wanted to write to him and Aunt Gudrun as soon as she had money for a stamp.

They were allotted to a farmer who had a big farm. The Präger Farm had looked more or less like this one, Mutti said. The farmyard was surrounded by living quarters, stables and sheds. That was why the farmer had to take in other people since he was rich and had many rooms. Another family lived next to the room where Lynette and her family were housed; both families shared the wash-bowl in the hallway.

Lynette put Baba's picture up on the windowsill and next to it she placed her chronicle, which she had packed in her bundle. That was all she possessed, apart from a few pieces of clothing. The Lauritsch grandfather had always said that Lynette would not need to worry about her dowry one day since she had everything already; it was good that he had not lived to see what happened.

They slept on straw which was prickly, stinging your skin. There were fleas, too, which weren't exactly of benefit to your skin either. In the night mice, perhaps even rats, scurried across the floor. When the winter came they had to break the ice in the well before they could fill their wash-bowl with water.

Their school was in Perleberg which was far away. The sun was just rising in summer when Lynette and her brother set out for their march to school. She wore the shoes she still had from Aussig. Mutti mended them again and again; they held together but bent her feet which was painful. She had become thin, much thinner than the sporty Gerda back *Home*. Aussig and her former life... that was *Home*: that was what she and her family had begun to call it now. Perhaps she had secretly always yearned to be slim and sylph-like but it came at a price since her skin broke out in festering boils which were caused by hunger and she was also losing her hair.

In the afternoons and evenings she and Heinz helped at the Russian Estate where Father worked. The Estate had not always been run by the Russians but nobody knew what had happened to the people who had once owned it. Father still wore his suit and tie; his collar, however, left a great deal to be desired since it lacked its former stiffness. Now, despite his one short leg, he was hoeing fields, though he had been sitting in an office most of his life, dictating letters. In the evenings he brought in a full cart that was pulled by farm horses. There was quite a bit of irony in it, Lynette thought: farm horses instead of the riding horses he had wanted to spoil herself and Heinz with. Father looked emaciated; his cheeks caved inwards and his eyes seemed to have become larger. But he had lost none of his energy; again and again he came across with his hoe to help her because she felt exhausted and tired though he had to till his own patch at the same time. Nearby an old man sat on a hay cart, conducting himself with his hands, continuously singing the well-known German folk song declaring that youth was a beautiful time. Yes, it was beautiful for him, Lynette thought, since for him it had become memory and did not hurt any more.

Lynette thought often of Herbert, though she did her best not to since it did not get her anywhere. Yes, she generally felt as if she had nothing to hold on to; she felt as if she was drifting and so she was glad that her days were strict, providing some framework to support her. Without it she would have gone under in all those strange sensations that she had not known so far and she would have got completely immersed in herself. It was as if she was under the spell of continuous April weather, an eternal change between rain and sunshine.

She tried to hide her moods and Mutti let her off when she did not succeed. Mutti had other worries. She worked as a seamstress and during the nights she mended Father's, Lynette's, Heinz's and her own old clothes, crouched forward beside a paraffin lamp which made the ceiling sooty. Cooking did not require as much attention as it had done at *Home*;

they had hardly anything to eat but bran. It was different when Lynette and Heinz sneaked up to the Russian Estate and got some potatoes or swedes. Mutti, however, did not like that at all, for thieving was a sin and what her children were doing was nothing other than theft. But that did not mean that she did not enjoy eating the potatoes and swedes.

For a while they were slightly better off since a Russian soldier who had been billeted with them made contributions from his food ration. He gave Lynette his mattress and slept on the straw instead. Sometimes he played something for her on his balalaika and he always had some sunflower seeds on him. He put them in his mouth and blew away the husks; this happened very swiftly. He taught Lynette how to do it and after a few weeks when the young soldier was transferred again she proved herself quite dextrous in this new skill. This was what she should have done with the sunflower seeds at *Home* instead of throwing them on the compost heap.

A big meeting was planned for May Day. There had always been a meeting on May Day but this time everything would be different since, instead of the red flag with the swastika, another flag would be displayed, which had a hammer and sickle as its emblem. A speech was on the agenda but nobody in the whole village wanted to volunteer. It was her brother who put his name forward. So on May Day, he stood in front of an assembly under a picture of little Father Stalin, a man with a grey moustache, immaculately combed back hair and piercing eyes, looking down watchfully at the assembled folk. Backed by this man, Heinz made his speech without consulting any notes and using expansive gestures to accompany his words. She had never thought that he would be capable of doing this, especially since he was always so downcast and had started crying more than once without any obvious reason. Now he stood on the rostrum in front of the village honoraries who applauded him enthusiastically. Perhaps one reason why they were so generous with their applause was that they felt relieved that none of them had had to go up to the rostrum to make a speech. Heinz, however, was clearly following in the footsteps of Uncle Franz who was a magnificent orator too. Yes, he had definitely inherited his talent from Uncle Franz, Mutti mused.

If he seriously meant what he had said in his speech it could not have been alright with Heinz that Mutti had begun to send parcels of clothes, cutlery, saucepans, everything they had been able to acquire bit by bit to Uncle Franz and Aunt Gudrun. The two of them and little Erika had their own flat by now.

One morning in summer Father did not go to the Russian Estate. Instead they all headed westwards from where the droning of the aeroplanes came, continuously flying from or to Berlin. Father had always thought about going to the West where the Americans were but they had never had the means to do so. They saved every penny and Baba sent them money too. Mutti had become acquainted with a clergyman who was in contact with a trustworthy man near the border who helped everybody fleeing to the West, albeit for a modest charge, considering that he risked his freedom, his life even.

On that summer day they went on a regular train to the border. From the train station Lynette and her family walked on and on across open fields till they found the small house near the border that the clergyman had described to Mutti. A bald, potbellied man stepped out of the house. 'My dacha,' he said, laughing, gesturing towards his house. Inside, Mutti counted several banknotes into his hand; he accepted them, nodding, and with a certain friendly reserve as if he was really out to do a favour for Mutti and did not think of himself. He put a stew on the table and he also produced a loaf of bread; he cut a slice for each of them. Now he explained to them in a roundabout way where it was best to cross the border. He advised them to go separately: the young ones together and the older ones. If one pair should be caught, there was still a chance for the others to get through. Besides, two people attracted less attention than four. They should wait till the patrol had gone; that would be their chance then.

Now, that called for a drink. The friendly man got a bottle of potato schnapps out of his cupboard; he had got it from a farmer who had left the Russian zone only a few weeks ago. So, all of them were treated to a small glass of schnapps and Lynette soon felt the schnapps making her head dizzy since she was not used to it.

They set out at dusk: Lynette and Heinz first. It would be difficult for the border guards to make them out in the twilight while they could just about see where they were going. They stopped after a while to get their bearings. The droning of the aeroplanes was more confusing than a real help since they flew both east and westwards. But there was the sparkling Evening Star to guide them; they only had to follow it. Branches snapped as they walked through the undergrowth. It seemed to Lynette as if this cracking noise resounded through the whole wood. Suddenly she was blinded by a beam of light and Lynette pulled her brother down with her so that they both lay flat on their stomachs. The man on the pillion turned his head in their direction but the motorbike drove on. They waited for a while; then they jumped to their feet and ran across the road. They could not see the Evening Star through the dense canopy of the trees any more. When they came to a barrier they did not really know where west or east was. They just walked on till they lay down to sleep, exhausted as they were. They were lost in the forest just like the brother and sister in the fairy tale. They carried on walking next morning till they met some forest workers. When Lynette asked, one of them said: 'You're lucky; you're in the West.'

Aunt Gudrun had kept all their parcels in a suitcase. One of the first things they did was unwrap them all. It was like Christmas, except that there was no surprise. Uncle Franz smoked a cigarette while Aunt Gudrun cooked some food. They had tinned sardines and potatoes and there were real coffee beans in the coffee. My God, the things they had here in the West.

Uncle Franz got a bottle of beer for Father and talked about his time as a prisoner of war. He had had a good time with the English who treated officers as officers. The English still had a feeling for differences whereas the French... Mutti should ask Karl to tell her if she did not believe him. Karl had been forced to run the gauntlet and the food was so bad that it was not fit for a dog. Yes, Mutti should go ahead and ask Karl. By the way, Karl had made a career for himself though it had hardly been his intention. The Americans were all obsessed with hygiene. That was why the people in the Western zones had to be made germ-free, which was called 'denazification'. Karl, who had never been a member of the Party, helped with this procedure. He had become influential and some people offered him whole houses to get his favour. But it went without saying that Karl was a person of integrity, who never took anything; he would probably have been in the Party in the first place if he had been susceptible to bribery of any kind. So, he carried on sitting over his files and in the evenings he sometimes went to a nightclub which had to replace the Café Falk, for Karl had still not married.

Now Aunt Gudrun wanted to have a word too after her husband had done all the talking. She had had quite an eventful time after she had set out from Aussig. Waiting for trains had been the least of her worries; it could take half a day sometimes and the train did not always go in the direction she would have wished for. Once the Russian masters had her hauling pianos. She left Erika on a bench and lent a hand. The pianos were stored in a wagon that was likely to go to Moscow or Leningrad. Erika screamed; it was no use. They raped her with Erika keeping on screaming in the background. Still, she had been lucky that she had not got with child then. Erika was quite enough, especially for Aunt Gudrun, who hoped to begin teaching again soon. Calm and peace were essential for any intellectual pursuit. A child, however...

'Perhaps we'll go to Hamburg,' Father said. 'Hamburg has a big port with a lot of trade.'

The two men remained sitting at the table. Lynette saw them from her mattress in the light of a lamp. Uncle's voice thundered out sometimes but she was unable to hear what Father was saying. Aunt Gudrun snored in the room next door, though she was soon enough woken up by little Erika. Lynette thought it strange that she suddenly found herself here together with Aunt Gudrun. She should really have got used to the fact by now that it was not her who decided what was going to happen. She was pushed about by something people called fate. All humans were ruled by it but did not admit to it and pretended that they were able to choose which path to follow. She had begun to watch herself: it was like seeing herself in a dream or a newsreel. An emaciated girl threw herself on the forest floor while a motorcycle carrying border guards droned past. She looked at this image now as she had looked at similar pictures from outside, strangely distanced. She had to remind herself that she herself had been this girl. Later, she did not know whether she was awake or dreaming, ships rose up in front of her, majestic, illuminated ships, ocean steamers – 'ocean steamers', the words had always sounded like magic to her. She saw a girl that was herself standing at the harbour and people waved down at her from the deck rails of an ocean steamer.

# 15

On one of the following days when they were having their breakfast, which was not quite as sumptuous as it had been at first, a letter arrived addressed to Herr Taussig. Father washed his hands before he opened it. He read it slowly, raising his eyebrows. Lynette and Mutti looked at him expectantly. Heinz had gone on a morning walk with Uncle Franz; he was in the habit of discussing politics, which they both enjoyed since they had completely different views. They could all hear Uncle Franz as soon as he entered the stairwell. 'It's good that Heinz is here too now,' Father said and read out the letter, which was from his former secretary, Fräulein Mandel. She had settled in Munich. Of course, it wasn't easy to get a place to stay but she would help them. As victims of the hideous regime, she and her half-brother now had quite a few privileges. She would be more than ready if he needed someone to speak up for him in court since he had officially been in the Party.

'Well, well, Fräulein Mandel... so they've thrown her out too,' Mutti said in amazement, adding acidly: 'The Czechs must have thought themselves quite lucky that they got the chance to rid themselves not only of the Germans but of the Jews as well.'

Within a week they were off to Munich, that splendid city of which Anne had always spoken so enthusiastically. Lynette's parents succeeded in getting a room. But it was too small for the whole family. Heinz found a place with a widow who had an empty attic and Lynette was taken in by a convent. She shared a room with two other girls, one Silesian and one Bavarian; the Bavarian girl came from the country and was doing an apprenticeship as a seamstress. In the evenings, she cried till her eyes were red since she was so homesick. Lynette and the Silesian girl looked at each other, shrugging their shoulders. Dear me, if that was so bad what should they have done? After all, the Bavarian girl still had a home to return to whereas Lynette and the girl from Silesia.... During the day the Bavarian girl was at the tailor's and the Silesian girl was away too. Lynette didn't mind that since it meant that she was alone and undisturbed when she returned from school in the afternoons.

When the sun was shining she went for long walks through the ruins around her and tried to imagine what the city had once looked like. She visited the cathedral; in its centre she saw a solitary pillar rise up into the sky, which was blue: a light, bright blue underlined by the clouds' white cotton balls. She strolled down wide boulevards that must have looked proud and magnificent before the fire storm caved in the houses, leaving mere façades. There were also fountains with spacious basins. It would take a while before water gushed out of them again. A jeep roared past; but otherwise the street was deserted. Further down, behind the triumphal arch, there were already a few new houses, bare, plain buildings betraying the hurry in which they had been erected. When Lynette walked down the road to the right, she came to a vast park, an undulating landscape with oak trees and birches. It stretched from the city's outskirts right into its centre. Aussig's Town Park would have been lost in it and so would the park in Prague. She climbed up to the small round Greek temple from where she had a good view of the torn-up cupolas and towers. A far-eastern pagoda made of wood stood not far away. She could imagine herself thousands of miles away in China or thousands of years back in time in ancient Greece, while still living at this spot in the present. This appealed to Lynette and she felt that she could almost be at home in this city.

Yes, she was not really unhappy and, all things considered, perhaps it was quite lucky that she had come here... though who could say really? She wasn't sure if she'd really been lucky. But she made an effort to convince herself of it and that made everything a bit easier and now she was already looking forward to going to the convent kitchen, which was Sister Benedikta's realm. Sister Benedikta was a very small person who had to stand on a stool so that she could stir the tall saucepans on the hearth. Lynette, to whom Sister Benedikta granted special favours, was allowed to lick out the saucepans. That felt like being in the *schlaraffenland* where you had to eat yourself through layers of food so that you were rewarded with even more food.

But this chapter in her life did not last for ever either, which was unlucky, since going to school only in the mornings had left her a lot of time for herself. Having time for herself: that had always been important to her. Now Father showed her a job advertisement from a pharmaceutical firm looking for a secretary. She had always been interested in medicine, and pharmacy was connected with it. But how could she apply for a job as a secretary when she couldn't even type? It wouldn't be a problem, she would just have to learn it, Father said, she should have confidence in herself and apply. Father was right; she started her job that autumn after she had done a typing course that was paid for by the firm.

Lynette sat upstairs on the fifth floor. The blinds were half closed so that the light snuck through the gaps, casting a stripy pattern onto the floor. Lynette sat in front of her typewriter; she tapped her fingers on the keypads until her shoulders ached. It was a long index that she had to type up, full of foreign words and medical terms. Many of the Latin and Greek words sounded familiar to her since she had discovered them in her medical book at *Home*. She felt bitter when she sometimes heard a pigeon cooing. No, this wasn't the surgery in Prague that she had dreamt about. But where was she to start? She didn't even have the money to study. After all, it was she who was earning the money for her brother to go to university, for Father had lost his job since his employer had fled abroad because of some distant quarrel in Korea; before he went, he dissolved his business and destroyed everything that Father had begun to build up patiently through his connections. So the whole family depended on Lynette who sat upstairs doggedly tapping at her typewriter.

She shared the room with 'Praline' whose longing for sweets was almost insatiable. This preference bonded them together and Lynette was getting quite round again after the long hunger years. Together they mocked the spindly, jumped-up 'Doctor Quick', who worked away and who was always in a hurry. Once he swept along the corridor with all the papers flying out of his file; Praline and Lynette helped him to pick them up and it took them some effort to suppress their amusement.

Losing all his papers because he was in such a hurry... that was typical of Doctor Quick, Lynette thought, as she queued at the cinema. Praline was with her and Heinz, who was out for some fun after studying. Everything American had become fashionable now and the women in the movies always looked perfect with their make-up on as if they were not made of flesh and blood. When Lynette compared herself to them she felt even plumper. But chocolate did not make Praline put on weight. Perhaps that was one of the reasons why her brother once put his arm around Praline's hips; since then Lynette almost felt a bit out of place and in the way. She was pleased when Father asked her to come along to some event in the conservatoire.

The floor and the stairs of the conservatoire building were made of brown-red marble and white marble shone from the walls. Fluted pillars lined the spacious entrance hall with its broad staircase. When she had got to the first floor, Lynette looked across to the Royal Square. It had been built by one of the Bavarian kings: he had wanted to resurrect antiquity by building edifices of beauty, distilled beauty, without any dirt or weaknesses, and in a way the square was an expression of his longing for the sublime. Likewise the conservatory building was a homage to the sublime; the rulers of the brown regime seemed to have modelled it after the same antique architecture. Lynette was just contemplating how ironic it was that the conservatoire had remained standing while most of the city had been reduced to rubble when she saw Father slowly climbing the stairs.

252

He had become quite corpulent. His cheeks were full and his chin soft and fleshy. His gait had become heavier and Lynette could hear him breathing when he arrived at the top of the stairs. The Great Hall was opened; it was panelled in plain wood, fitting in with the sober style of the time. The builders had finished work here not long ago. Now the pupils of the master classes appeared on the stage; the women were slim and blonde and wore black. The music they performed sounded dazzling but sometimes Lynette would have wished for the occasional mistake and a more intimate tone. Father, who was employed again by now, and had purchased an instrument made by a South German master violin maker for himself, was full of admiration: it was quite something what these young people were capable of, he thought, and nodded approvingly.

After the break, a piece of chamber music by a contemporary composer was to be performed. The composer was still quite young and had finished his studies a few years before at this very conservatoire. Lynette half-expected to see Herbert stepping forth when the composer was due to appear on stage after his piece had been performed. Instead, a broad-shouldered young man with a full mane of blond hair came onto the stage, reminding Lynette more of a circus than the darkened world of concert halls. He bowed, received a bouquet given to him by a girl and strode off again with steps of such self-assurance that it was clear to everybody that not even the greatest success could shake him. The piece was atonal, as it had to be in those days if a young composer wanted to get some attention. For a while Lynette had felt as if she were back in the villa of the Domansky family, when Herbert had played similar jagged music with his eyes closed. Seen from now, this brief performance seemed to have foreboded her childhood world being broken up, its sharp pieces scattered like smashed glass. If things had turned out differently, she might have been with Herbert now; it was more likely, however, that everything would have developed in a completely different way still. How? Well, it didn't really matter since knowing it would not change anything.

Here in this city there was somebody else who did not feel indifferent to her. It was young Lenz, who lived in the neighbourhood and whom she saw sauntering through the streets, clad in a red scarf, a dark coat and a beret, which altogether gave him a somewhat mysterious aura. Her brother had talked to him in the street and she asked him who he was. She found out that his name was Max Lenz, a fellow student of her brother's. She often thought of Lenz in his red scarf when she sat in front of her typewriter, copying lists. Her brother and Lenz had become friends and so she began seeing more of him. One day he asked her whether she wanted to go to the theatre with him: *Faust*, of course – he wouldn't have any lesser play. Afterwards, he accompanied her back to the entrance of the house she lived in (she had moved into a shared flat with Heinz and her parents by now). Lenz told her that he wanted to become a writer. My God... she always seemed to end up with some creative type, be it a writer or composer. She was surprised at herself when she married him: everything had happened so quickly. They did not marry in just any old town church; that would not have been like Max, who was very much the Romantic. No, the wedding took place high up in the Alps, in a remote mountain chapel. It was he who furnished their new flat since he had a certain 'flair' for it, as Mutti would have said, and when it was finished it looked all stylish in an artistic-negligent sort of way. In the evenings, when Lynette came home from work, he dictated his doctoral thesis to her and she typed it all up for him, while he leaned back smoking and drinking red wine. Yes, he had the way of a true Bohemian though he and the generations before him had all lived as pillars of respectability in this city. His mother was a proud householder and could not understand why he had picked up a girl from nowhere, a pauper, and she never stopped referring to Lynette as 'the refugee'. Perhaps this made Max like Lynette even more and he was quick to take up her Balkan habit of eating slices of bread spread with garlic, enjoying it when the people on a bus, especially North German holiday-makers who had begun coming to the South, complained about the unbearable stench. When Max got his doctorate, he found a job with a publisher and got to know many writers and painters but the everyday work itself was too dry, dull and outright boring for a Bohemian like him.

One night when Lynette returned to their flat, worn out from work, she was greeted by a bouquet of red roses. Next to it lay a card. She opened it and read that he had not been able to stick it with the publisher any longer and had left for the south of France to write a novel. But two weeks later he returned, without a novel. Things like these exasperated her, of course, for she liked nothing more than having a calm and quiet life. Yet Max thought it unforgivably bourgeois to go to work day after day. She may have been bourgeois, according to him, but it was she who brought the money in so that he was free to follow his Bohemian inclinations. As far as his affairs with women were concerned, she was not bourgeois and possessive at all but generous and turning a blind eye. Some of his lady friends were nice, that she was ready to admit. Of course, they were all some kind of artist or gifted in other ways, not simple drudges like herself, though she had risen lately thanks to her reliability and diligence and she had her own room now, sitting in front of her boss's office.

But then Max decided to take on a new job in the Far East. There, working for the cultural institute that was named after the Olympian among the poets of the German tongue, he hoped to find the freedom that he seemed to need so much. It was a branch where he would have a free hand to do as he pleased, far away from the central office in the Palais Bernheim. This would be quite a challenge. And while his wife gave birth, he enjoyed the laid-back life on the deck of a banana steamer. The sea voyage had been recommended to him so that he could get used to the different climate slowly.

Lynette would come later by air, as soon as the baby was strong enough. It was the same patch of the world that Herbert's ancestor, his great uncle who was an explorer, had once been to. Whatever had become of Herbert? Not only her memory of Herbert but all her memories of *Home* were fading more and more. But that was probably a good thing really since everything moved on. She tried not to think about Baba whose picture she had saved and now kept on her bedside table. Baba had left Czechoslovakia in the end and settled near her daughter, Aunt Bertha. But it was not long before she died. Minute changes, deep inside her body, felled this strong, courageous woman. Of course, Mutti, who said that she should not have eaten so many geese, was right; ultimately it was all down to goose fat.

Uncle Karl and Uncle Wenka had passed away too. Wenka had never recovered after he fell into the icy river when partisans had blown up a bridge. He was almost the only one who got out of the river alive. After the war he succumbed to a minor illness and left Aunt Bertha a comfortable pension as a war widow. Karl finally developed a heart condition since he was working too much, aggravated by cognac and wine. He never went to physicians but to non-medical practitioners instead. He was told that there was something wrong with his spleen and that he had to get out of bed, though he was really in urgent need of rest. When he was laid to his final rest, the cemetery was crowded with people as if it were the burial of some well-known artist or statesman.

Seen from here, where traders called out the names of their merchandise in a foreign language, over there on the other side of the banana trees, her family's fates seemed strangely unreal. All that belonged to a different life that was detached from the life she was presently leading. But her present life was made up of distant pictures too; they moved continually across her inner eye, so that she was able to tell Mutti and Father about her life here. She sat at a table by the open window which was covered in a closely knit mosquito net, writing a letter that got longer and longer. She wrote about her chores and duties, about little Markus who was thriving in this tropical hothouse, about her husband's achievements at work. But she kept quiet about him still having affairs with other women and that one of her rivals was expecting a child by him, as well as about the eruption of Gunung Agung; all that would have worried her parents unnecessarily. Day turned into night when Gunung Agung erupted; the ash raining down from the sky eclipsed the sun.

Max would not even consider returning. He really enjoyed it here, had put on a lot of weight and soon looked like a *Tuan*, a real Lord. And that was what he was now, for how many people back there got a reception with Balinese princes and ruled over half a dozen servants, 'boy' and cook included? But Lynette felt her longing rise for clear air that caressed your skin like velvet and a crisp winter's day. When he had two of her new women rivals, who were twins, move in, she decided that enough was enough and packed her suitcases.

Perhaps she should have done that much earlier instead of accepting everything. Max was somebody who only thought of himself; there was something wild and unruly in him, which must have attracted her to him since it was missing in her. She moved into a flat with her parents; she began working as a secretary in the firm again and it almost seemed to her as if she had only left her typewriter yesterday.

Praline had left, of course; she had married Heinz before Lynette had gone away. She missed Praline in the evenings when she had nobody to go out with. Praline seemed happy though; she had one child and another one was on its way. Who would have thought that Heinz would make such a dedicated father? On her visits, Praline showed her photos of Heinz pushing his little daughter in a pram on Sundays. In another picture he had his daughter sitting at his desk with him, a whole wall of books behind him. The photo showed Heinz wearing a tie, a jacket and a white shirt. He was looking out of the photograph at the perceived beholder with self-assurance and aplomb. Yes, a lot had happened since he crossed the border with her, penniless and shaking with fear of the Russian border guards. He had risen in the municipal administration; without any doubt, he had had the right political instinct and had joined the right party. From his aloof position he looked down on the world, liberally dropping names that Lynette only knew from the papers. Yes, Heinz had made a career. Perhaps it was not all that surprising since he had not even been afraid when still a child of getting close to meetings, gatherings and speeches of the youth organisation of the Party which was in power then.

Lynette, however, felt that she was a drudge. But that was alright. She could just close the door in the evenings and leave behind all her worries. At weekends she went to the Englischer Garten, if only to see what was now in fashion; you had to walk along paths between tidy areas of lawn and you weren't allowed to step on it. The nearby Luitpold Park was better for Markus since there was a large playground where Father often took him. Lynette would have liked it if Mutti had gone out into the open air with the boy too. But she didn't leave the flat any more; she got so worked up by having to make a decision about what to wear that Lynette had stopped mentioning it to her. She preferred to sit in the flat all day, cooking Bohemian dishes, baking Bohemian cakes, which didn't do her heart any good. Of course, it was really sorrow that gnawed at her heart; she had never got over what had been done to her and the city all around her remained alien to her. She was getting weaker and weaker, dipping into a delirium at the end where there shone a world where it didn't matter what language you spoke. On the gravestone she was called 'Anny', a name she had liked much better than Antschi.

Not long after Mutti died, Lynette married again. It was a quiet wedding, without any pomp; perhaps that would make it last longer, she thought. During a meeting Doctor Quick had brushed away a small speck from her pullover and said that he would marry her. This surprised her just as much as it did the others who were present in the meeting. But the more she

**259**

contemplated it, the more she was reconciled with the idea. She had had enough of the arty type. Helmut would give her safety and a firm ground to stand on; that was important to her. She was alone and this loneliness had become even more painful when she had realised that there had been no common ground with Max, though she had always convinced herself that he cared for her. At least with Helmut she knew what she was letting herself in for; with him everything was clear and open as in a mathematical formula. Yes, that was how it seemed to her. At the weekends he worked away in the garden or busied himself with an electric drill and a hammer while most evenings during the week he spent in sport halls where, with like-minded folk, he whipped his hand hard across volleyballs so that they bounced up from the springy floor. Urged on by him, she also began to do exercises and chocolate was completely banned from the house. She did not get as slim as Helmut but her figure improved nevertheless so that she looked quite attractive... which meant she looked more or less as was required by the fashion of the day. For the first time she had the feeling that she was pretty, though she wasn't young any more. But perhaps age made her more lenient towards everything, including herself. By now she wore glasses and when she looked into the mirror she was happy that she had lost her young, girlish face; her features were not empty any more but all the years she had lived had left their trace, transforming her face into something quite unique. All things considered, she was more or less happy with her life as it was now. The only thing that worried her was Helmut and Markus not getting on. Markus was so dreamy and always seemed far away, which reminded her of herself; such a pensive temperament required a lot of patience and forbearance. But

Helmut was brusque in his ways, which hurt Markus, who withdrew more and more into his shell. Markus's withdrawal and his melancholy moods irritated Helmut even more. He couldn't stand it when Markus was reading or listening to music; he didn't need either and thought that Markus should become like him. For Helmut permanent activity was all-important; you had to be able to assert yourself. Yet Markus preferred to dodge things, to give in. Father seemed to understand her boy much better. Father had been a cultured businessman; such a combination was rare these days.

Father's death coincided with her son leaving. This seemed not all that surprising since both had been so close to each other that Father had been worrying half a year before Markus actually left. For Markus, Father would never die; that was also why he was interested in the past and loved to be told about the land from where she and Father came. Was there not a river in ancient Greek mythology that induced forgetting? By asking about the past and making her remember it, Markus ensured that there was a bridge over that river.

'I'm going out now; you only need to reheat your food,' said Lynette, opening the door.

'Yes, that's fine,' shouted Helmut who was in his underground workshop, banging something into the right shape. She took the bus and later the tram. She was not in a particular hurry and was able to see more than if she had taken the underground that zoomed through narrow tunnels. It was a beautiful summer's day; on such a day there was a decidedly Mediterranean atmosphere in the city with its colourful houses, fountains and Venetian turrets. Trees spread welcome shade on the banks of the Isar. Above the trees rose the hill where folk made their pilgrimage before spring arrived to get some energy from strong, nourishing beer to last over Lent. But these days hardly anybody fasted during Lent and the strong beer was a kind of extra.

She entered the hall in the middle of a speech. There weren't that many people here this time. It was probably because of the weather; when the weather was like this many thought twice before coming and settled for a trip to the lakes instead. A fairly old man sat at an empty table that had a small flag with the inscription *Schönpriesen* on it. No, she said, she did not come from Schönpriesen but her mother had been born there. Then she left the hall again in the hope of getting some coffee in the beer garden. The journey and heat had tired her out and she needed something to refresh herself.

As she walked across the gravel she saw a woman whose face looked familiar and unfamiliar at the same time. The woman seemed to feel the same way for she stopped, gazing at Lynette, trying to make out who she was. It took quite a while before the woman said: 'Lynette? Is it you? My God, what a surprise after all these years!'

They sat down at one of the outside tables. Anne liked the sun. My God, what had she been doing? It was almost a lifetime since they had seen each other last. Anne hesitated, smiling. She looked good; she had pushed up her sunglasses which now sat on her hair and the features of her face had become firm and almost masculine. She didn't know how to start, so she began with Herbert: 'He lives in Mainz now. He has actually become a composer but not as he had imagined. He writes music for television; I'm sure you've seen his name?'

Lynette didn't watch a lot of television. It was a waste of

time since there was so much else to do and Helmut usually kept her busy anyway. She had more than enough work, though she had given up her job after her marriage and had become a full-time housewife.

'Herbert writes music for television to make a living,' Anne said, 'but he writes other music too; you know how things are with serious music... nobody wants to listen to it. In his circles, among composers, he is well-known. Yes, and he's married; it still surprises me to think that because there's always been something quirky about him....'

Lynette was glad that Herbert had become a composer after all. When she heard that he had a family she felt a slight discomfort in her stomach; she would have preferred it if he had not married. And what about her, how had things turned out for Anne?

'For me,' she said waving her hand as if to express that there was really nothing worth talking about, 'just the usual things, you know. I live in Frankfurt; I'm married and my husband is an architect, quite a successful architect; I've got two children who are grown up. That's it really.'

Anne wanted to have some beer; after all she had not come to Munich to drink coffee all the time. Lynette allowed herself to be persuaded to keep her company by having a shandy. When Anne had drunk about half the beer in her litre glass she became more talkative.

She spent most of her time out of the house as far as possible. When the unrest at the universities started she began a teacher training course. She never became a teacher in the end but she really enjoyed the liveliness and excitement of those years. Of course, she had always remained on the periphery, watching, for she didn't like getting too close to things... even when she had still been at school she had not liked it. Times had become quieter now. But she still liked going where something was happening. With her husband she was the conventional architect's wife but when walking around Frankfurt's city centre, hobos called her by her first name, asking her whether she'd got some spare money. Of course, these were masks she put on. The true Anne... where was she? Perhaps it was the Anne who had shared the school bench with Lynette. Anne felt that she had missed out on a lot: life had slipped through her fingers. Yes, that was how she felt at times.

'But what about you; I've talked all the time about myself... what have you been up to?'

When Lynette had told her story (it was not a long story either) Anne scolded her that she was too soft with the men; she should not put up with everything. Her son, Markus, what was he doing? She began to talk about the country where he now lived. She had visited him several times. It was a hilly country with towns and villages strewn in between the hills; it sometimes reminded her of *Home*. But there was no big river like the Elbe. Instead, there was the sea which surged up against grey cliffs that were covered with bright yellow gorse. He seemed to have settled there as far as he was able to settle anywhere. The foreign country did not seem to bother him, for he had always felt alienated and disconnected. At school he made few friends, so that Helmut was concerned and warned that he might turn out to be a loner all his life. And at university Markus suffered from the competition of his bright fellow students who tried to outdo each other, as well as from brash lecturers (he had told her that one lecturer, for instance, read out the most intimate passages in Stifter that would hardly have borne a whisper in a loud, mocking voice, making the whole lecture theatre bray with laughter). Perhaps living abroad gave him a good reason for his alienation, whereas it would have tormented him in the city where he had been born. He spoke Welsh quite well by now as far as she was able to judge. Welsh was an ancient language that, together with the standing stones, had lasted for hundreds of centuries in the open landscape of fields and hedges. The government in London had not always been very keen on this different language and there had been many disputes. All this sounded so familiar. Perhaps what happened didn't form a line that stretched from the past to the future but went in eternal circling movements and everything kept re-emerging in a different form. Thinking this, she realised how similar she was to her son. Helmut would never have racked his brains over something so vague; for him things were only important if they could be counted or measured.

'We could go to Aussig almost straight away; everything has got so much easier since the Iron Curtain disappeared,' said Anne, putting her hand on Lynette's. 'It would be interesting to see what it's like there now; we hear about it but it's better to see for yourself. Do you want to come?'

Lynette withdrew her hand and said that the beer had made her tired. It was already quite late and she liked to get home while it was still light since there were often shady characters roaming around at night. Anne was disappointed that she left so early; she was only there for the annual Aussig gathering. It was the first time she had come; so far she had not been able to bring herself to join for political reasons. But the political climate had changed and many things that people had frowned upon before seemed acceptable now. She had a room in a cosy pension and tomorrow she would be going back on the train, one of those very fast ones; not that she was in a hurry but she liked the feeling of flying through the landscape along the rails. Lynette should visit her in Frankfurt one day.

So they said goodbye to each other and it seemed to Lynette that a wide gulf had opened up between her and the old friend from years ago. She preferred to go to Aussig on her own if she was to go there at all; or with Markus, yes, that was an idea, why not? He would be able to spare a few days; after all he had a wife who could look after Llinos while they took the trip. Llinos was a Welsh name and meant 'linnet'. She quite liked the name, if only for the fact that, when translated, it was a distant echo of her own name. Once she had looked it up in a dictionary where it said: 'the linnet's pleasant song contains fast trills and twitters'. Perhaps Llinos would be a singer one day... who knew? In any case, Markus had always wanted to go to Aussig where his grandfather had lived more than half of his life.

# 16

Lynette and Markus arrived in a train that was called *Carl Maria von Weber*. They had spent the last day in Dresden and now they were in Aussig. The station with its grey concrete pillars was probably new, though she was not completely sure; it was all such a long time ago and memories faded.

When she looked out of the taxi she felt quite shocked: there was hardly anything familiar left in the streets. If there was an old building it looked blackened and dilapidated as if the fire storm had only descended over the town yesterday. One old row of houses was crumbling away, its windows boarded up. In the middle of the town was an empty area covered with weeds and sunburnt yellow grass. The hotel, in contrast, was very grand: a huge box made of grey concrete. Outside, as they walked from the taxi to the hotel, the weather was thundery and close. She felt the sun stinging her skin. Beads of sweat were running down her forehead. There actually sold anything at all. Herr Filip's corner shop had disappeared, which was not so surprising after all this time.

She was glad that she was still able to find the Town Park without Markus having to look at the map. She had walked this way so often; it seemed to have left an indelible trace in her memory. The roses that grew in beds laid out in the middle of the path seemed to greet her familiarly. Yes, the roses were still there. The pavilion had been left too, in the middle of a rotunda of stone. But it didn't look as if a band still played there on hot summer days; the roof looked weathered, decayed. The further she and Markus got into the park, the more overgrown it became; trees and bushes were all tangled up with each other and only here and there was the sunlight able to shine through, casting bright spots on the ground. A grandiose memorial rose up in a corner close to a thicket; it had been erected in honour of the Soviet heroes but it did not seem to have been maintained over the years and it now looked quite dilapidated. Whether it was because of this memorial or the rampant growth of the plants, for her the Town Park had something oppressive about it and had lost the charm which it probably never had except in her memories.

She was happy to step out into the light again. On the other side of the road she saw an old house that was painted a fresh purple. She felt better for it since she realised that not all the old buildings had been left to decay. The wooded hilltop of the Ferdinand Rise loomed up at the end of the street in the hazy distance. Markus seemed surprised; it was almost like a resort in the Alps, he said, where mountains towered around you, though – mountains?... well, maybe not quite. Whatever, the streets shimmered in the glistening sunlight and everything looked friendly and soothing.

was no need at all to have brought the thick jumper. She was now like her own Mutti, who had always been so careful, yet when she was a child she had mocked her mother for being so fussy. Clouds were gathering and Lynette felt that everything that had been bottled up would unload itself soon in a terrifying thunderstorm; then would come the calm.

They each put their suitcases in their rooms. The hotel porter was very young and spoke a few words of German, though his English was better. He wished Lynette and Markus a nice stay; smiling, he accepted the tip she gave him for helping with the luggage. She hung her clothes up in the wardrobe and went to the bathroom to splash her face with cold water. Then she walked down to the lounge where Markus was already waiting for her. She felt her heart pounding with expectation and was annoyed at herself at the same time: it was almost as if she was a schoolgirl again and did not have the decades of experience that should have made her more blasé.

She wanted to go to the house where she and her family had lived straight away; she hesitated, looked around. She was grateful that Markus had brought a town map; it was from nineteen hundred and thirty-six (they had not been able to get another map) but the layout of the streets had not changed, only the houses had been replaced by new ones. Her house, however, a corner house, was still there. Indeed, the whole street had been preserved, including the neighbouring house with its mighty arches, which Lynette once thought had been lived in by titans from the Giant Mountains. Cars, mostly Škodas, were parked at an angle all along the pavement, their rears jutting out into the road. There were several shop signs at ground floor level but everything looked barred and locked up and she wondered whether these shops

The façade of another old house was painted a yellow that was as intense as the sun itself. The year nineteen hundred and ninety-three was engraved above the depiction of a vase with stylised leaves and blossoms. But surely this house must have already been here when the Emperor Franz Joseph came down the Elbe for his visit, Lynette thought. Perhaps the people who lived in the house felt uncomfortable since they did not know what had happened to the former inhabitants; that was why they pretended that the house was reborn with its renovation... quite understandable really, maybe Lynette herself would have done the same under similar circumstances.

Next stop on their sightseeing tour was the school building which they peered at only from the outside. So she carried on, leading Markus around in the role of a tour guide, following the traces of that distant person that she had once been. Pity that Helmut had not come. But he had not even been back to Königsberg where he had been born. His brother and sister had flown there; they brought back a broken branch that he kept in his room. It was from a tree that had been planted by his mother, and Helmut's brother and sister had just arrived in time to see it being felled. Lynette had been fond of Helmut's mother and liked remembering her. Lynette's mother-in-law had been a practical woman, cast in the same mould as Baba. During the bad years soon after the Great War she was in charge of a lemonade factory and delivered the lemonade herself; before that she had sat in cinemas and accompanied silent movies on the piano. The place where she had been born, called Heidekrug, had disappeared long ago. Lynette's mother-in-law took it with the same calm composure that she always showed. Once, when a bowl of sugar slipped out of Lynette's hand, so that the contents were spilled everywhere, she had only laughed: come on now, it's not the end of the world. She enjoyed being driven around the Bavarian highlands and she could never get enough of looking at the balconies that were covered in flowers. But whoever sat behind her on such a trip had a somewhat restricted view for Lynette's mother-in-law was in the habit of wearing hats with an enormously wide brim which she steadfastly refused to take off during car rides. Jokingly, Helmut used to call her hats *kalabreser*, slouch hats. Because Lynette was thinking of her mother-in-law she said *fejucheln* when she pointed out an old lady who strolled past. Of course, that was an East Prussian dialect word and meant something like 'to be out and about'. But Markus would understand; he had grown up with exiles who all spoke a somewhat peculiar German. Perhaps it was not all that surprising that he had gone abroad and had said that he did not feel that he belonged anywhere, not even to the city where he was born.

Though this branch of a Königsberg tree lay in Helmut's room now, he always pretended that he had no interest in anything to do with his origins. Even more, he showed a considerable amount of self-hate for being German. He watched football matches, for instance, hoping that the German side would lose, yes, they should lose, they deserved no better. If the German football team lost, he walked into the kitchen and expressed his joy with such fervour that it almost seemed uncanny to her. On such occasions it dawned on her that there was an abyss behind the control and rationality he showed during the day. She had to think of the figures in Kleist where iron discipline could spill over into an emotional deluge at any moment. When they still lived in the Eastern Sector she had read Kleist, together with Storm and

Schiller in old, tattered editions. It had been Father who had got the books for her, somehow.

When she thought of Father now, she realised that he, too, had never wanted to hear anything about Aussig or Prague. Father never uttered a word in Czech, not even when Markus asked him to since he was interested to hear how the language sounded. But there was nothing of Helmut's self-hatred in Father, who was not ashamed of his nationality. Mutti, on the other hand, had never been able to put an end to it all. She ordered picture books about her homeland from her book club and she kept leafing through them. Every day she stood in the kitchen for hours cooking Bohemian dishes. Sometimes she talked about some old Aussig acquaintances as if they just lived around the corner. But then she was suddenly sorrowful when she realised that she was not at *Home* after all. Father had done the right thing really; he had resolutely shut the door behind him and kept walking straight on. For constantly looking back in a direction where there was nothing left destroyed any joy in life and gradually extinguished the heart. So it was not surprising that Mutti died of heart failure, just like her brothers, Karl and Franz.

Lynette had seen Uncle Franz frequently in Munich where he would meet his *pfeifendeckel*, as the batman had been jocularly called in the old Austrian army. He still loved debating and the older he became the more adamant were his views, which he expressed with his usual vociferousness. His end, however, was peaceful: his chin had sunk on his chest when Aunt Gudrun got up from a bench to continue their uphill walk. Aunt Gudrun was the only person of that generation who was still alive, with the exception of Auntie Bertha of course. Auntie Bertha was well looked after by the nuns. As in Aussig she had still come on a yearly inspection visit to check that things were right and proper but even these visits had ceased now. When Lynette went to see her, Auntie Bertha complained non-stop; she complained about the world becoming more evil by the day and her life that would not end, would not end. As she complained she peeped, out of the corner of her eye, at the next chocolate; complaining, it seemed to Lynette, was part of Auntie Bertha's *joie de vivre*.

Of course, Auntie Bertha was on the list of people to whom she was going to write a postcard. They sat down in a restaurant that was called *Europa*. Walking along the hard pavement hurt her feet and the heat made them even worse. Apart from Auntie Bertha, she also wrote postcards to Helmut, Heinz and Aunt Gudrun. They were the same postcards since there was not a lot of choice. Perhaps she should have sent greetings to Anne too... but no, that would have upset her, after all, she had wanted to come here with Lynette. Now here she was with Markus, who was sitting next to her studying the menu with the help of a dictionary. There was not much to be had apart from pizza but it could not do any harm to know what the topping was. She knew quite a few words when he asked her. She was surprised at herself but somewhere at the back of her mind some Czech seemed to have outlasted the decades. She had to shout almost so that he could understand her. Music from a radio was raving mercilessly; Father would not have called it music but noise. When it came, the pizza base was so hard that pieces kept flying off the plate when she tried cutting it. The occasional fingernail-sized mushroom could be found hiding between watery tomatoes. This was the 'international cuisine' that, by now, was more or less successfully practised here too.

273

When they came out, the wave of silence was a relief to her. Cars swished past from time to time but it was nevertheless silent in comparison to the restaurant where she had been tormented by the music's incessant beat. Markus wanted to go back to the hotel. He was tired, he said, but she knew that it was the books he had bought yesterday which enticed him back. It was alright with her since she did not have to play the tour guide any more and could pay closer attention to everything. When he had gone back to the hotel, she carried on on her own.

A man went past pushing a buggy with a strapped-in child sitting under the see-through plastic roof. He was wearing sunglasses and was chewing gum. Next to him a woman minced along on high stiletto-heels, wrapped in tight jeans and with a profusion of platinum-blonde hair. When Lynette saw this pair, she felt as if she had walked straight into an American film. But if it had been an American film a car would have stopped by now, its tyres screeching, or the man would have hurled away his chewing gum, making some sort of wild gesture with both his arms, for in American films something had to happen all the time and there was little room for contemplation.

On the roof of one of the houses behind the wasteland that she had already seen from the taxi a sign said, under the Czech words, CONFECTION COMPANY in English. Three adolescents, their shoulders bared, gallivanted past, belching and saying in German 'Little piggies, little piggies...' What was all that about, Lynette thought. A man clad in leather from top to toe stood in front of the station holding a whip in his hand. He did not even walk up and down, only stood there as a bizarre monument or an embodiment of the notorious Western decadence that was spreading here unhindered now after the citizens had been guarded from it by barbed wire and watch towers for decades.

None of the passers-by paid this figure any attention. Everybody was hurrying past with bags and briefcases, all of them pursuing their own business. They were all Czechs, most of them pale-skinned, but a few with a very dark complexion. Again and again she ran into Germans who had come across the nearby border for a little outing. A white-haired gentleman said to his two companions in Saxon dialect that he was dying for a good cup of coffee but was not sure where to get it here. Two old women stood near the Town Church. The beams propping up the church tower had gone but it was still leaning to one side, which Lynette clearly noticed when she compared it to the straight wall of the building next to it. One of the old women said that the Town Church had lasted well over a thousand years and it was nothing less than a miracle that it had been saved during the bombings. Old women, Lynette thought when she saw two girls pushing their bikes past, yes that was how she had referred to the two ladies in her thoughts but now she felt uneasy about it, comparing the young girls to herself. The two girls were probably still at school, going on a bicycle tour and stopping in this town before they rode on. They had a good look around but for them the houses and streets were nothing more than the houses and streets of a foreign town where Germans had once lived and perhaps this spelled hope for the future since they did not seem to bear any grudge or feelings of resentment.

She walked on to the Market Square. Looking at it she felt saddened. Once there had been houses that had had some character to them but now the square was bleak and empty.

On the other side of the square, however, plaster had been removed to show a very old arch; a sign in decorative golden writing explained in Czech and German that this arch was part of the arcades that had once encompassed the square. In the days when this arch had been built the houses had been solid with thick walls and broad arcades similar to the houses that still stood in Burghausen and Wasserburg on the river Inn. The arch made of old brickwork and stones was just one layer bearing witness to the past and the present too was not much more than such a layer. The sign said that the town administration had uncovered it after it had been walled up between nineteen thirty-nine and nineteen forty. One of the few things that were an improvement in this town, thought Lynette, since it meant you could look back through time.

However, her mood sank again when she arrived at the Materniplatz (she still called the square by its old name). Though there were plants growing in beds once again, the slowly decaying concrete slabs in between were hideous. An iron bar had been rammed into the ground in front of the Town Theatre; this iron bar was part of a new fountain and she recalled wistfully the old Elbe Fountain. The Town Theatre had been renovated and looked neat with its candelabras and Greek-style masks that decorated the front which had been freshly covered with white paint. The ornamental shield above the theatre's entrance had remained empty.

As she walked on she came to another open space where three long strides led up to a platform set against a background of juniper bushes. It seemed as if it were these bushes that were supposed to attract the attention of the passers-by. Lynette, however, saw for a moment the cast-iron bust of Master Wagner still dominating the square.

She came to streets that were narrower; some corners seemed familiar at first but when she looked closer they looked alien to her. Perhaps it was because of the neglect since the façades often had cracks in them and the road signs had unfamiliar road names in Czech written on them. In a small road, however, was a shop that had a sign saying BUCHHANDLUNG. The wooden floor creaked when she entered and a young man who was busy writing something behind the counter looked up at her through his glasses. She tiptoed around more carefully since she felt that she had disturbed him. Though it pretended to be a bookshop there were also plates showing wintry still-lives and the inscriptions read *Weihnachten 1938* or *Weihnachten 1944*. There were boxes full of German passports and a savings account from the Municipal Savings Bank with a stamp after the last entry in February 1945; the balance read 10.321 RM and *33 pfennig*. The account booklet had belonged to a *Herr Wolfgang Schmidt*. What had happened to the owner of this booklet, the owners of the passports, all those Germans? Lynette had read the most gruelling reports of Germans being set alight and hung up on street lamps, of children being driven out into the snow-covered mountains to perish, of women being hacked to pieces by just and righteous avengers. But who knew whether any of it was true since the most absurd things could be said about the past, which remained a foreign country and ultimately out of reach. And there was always this pleasure people took in telling powerful tales, just as Odysseus had done after his long wanderings. So it was best for her to stick to what she had experienced herself, she thought, turning away from the boxes and to the bookshelves. She got engrossed in a guide book detailing walks along the Elbe. Another book was of a political nature and argued how very wrong it had been that the Czechs had always sided with the French, English and Russians against the Reich; the book had been published in 1943 in Prague, Amsterdam, Berlin and Vienna. Then she found a book of folksongs called *Lieder unserer Heimat*, Songs from Our Homeland. It seemed to be a book which had been used in a school since the owner's name pencilled in on the first page was followed by the form details. Lynette leafed through the yellowing, musty pages that had some brown patches. Yes, there it was: the song of the wild Waterman. She wondered whether she should buy it since Markus had asked her about the song. But then she decided against it, for it did not feel right to her that the young man should be selling the belongings of Germans who had been robbed of these things back to the same Germans or their descendants. She would get an edition when she was back in Munich again and probably a better one too.

It was not far from the shop to the Elbe which kept flowing past the Schreckenstein as it had always done. The Bila was also still there; the same Bila in which Father had almost drowned. It carried red water that mixed with the Elbe water. The bridge over the river had not changed either; it was the same bridge she remembered, with its concrete pillars and mighty steel arches. This was the bridge where the massacre had taken place. Many months after the end of the war when Lynette was already in Perleberg many of the remaining Germans who had to cross the bridge on their way from work were attacked here on this bridge and killed with wooden beams or shot; then they were thrown into the river. Perhaps the red water was a reminder of what had happened, she thought, realising of course that it was the sewage from some nearby chemical works.

The sun was hot and stinging. She felt it on her skin and

thought it better to return to the sheltered town streets where she could walk in the shade of some houses. She felt tired too and thought that she had seen enough. Slowly, she wanted to make her way back to the hotel. She walked past the façade of the monastery church with its figurines and rich décor, which was a contrast to the plainness of the Town Church. Surprisingly, the monastery church had been left intact in all its splendour; its walls looked old and worn but this added to its charm. Next to it the clean and futuristically glittering building of the National Bank rose up in which the God of our times, Mammon, was worshipped. Two policemen strolled down the alleyway between these sacred buildings; one of them took off his cap, wiping the sweat off his forehead.

She passed the hotel; she could have gone up to her room and put her feet up. Instead, she found herself walking on to the road where she had lived. It had not changed much from the morning when she had been here with Markus, except that the iron shutters had been removed and the shop that was in the same building as her former flat was now open. She looked up to the windows from where she had once looked out. But the net-curtained windows retained their secrets; even those that were uncurtained shut her out by reflecting the sky and trees. A grey, silvery-haired man walked up to the entrance door. He had a moustache and looked her up and down from top to toe till the entrance door was opened. Then he disappeared with a quick, elastic stride, shutting the door behind him as he entered the dark interior. Lynette felt that he must have noticed that she was German, just as Herr Novák had back in Prague, though she was not wearing white stockings but a light summer costume. Father had been right when he had decided to leave; even after the pogroms had ceased everybody would have looked askance at Lynette and her family for being German. She read the street sign and found that her former street was now called *London Street*. It ended in Masaryk Street which, as she knew from Father, had once been named after the notorious Leader of the Reich. Diagonally branching off from this main street in a straight line on the other side was *Churchill Street*, with *Roosevelt Street* beginning next to it and meandering through vast tracts of barren land. Yes, these had been the men who had made it all possible. It seemed only fair that they were commemorated. But Lynette was unable to find the third man who had also made his contribution at the same glorious conference. No street seemed to be named after him any more, though it must have been different four or five decades ago. What names would these streets bear if, God forbid, in a hundred or two hundred years new wars and pogroms descended on this town? For the time being, however, there was peace and peace was hard enough to maintain since it was so much easier to tear things down than to live patiently from day to day.

By now her feet were so painful that it felt like heaven when she was able to slip her shoes off in her hotel room. Sitting in a comfortable chair and drinking a cool grapefruit juice, she leafed through the chronicle that she had begun to write in this same town almost a lifetime ago; yet it felt like yesterday. She had written the first entry in large, meticulously drawn letters. Later she seemed to have become more careless; whole sentences had been crossed out and in one place the ink was smudged, the page warped, bearing witness to some spilled lemonade or juice. Now she began to write down today's impressions, putting the chronicle on the small table at a fair distance from her eyes so that she could see alright without reading glasses. She began again where she had left off as if there had not been almost a whole life in between. But when she thought about this passage of time, it kept shrinking till the thousands of days seemed not much longer than one single one. Strangely, the years that she had spent here, that is at *Home*, appeared to be long to her, so that her life tilted backwards to its beginning. She thought of the toy spinning top she had as a child moving faster and faster till its many colours were all blurred, only to be brought to a sudden halt by a merciless hand. Yes, that was how it was more or less, Lynette thought, writing FINIS in big letters in the large black book with its red spine and red corners.

Outside, the sun still poured heat into the streets, though it was already sinking into the forested hilltops. The clouds seemed to have been sucked up by the sun; perhaps the necessary thunderstorm that purified the air would come tomorrow. Lynette felt exhausted; the closeness of the weather as well as walking endless hours on the hard pavements had made her tired. She pulled the curtains so that the room was filled with pleasant twilight. When she lay down on the bed, she felt a sensation of comforting warmth streaming into her legs. This sensation was so luxurious... there was no sensation more beautiful. And she had earned it after all. She shut her eyes and there was a flickering which became stronger and stronger till Baba ascended from it, holding some flowers. She wanted to give them to Lynette. But for some reason Lynette was unable to bring her hands to the front, however much she struggled; her hands seemed to be tied together behind her back. Baba opened her mouth and began talking. But Lynette did not hear a sound. She nodded eagerly so as not to annoy Baba. Baba held the flowers up, pointing with them towards the curtains. There Heinz knelt in *lederhosen* playing with his lead soldiers. Lynette was surprised that she had not noticed Heinz earlier. Where can I find an apple here, haven't you got an apple, shouted Wenka who sat next to the small table. Mutti walked up and down the room, her hands in the pockets of her apron, looking everywhere for an apple. She even crawled under the bed from where she retrieved a dusty white stocking which she held up reproachfully to Lynette. Uncle Karl stood at the door playing with an apple. He kept throwing it over his head, from one hand in the other. He moved very dexterously while doing it, almost like a professional juggler in a circus; and in the short intervals when he had tossed up the apple he quickly put his glasses straight because they kept slipping down. It was not long before Uncle Franz appeared on the other side of the room. Now the apple flew high through the room, going back and forth between the two while poor Wenka, the *muschig*, tried to catch it by jumping after it like a little dog. This was a cruel game. Auntie Bertha sat in the comfortable chair watching her husband. Instead of helping him and telling the others off, she only sighed: Oh dear, oh dear... the Lauritsch grandfather tried his best to intervene; Lynette could tell from his lips. But however much he tried, you could only hear some stammering; he seemed to have forgotten how to talk. Grandmother began to count the eggs in her basket and discovered that one egg had got lost. Well, well... how did that happen?... there wasn't a hole in the basket, was there? Careful everybody now that you don't step on the egg, Grandmother shouted. Father checked the floor before putting up his music stand in the middle of the room. He got a violin neck out of his jacket pocket and began to play on it as if playing the violin itself. He ignored Franz and Karl who kept throwing the apple back and forth. When poor Wenka knocked against the music stand in his attempts to get the apple Father just righted it again and carried on. Aunt Gudrun started a row with Lili. Lili seemed to have said to her that she was ugly since she did not have any freckles or something like that. My dear ones, please try to get on with each other, Mutti intervened. There was such a mess and noise everywhere: the room had been turned into a fair. Through this mess Fräulein Pechwitz fought her way holding a tray; she was quite lucky that she was able to hover above the ground so that it was not too difficult. On her back were two silvery wings that reminded Lynette of one of the angels that had always hung from the Christmas tree. Fräulein Pechwitz was able to stay completely still in midair like a dragonfly and, with her wings whirring, she picked up a glass of Tokay for Lynette from her tray. Lynette was about to take it when there was a knock at the door. The room went silent straight away. Father put back the violin neck in his jacket pocket and raised his head; Karl hid the apple behind his back; Heinz did not resurrect his soldiers any more after the last shoot-out. Even Baba stood paralysed and silent though she was usually resolute. There was another knock. Lynette felt a powerful pressure behind her eyelids. She had fallen deep and now she had to pull herself out of this abyss.

'It's me,' she heard Markus shout, knocking again on the door. Her eyelids seemed to be glued together but in the end she was able to open them. She had already thought she could never set herself free again; she had felt increasingly vexed as if in a dream where you hoped to get close to something that constantly moved away from you. She looked around her; it was dark in the room. She must have been nodding off for quite a while.

'Yes, I'm coming,' she said and got up slowly.